THE WIDOW'S CHRISTMAS SURPRISE

THE WIDOW'S
CHRISTMAS SURPRISE

JENNA JAXON

THORNDIKE PRESS
A part of Gale, a Cengage Company

**LIBRARY OF CONGRESS CIP DATA ON FILE.
CATALOGUING IN PUBLICATION FOR THIS BOOK
IS AVAILABLE FROM THE LIBRARY OF CONGRESS.**

ISBN-13: 978-1-4328-8424-6 (hardcover alk. paper)

Published in 2020 by arrangement with Zebra Books, an imprint of
Kensington Publishing Corp.

Printed in Mexico
Print Number: 01   Print Year: 2020

THE WIDOW'S CHRISTMAS SURPRISE

PROLOGUE

The candle's flickering light cast ominous shadows onto the piece of foolscap on which Alan, Lord Kersey, was scribbling his last will and testament in the early hour before dawn. Pausing to peer into the gloom of his study, walnut paneled and dark on the sunniest of days, he laid down the quill and stretched his cramped fingers. Writing for any length of time hurt his fingers horribly. Not something one wished to do before a duel, but the document must be exact in the wording that spelled out his final wishes. Although the bulk of his estate was entailed and would ultimately pass to the heir his wife, Maria, was hopefully carrying, other bequests that did not fall under that settlement were his to make.

He'd suspected for years that such a moment as this would come. Living his entire adult life as a rake and a cad had given him enormous pleasure. The insatiable taste for bedding women he'd acquired at the early age of fifteen had never abated. Even though he'd sworn to change his ways eight months ago, to his uncle who lay dying in the upstairs chamber Alan now called his own, he'd managed to refrain from his debauched ways for only a few weeks. Then he'd resumed his habits with a vengeance. The addition of the title Earl of Kersey had been amazingly helpful in drawing women to him who would not have cared a jot to bed plain Mr. Alan Garrett. The title had been good for that, he had to admit.

Even now, when he might have only an hour or so left to live, he still could not summon any regrets, save that he wished he'd become a better shot over the years. Luck only lasted so long, and his had apparently run out in a spectacular way at Lord Remington's manor two weeks ago. Lady Remington's assertion that her husband had gone off to a final fox hunt in Scotland had been more wishful thinking than absolute truth, with the result that in approximately one hour Lord Remington would be aiming a gun at him and not some wretched animal.

Alan picked up the pages, perusing the words he'd been writing for the past two hours. There were mistakes here and there, crossed out in tiny *x*'s, and one section where he'd decided the wording would not do at all and thus he'd blackened it out entirely. The resulting document was neither neat nor very pretty; however, he believed it would be accepted by the family solicitor, Mr. Hezekiah Clarke, and carried out in the event of his death. Picking up the pen, he mended it neatly, then signed his name.

A hollow knock sounded on the door, making Alan flinch. God, he needed to steady his nerves if he'd any hope of surviving the coming ordeal. Glancing to his right, he looked longingly at the decanter of excellent cognac that his butler faithfully refilled every morning. It stood at a third full, more than enough to take the edge off him, but he shook his head and, pulling a blank sheet of paper over his document, rose. While a drink might steady him, it might also take him off his aim just enough to keep him from disabling his opponent before he could kill Alan. A sober head was needed, no matter how much he thirsted. "Come."

The door opened and Hugh Granger, the steward he'd inherited from his Uncle Kersey back in August, strode into the room. Granger had been a good man all these months. Apparently his uncle had hired the man years ago, as a favor to the steward's father. A favor that had worked out well, for the Kersey estate had run effortlessly in Mr. Granger's capable hands, at least for the time Alan had been in residence. Hopefully it would continue to do so.

"I saw the light, my lord, and wanted to take my leave of you." The man nodded deferentially. From his initial interview with the steward, Alan had discovered Granger was a second son to a very prosperous landowner in Suffolk, his uncle's friend who had died several years before, leaving Granger's elder brother the entailed estate. A rather uncomplicated man, Granger was excellent at management, having a bent for organization and attention to detail. "I'm for London to see to the repairs to the townhouse. You'd asked me to oversee them."

"Yes, I remember." Bad timing, that. Should something untoward happen this morning, Kersey Hall would need a steadying hand here. He shook off the image of himself lying on the damp ground, a bullet in his head, which unexpectedly popped into his mind. Perhaps ask Granger to remain until tomorrow . . . .

His gaze fell on the pages he'd been writing. No. Better Granger leave and *post haste.* Alan would have no better emissary to deliver the will safely into the solicitor's hands. "I have an additional task for you when you get to London, Granger."

"Yes, my lord?" The man's dark gaze gave no indication if he knew about his master's indiscretion and the coming consequences, although Alan suspected he did.

"Can you summon Chambers, please?"

Granger blinked, but moved back to the door and then into the corridor. He returned in a moment, followed by the butler, another holdover from his uncle's staff, impeccably dressed and ready to begin the day's duties, even at this ungodly hour. Did the man ever sleep?

"Good morning, milord." Chambers stood straight, his eyes slightly averted.

"Good morning." Alan adjusted the piece of paper covering the will, leaving the blank bottom half of the document uncovered. "If you will, Granger, Chambers, I would like you both to sign the paper here on the desk."

Chambers's eyes met his, somewhat larger than before, but he nodded. "Of course, milord."

"Very good. You first, Chambers. Mr. Granger will sign after you."

The butler stepped forward, bent over and

grasped the quill with suddenly awkward fingers. With hesitant strokes, he scratched out *George Chambers*. He then placed the pen carefully next to the paper and righted himself.

"Thank you, Chambers. Direct Lawson to bring the carriage around."

"Yes, my lord." With one fleeting look at Alan, the man bowed and left.

"Granger." Alan nodded toward the desk.

The steward met his gaze, his lips firming into a straight line. He opened them, then closed his mouth without a word and took up the quill. With a bold hand he wrote his name, then laid the pen down and stepped back.

"Thank you, Granger." Alan sanded the ink, waited a moment to make sure it had dried, then folded the document. He dripped black sealing wax onto it, then pressed his signet ring into the warm blob. Under the circumstances, this was the best he could do. Of course, his best had often fallen short of what had been expected of him. He hoped this would not. Turning back to his steward, Alan held the document out to him. "Take this directly to Mr. Hezekiah Clarke of Messrs. Grimes and Clarke, Solicitors, in Milford Lane in London." He gripped the foolscap sheet until it crackled.

Pray God this would remain nothing but a precaution. "Put it into Mr. Clarke's hands directly."

Mr. Granger looked at him askance, but nodded and grasped the document. "I will, my lord."

With a nod, Alan let go the paper, sudden regret filling him. This was a sorry business, and totally of his own making. If he survived, perhaps he could turn over the proverbial new leaf, as he had promised his uncle as he lay dying. He shivered. Goose walking over his grave. He straightened his shoulders. Then so be it. "That is all, Granger. Safe journey."

"Thank you, my lord." The steward looked as if he would speak again, his gaze shooting directly into Alan's eyes, a gleam of sympathy — or more likely pity — in the blue depths. Granger must have thought better of the comment, for he simply nodded and left.

Clenching his jaw, Alan went to the window and pulled back the blue and black damasked drapes. The seemingly unrelenting darkness had lightened several degrees. A glimmer of the approaching dawn shone in the east through the trees that had just begun to bud. Time to meet Beauchamp, his second, and get this farce over with.

With a jerk, Alan turned and strode back to the desk. From a deep drawer he withdrew the polished mahogany box that contained a set of French dueling pistols. Why his uncle had bought the guns was a complete mystery to Alan. He'd found them when he first took stock of the estate after his uncle's death, looking brand-new, as though they'd never been taken out of their case. Now both pistols had been fired repeatedly. Beauchamp had informed him yesterday that Remington would not, under any circumstances, accept an apology. So Alan had practiced as best he could out in the yard until it had grown too dark to see.

Securing the smooth box under his arm, Alan glanced once more around the familiar room; then, raising his chin, he turned and strode out of the room to face his destiny.

CHAPTER ONE

May 1817
Kersey Hall, Essex

"I can't do this. I can't. I — Owww." In the grip of an exquisitely painful contraction, Maria, Lady Kersey, squeezed the already mangled hand of her cousin Jane, Lady John Tarkington.

"Stop talking and breathe, Maria." Jane smiled at her through clenched teeth, wiggling her fingers against the death grip.

"You're almost there, my lady." Mrs. Middleton, the village midwife, looked up at her, a fine sheen of sweat on her brow.

The birthing room had been prepared for the delivery, the windows closed off, dark coverings erected over every wall, so the fireplace and the myriad candles burning gave off incredible heat. The airless chamber was suffocating, though by now Maria had ceased to care.

"I'm going to need you to push with the

next one."

"I've been pushing forever as it is." Lying on her left side, Maria had been instructed to draw her legs up toward her stomach, a position she'd been in for several hours. Comfortable at first, her body now seemed ready to split in two. The pains were almost constant, one long, searing cramp after another. "When is this going to end?"

"Very soon, my lady." Leaning forward, the midwife, a local woman from Kersey Village, shifted Maria's stained and sweat-soaked nightgown away from her body.

"You'll have your son in your arms before you know it, Maria, and you'll forget all about the ordeal." With her free hand, Jane wiped a cool sponge over Maria's hot skin. "Trust me. I know."

Her cousin should indeed know. She had birthed four children in the years before her husband had been killed at Waterloo. How on earth had she managed it? Right now, every inch of Maria's body seemed on fire. If she survived this nightmare, she'd never have another child as long as she lived.

Gritting her teeth in preparation for the coming pain, she forced herself to think only about her son. The one duty she had left to accomplish for Alan. Her husband was dead — she still could scarcely take that in. There was so much she'd had to endure the past month, from the disagreeable effects of late pregnancy, compounded by the shocking discovery that Alan had been unfaithful to her, to the equally stunning news of his death less than a month ago. Anger had fought with despair the past few weeks, leaving her exhausted, morose, and weak even as her time had drawn near.

Pain seized her belly, threatening to tear her apart, and she sat up in the bed, shrieking.

"Push, my lady. Now. A big push." Face eager and intent, the midwife crouched closer at the end of the bed.

"Nooo." The sharp agony in her belly mirrored the one in her heart. She'd loved Alan, and he'd betrayed that love in the bed of another woman. When she'd learned of it she'd wanted only to die. Perhaps now she would get her wish.

"Almost there, my dear." Jane had disengaged her hand and now slid an arm around Maria's shoulders, steadying her when all her strength seemed to have drained away. "Just a bit longer and your baby will be here."

Her baby. Hers and Alan's. He'd been so pleased as her pregnancy had progressed. So proud to have sired a child to carry on after him. Despite her fury at Alan's betrayal, she owed it to him to bring his son safely into the world so the Garrett line could continue here at Kersey Hall.

Another pain swept through her body, forcing a cry from her lips as she instinctively bore down. There was a moment of pure agony, then Maria sagged back against the pillows.

"Good, Maria, good." Jane smiled as she peered over at the midwife. "I believe that did the —"

A piercing wail cut off Jane's words. Maria raised up as Mrs. Middleton stood, the shrill squalling continuing to emanate from the swath of white cloth she carried. "Well done, my lady. Very well done, indeed."

Her heart beating strangely as the woman crossed to the head of the bed, Maria stared helplessly as the woman placed the wiggling bundle into her arms. The baby's red and wrinkled face below a shock of almost black hair ceased its crying for a moment and stared directly at her, its eyes round and blue. Maria's heart melted. Every inch of her exhausted body pricked with excitement, her pain forgotten. "Oh, look at you. You are so beautiful, my love."

The baby opened its mouth and screeched anew.

"He's likely hungry, my dear." Jane bent over, adjusting the pillows so Maria sat more fully erect. "Why don't you put him to your breast?"

Smiling broadly, unable to take her gaze from her son, Maria nodded and Jane adjusted her nightgown, opening the placket at the neck. Carefully, Maria moved the baby to her nipple and gasped when he latched on with a vengeance.

Jane smiled, pushing a stray wisp of hair out of her face. "Oh, he's a grand one, Maria. Not all babies catch on so quickly."

"It's quite, um, startling, isn't it?" The baby's deep pulling on her breast was a strange, yet satisfying sensation.

"You'll get used to it quickly, my lady." Mrs. Middleton had finished cleaning up evidence of the birth and was washing her hands at the basin. "It helps your body heal itself from the childbirth." She shook her hands, then grabbed a piece of clean toweling to dry them. "And the longer you have the child at the breast, the longer it'll be before you'll conceive again."

The midwife turned white, Jane gasped, and Maria clenched her jaw. The pain of Alan's death, mixed with the equal anguish of his infidelity, shot through her. Her body tensed and she flinched, as from a blow. The movement pulled her nipple out of the baby's mouth and he set up another hungry wail.

"Beggin' your pardon, my lady." Mrs. Middleton wrung her hands. "It's just that's always been my advice to new mothers, so it just popped out. I'm that sorry to upset you."

Though Jane looked daggers at the woman, she nodded. "That will do, Mrs. Middleton. I believe I can carry on with Lady Kersey from here."

Taking a deep breath, Maria nodded as well and steered the baby's mouth back to her breast. "Thank you for your help, Mrs. Middleton."

The midwife dipped a curtsey and turned toward the door.

"What shall you name him, Maria?" Jane bent down and ran a gentle finger over the wrinkled brow of the sucking child. "Have you decided?"

"I haven't fixed on a name yet." She hadn't wanted to admit it, but secretly she wanted to name the child for Alan. Jane would object, with good reason, and Maria suspected that such a reminder of her husband would haunt her for the rest of her life. Still, this was Alan's son. If he couldn't have the raising of him, at least the child could share something of his father.

"One more thing, my lady." At the doorway, the midwife had turned back toward her.

"Yes, Mrs. Middleton?" Maria looked up expectantly. Some additional piece of advice for newborns was likely on the woman's mind.

The midwife clenched her hands. "About the baby."

Fear shot through Maria, making her clutch the child closer to her. Was there something wrong with her son?

"What about the child, Mrs. Middleton?" Jane's voice cut the sudden silence like a reaper's scythe.

"It's a girl." The midwife nodded her head toward the baby rooting happily at Maria's breast. "You have a daughter, Lady Kersey."

Several hours later, after some much needed sleep, Maria awakened to the clatter of silverware on a tray. A maid had set a tray on the bedside table and Jane was now directing her to pull the dark wall hangings back, allowing the afternoon sun to blaze into the chamber.

"What time is it?" Maria sat up in bed, then winced. "Owww." The child. Her gaze darted around the room, but there was no cradle to be seen. Panic flared in her muddled mind, adding urgency to her voice. "Where's the baby?"

"Ah, good." Jane turned toward her, smiling despite the dark circles under her eyes. She'd been up half the night with Maria, never leaving her side throughout the excruciating ordeal. "You're awake. You need to keep up your strength. I've had Cook fix some broth, tea, and toast, and later, if you can manage it, you can have some blancmange."

"The baby, Jane. Where is she?" A sudden premonition that Jane was hiding horrible news and was trying to distract her with food made Maria's mouth dry as cotton.

"In the nursery with her nursemaid." Her cousin came forward and adjusted the pillows before pulling up a chair. "You would have been of no use to her after you fell asleep, so I had Nurse fetch her." She picked up the cup of broth. "Once you've eaten, I'll have her brought back to you if you like."

Slumping back onto the pillows, Maria burst into tears. "I thought she had died."

"Don't be ridiculous." Jane returned the cup to the tray, then patted Maria's hand. "It's all right. New mothers get these notions." She blotted the tears with a handkerchief. "I remember with Robert, my first, I was convinced the wet nurse was starving him. I changed the women three times before Tark put his foot down. He said all the different women were upsetting the baby and I suspect he was correct." Her cousin smiled at the memory. "Once I gave the woman a chance, Robert settled down and put on so much weight he looked six months old at three months."

Maria rubbed her eyes, trying to stem the tide of tears. So much had happened in the past six weeks. A lifetime of sorrow compressed into such a small space of time. "So many bad things have happened to me, Jane, I can only think my wretched luck will continue. As though I am cursed."

"You are not cursed, my dear. Far from it." Jane picked up the broth again and held it to Maria's lips. "Here, take a sip of this."

Obediently, Maria took a tiny sip. The rich chicken broth exploded on her tongue and her stomach growled.

"I believe you can manage this by yourself." Jane relinquished the cup.

Maria took a larger mouthful. Now she was ravenous. "You said there is toast?"

"Yes, right here. Very good, my dear."

Too soon the cup was empty, the plate of toast bare. "Can I have more, please? I'm still frightfully hungry."

"The midwife said not to overdo with food. Let that bit settle and we'll see what you can manage this evening."

"I hope Mrs. Middleton does not intend to starve me." More rumblings from her stomach, despite what she'd just eaten, attested to Maria's fear. Advice she'd been sent from the other of her formerly widowed friends, had spoken of keeping to a bland diet until she'd been churched, some six weeks from now. When she'd read that, she'd supposed it was because new mothers had no appetite. Apparently that was far from the truth, at least for her.

"Well, my dear, you were the one who insisted upon a midwife rather than an *accoucheur*." Jane's rueful words were said with a pucker of the mouth as she settled onto the side of the bed. "I could easily have had Dr. Gilliam come attend you instead. Hopefully he would not have made such an inappropriate suggestion."

Avoiding Jane's gaze, Maria tucked her arms beneath the covers. "I suppose I could have done, but Mama was so adamant about having a midwife attend me, and since she could not be here, I felt that I should at least take her wishes into consideration." Jane was a dear and had been by

24

her side ever since the revelation of Alan's infidelity. Still, a woman wanted her mother with her at such a time as childbirth. "Besides, having Dr. Gilliam attend me would not have changed the fact that Jane is a girl."

Her cousin's eyes lit up. "You have decided on a name, then?"

"Of course she must be named for you, Jane." Maria pulled her arms free of the covers and sat up to hug her cousin. "You have been my staunchest supporter these many weeks." She sighed and leaned back on the bed. "And now you must help me decide what to do."

"What do you mean, Maria?"

"Jane cannot inherit the Kersey title and estates, so another heir must be found." Alan had impressed that upon her, the need for this child to be a son to secure the line. "When he is located, Jane and I shall quite likely be made to leave."

"You don't know that, Maria." Though Jane surely meant to be comforting, her downcast eyes spoke more eloquently than her words.

"I must be prepared for it. Whether or not he meant to torment me, Alan made my options perfectly clear only days before he —" Oh, but she didn't want to cry for the wretch again, but here were tears trickling down her face once more. She sniffed them back and wiped her eyes with the sleeve of her white gown. "He told me if he survived there would be nothing to worry about. But if he was killed, I had to pray hard our child was a son, because if it was not I would likely be turned out by the next Lord Kersey, who had no obligation toward me."

"What a horrible thing for the wretch to say. And at such a time as that." Narrowing her eyes, Jane looked as though she itched to plant Alan a facer if only he were here. "But what about your settlements? Your dower rights? My father negotiated a jointure with Tark before our marriage, which is why I am in no hurry to remarry." Jane frowned. "Surely your father made arrangements for you and your children in your settlements?"

For the thousandth time, Maria admitted to herself that she had been a fool for Alan Garrett in more ways than one. "I have none."

"What?" Jane sat back, her mouth agape.

"If you remember the circumstances, I had just discovered I was with child when I arrived at Charlotte's house party last October. Alan had been beaten almost senseless by Lord Wrotham. I still have no idea why." She glared at Jane, who looked away. "He was unceremoniously thrown out of the house and so I went with him. By the time we reached London he had agreed to our marriage, but I was so afraid he would change his mind if we waited even a day, that I encouraged him when he said he would get a special license so we could be married at once. My parents didn't know about the marriage until after I was Lady Kersey. They were thrilled, make no mistake. But because of my haste there are no settlements, no dowry, no jointure." Tears welled again. "There are only Jane and I, with nowhere to go."

Jane sat still, her brow furrowed as if in deep thought.

Could her cousin come up with some way for Maria and her daughter to remain here at Kersey Hall? That would be a miracle indeed.

"Did Lord Kersey have a will?"

The question caught Maria off guard and she stared at her cousin. "I . . . I don't know. Would that matter?"

"Oh, yes. Very much so." Jane smoothed the covers down. "If he made a will after his marriage, he might very well have left you money or jewels or property for your continued maintenance."

Maria frowned. This had never occurred to her. "I thought everything went to the next Lord Kersey."

Jane shook her head with vigor. "Oh, no, my dear. Only the title and any lands or property that are part of the earldom's entailment. If there is anything unentailed, even though it was inherited from the previous Lord Kersey, it would have been your husband's to dispose of."

Hope rose in Maria's heart for the first time since learning her child was a girl. "How do I find out if he made such a will?"

"The family solicitor would have it. Did he not contact you after Lord Kersey's death?"

"Well, yes, he wrote to tell me that we needed to wait until the child was born before he could make any determination about the estate." Mr. Clarke's message had confirmed Maria's suspicion at the time that if her child was not a boy, she'd be in dire straits indeed. She frowned at Jane. "That does not sound as though I am to inherit anything."

The lines around Jane's mouth tightened. "I admit it does not. Still, you must write to him now to advise him about Jane's birth and to inquire directly about any will or provisions Lord Kersey may have made."

"I shall do so first thing tomorrow." Despite the recent food, Maria's strength was waning again. She stifled a yawn. Another nap would not be amiss.

Rising from the bed, Jane shook her head and straightened the covers. "If the worst comes to pass, can you not go home to your mother and Cousin Edward?"

"Father has been ill for months. Mother attends to him night and day. That's why she couldn't be here for my lying-in. I could take the baby and move in with them, but it would be an increased burden on them." She looked hopefully at Jane. "Might I stay with you, Cousin? At least until I am out of mourning." The ghastly crepe awaited her after her confinement. She'd only worn the deep purples and dark browns of half mourning since Alan's death. Her mother had feared wearing black would harm the child. "Hopefully by then I will be able to figure out where to go. What to do."

Jane's pained expression foretold what her words would be. "I am afraid I can offer you no sanctuary, my dear. When in London I still reside with my brother-in-law, although the marquess is a gravely ill man. I am not quite sure what I will do if he succumbs to this odd sickness Fanny related to me at her wedding." Clasping Maria's fingers, Jane looked deep into her eyes. "I stayed in London only briefly before coming here, but long enough to tell you that even if I did have a place to offer you, I would not do so."

"What?" Her cousin's statement startled Maria more than anything else she'd said. "Why not?"

"Because I must advise you, whatever you may do, do not to go to London."

Why on earth would Jane say such a thing? "I don't understand."

Drawing a deep breath, Jane paused, as if words failed her. When finally she spoke, she did so very unwillingly. "I have kept this from you because of your condition, but now you must be warned about what the *ton* has been saying. About Lord Kersey and about you."

"Members of the *ton* have been gossiping about me?" Such a thing was baffling to even contemplate. "No one in London ever gave a fig about Maria Wickley."

"But they all give a fig about Lady Kersey and her husband's scandalous infidelity while she was carrying his child. And they care even more about his death in a duel by a man defending his wife's honor. Even though the woman had none, to be sure."

Maria hitched in a breath. Alan had been

30

discovered in Lady Remington's bed by Lord Remington, in such a way, she had gathered — certainly no one had breathed a word of what had actually happened to her directly — that there had been no doubt whatsoever what they had been doing there. "So Society is reviling my dead husband. I can understand why they would. *I* have done so, ever since I discovered what he had done." She had rung a peal over his head while he lived and, after his death, had done the same to his empty bedchamber. "But that should have nothing to do with me. I am the woman wronged in this whole horrible mess."

Jane shook her head. "Unfortunately, my dear, the *ton* is made up of some of the ficklest people on earth. They have concluded that you were no better than you should be — believe me when I tell you they have been counting the months since your wedding and the numbers do not add up to a child conceived in wedlock. They are saying you trapped him into a marriage he did not want, as evidenced by his infidelity so soon after the marriage." Jane ducked her head. "There is even one hideous *on-dit* that claims the child is not Lord Kersey's."

Maria gasped, her stomach clenching on the food that now threatened to come back up. "How dare they! Jane most certainly is Alan's child."

"Shhh. You mustn't upset yourself. This is exactly why I did not wish to tell you what has been said in Town before now. But they have torn your reputation to shreds along with Lord Kersey's." With nervous fingers Jane picked at the edge of her sleeve. "Compound that with your husband's scandalous death, and you are now considered *persona non grata* in London. How long that will last I do not know. It may be that your disgrace will be displaced by the next outrageous *on-dit* that comes along. But until then, you must stay well away from London, lest you receive the cut direct whenever you show your face."

Maria sagged against her pillows and closed her eyes, not wanting to think about the devastating news Jane had just delivered. Even though she had not truly thought of going to London, unless to stay with Jane, to be told that she could not go unless she wanted to endure the worst Society could do to her made her want to give up completely. What use was it to try to go on?

"My lady?"

The strange voice brought Maria up instantly to a sitting position, her gaze on the tall older woman in the nurse's uniform standing in the doorway, a swathed bundle in her arms.

Jane. Her daughter.

"Lady John gave instructions for me to bring Lady Jane to you at exactly three o'clock." Nurse hesitated, but Maria opened her arms and the woman laid her sleeping child in them. Her baby.

"Thank you, Nurse. That will be all." Jane dismissed the woman, who left the room, then rose. "I will leave you with my namesake for a while. Try not to worry. It will likely take the solicitors time to find the new earl. We will think of something before then."

"Yes, we will." Maria gazed down on the angelic face in her arms. The petite nose, the delicate dark brows, the soft rounded cheeks. No one would take her daughter's birthright from her. Lady Jane Garrett would have her come-out in Society one day and nothing her parents had done was going to stop that from happening. Whatever it took, she would make certain that her daughter, hers and Alan's, had every advantage socially possible. So help her God.

CHAPTER TWO

Mid-October 1817

Golden-yellow leaves swirled against the windowpanes of the cozy drawing room, making Maria smile as she poured tea for her and Jane. Autumn had always been her favorite season — the crisp air, the colorful leaves, the sweet taste of roasted chestnuts. Few things had made her smile in the past months. Her future was still as uncertain as it had been when Jane was born.

"So you have still had no recent word from Mr. Clarke?" Jane tasted her tea and sighed with pleasure. "Is this the new tea from Jackson's?"

"No, I haven't, and yes, it is." Maria dropped a lump of sugar into her own cup and stirred it briskly. "I finally decided to order the tea just last week. I feel odd spending money that truly isn't mine, but we have to live until the heir is found." She gritted her teeth to keep from tearing up each time she thought of her precarious circumstances. "My last letter from Mr. Clarke, which I received a fortnight ago, assured me that he had set every available clerk to searching Alan's lineage to find the heir. He mentioned that these inquiries sometimes take a very long time to complete. Years, he told me, in some cases." She truly didn't think she could live for years with the uncertainty of eviction hanging over her and Jane's heads. Her inquiry as to whether Alan had made a will benefitting her or her daughter had been met with a dignified but firm "no" from Mr. Clarke in June. "So I try to maintain as frugal an existence as possible."

"You are a model of frugality, my dear." Sipping the fragrant tea, Jane nodded, and Maria relaxed back a trifle. "You have been putting that purchase off until I believed we would need to steep the leaves three times ourselves."

"I simply feel that as I've been left in charge of the estates, it is my duty to Alan's family name to keep the Kersey legacy in the best manner I can." It was her daughter's legacy as well, even though once the heir took possession of the title little Jane might not get a farthing of help out of him.

"You are conscientious to a fault, Maria."

Jane set her cup down, her face betraying a tinge of surprise. "You have come far since this time last year."

"Being widowed twice in almost as many years may have had something to do with that." She couldn't help the forlorn tone in her voice. It had only been three years ago that she and William had been running and laughing through the falling leaves on his father's estate in Oxfordshire, without a care in the world save to make sure they came home in time for supper. If only she could get back to those carefree days, with a man she loved and who loved her by her side. If she and William could have waited, could have grown old together, with children of their own, she never would have made the horrible mistake of marrying Lord Kersey.

"You needed to grow up very quickly, my dear," Jane said, patting her hand. "I am sorry for that, I truly am. You should have been allowed to stay in the schoolroom longer, should have had your come-out, rather than be consigned to crepe at the age of sixteen."

"At least that indignity is over now as well. I would never have dreamed I would be wearing these clothes again." Maria smoothed out her half-mourning gown of gray silk. "I am surprised Mama hadn't already sent them to the church for an overseas mission. When I realized I was about to need them again, I wrote and asked her for them. They arrived two days ago. Just in time."

"Well, they still fit marvelously well to judge by this one." Jane smiled and added more tea to her cup. "Not every woman keeps her figure after having a child."

"What will that matter?" Leaning back in her chair, Maria poked out her bottom lip. "Even when I can put aside this half mourning, I still won't be able to go back into Society unless . . ." She looked up hopefully. "Have you heard from your friends in London?" If the gossip had died down there was a chance she might be received by the *ton* once more. "Has the scandal of Alan's death been forgotten?"

Slowly, Jane sipped her tea, avoiding Maria's gaze. "When I last heard from my sister-in-law, she did mention that talk had begun to die down, however —"

"It has?" A thrill of excitement shot through her. Over the past months she'd brooded over what was to become of her if she were asked to leave Kersey Hall. Unless she wanted to move back to her parents' home — a prospect that filled her with despair — the simplest thing she could do would be to marry again. Not that another marriage was what she wanted at all. If Alan had taught her anything it was that men could be the worst deceivers. But in her straitened circumstances, a husband meant security for her and little Jane. If Maria could be accepted in London once more, she could perhaps meet a man with similar needs — a widower, in search of a wife and mother for his children. Not an ideal match, but one she could perhaps come to accept in exchange for the security it offered. The first step, however, was to be allowed back into the *beau monde.* "What did Lady Theale say?"

Looking uncomfortable, Jane replaced her teacup in its saucer, then rose and stalked toward the fireplace, where a fire crackled merrily. "I am afraid the length of time it has taken for the solicitor to find the Kersey heir has brought the matter of the duel and its outcome to the attention of the *ton* once more. *On-dits* flying around about claim state that there is no heir and that the estates will be forfeited to the Crown."

"Dear lord!" Maria's hand flew to her throat.

"It is nothing more than rumor, but, of course, with nothing substantial for people to turn their minds to, they will dredge up old scandals and give them a new coat of paint." Jane scowled, her frown almost reaching her nose. "If the wretched heir could have been found two months ago, all the talk would have been laid to rest once everyone's attention had focused on the new earl." She made a snort of disgust, then turned kind eyes on Maria. "Do not worry overmuch, my dear. It will take years before the property is forfeited."

Clutching her cup, Maria's heart sank. The longer it took to find the heir, the longer it would take for talk to die down, which meant she couldn't show her face in Town and so could not find another husband. Of course, as long as the heir was absent, she could live quietly here at Kersey Hall. At least she hoped she could. Her gaze met Jane's. "So I could stay here all that time?"

"That, I'm afraid, is a question for Mr. Clarke." Jane shook her head. "Such things are far beyond my knowledge. But I assume if your steward can keep this estate running properly, and you require the other properties to give quarterly reports to him, that you can manage them yourself with . . . What is your steward's name again?"

"Mr. Granger." Maria had already come to rely heavily on the handsome young man in the past few months. He managed the day-to-day business of the estate and the outlying tenant farmers with ease, consulting her from time to time when he felt it warranted, but generally doing what he deemed necessary with great efficiency. "Alan said he's been here for quite some years, and knows his work exceedingly well. I frankly don't know what I or the estate would have done without him these past months."

"Well, thank goodness for that." Her cousin nodded as she set her cup on the table with such force it clattered into the saucer. "Speak with him about taking over the management of the earldom's other holdings. He may be doing so already." She paused. "Do you know how many there are?"

Maria shrugged. She and Alan had never spoken about business at all. He had been so young there didn't seem to be any rush for him to explain to her how the earldom operated. That was something he would do with his son one day. By the time the duel was imminent, they spoke only briefly, but she'd been so angry at him they hadn't talked of anything save his infidelity. "I'm sure Mr. Granger does. Alan seemed to depend on him quite a lot, so I expect he knows all about the other properties as well."

"If I were you, I'd seek him out and make sure those properties are also being managed as well as possible. Oh, and I had another thought you can ask him as well."

"What is that?"

"Ask if there is a dower property on the estate."

Maria frowned. "What is that?"

"Last night I remembered Letitia — Lady Theale, that is — talking about her mother-in-law moving to the estate's dower house when Lord Theale brought Letitia home after their marriage. It's a smallish manor some estates use to house the previous lord's widow. She becomes the dowager countess or marchioness, or what ever her title is, so there will be no confusion with the wife of the current lord. With the lord's permission, the widow can often stay there until her own death."

A small ray of light in a pitch-black tunnel. Maria clasped her hands together, pressing them so tightly her nails bit into her flesh. She didn't want to hope again only to have it dashed, as previous expectations had been. "You think the baby and I would be allowed to stay there?"

"It is a possibility. If there is indeed a

dower house on the property." Jane rose. "I must write to Lord Kinellan and postpone my journey to Scotland once more."

"I am so sorry, Jane." Maria's cheeks stung with heat, distracting her from this newest chance at a future. She'd kept Jane with her these many months as a companion and friend and as a result, she'd come to depend on her very much. Jane had time and again put off her trip to see Lord Kinellan, for whom, Maria understood, her cousin had a bit of a *tendre*. Maria hated to impose on her so, but she would be completely lost without her excellent counsel.

"It's no great matter." Jane's eyes held a glimmer of sadness before she put on a smile and turned toward the door. "I suspect he will be disappointed, at least I hope he shall be. But my duty is here, at least until things are more settled."

Maria jumped to her feet and flung her arms around her cousin. "You are too good to me, Jane. I declare, I do not know what I would do without you." She leaned back to face her cousin. "Do you think Lord Kinellan will be terribly angry?"

"If he is, all the better." Jane tossed her head, a confident smile on her lips. "If the mountain will not come to Muhammad, perhaps Muhammad must come down from

Scotland."

"Why doesn't the mountain invite Lord Kinellan to visit?" Maria linked arms with her cousin and they strolled out into the corridor.

"That could perhaps be done. Although it would be much better if he simply appeared out of the blue as though he couldn't stand another day without me." Jane gazed down the staircase, a satisfied smile on her face, as though she could see Lord Kinellan striding up the stairs in search of her. "Yes, that would be quite satisfactory."

Tears pricked Maria's eyes. If only her life could be handled so easily. Determined not to become a perpetual watering pot, she blinked back the incipient downpour and started down the steps.

"Where are you going?" Jane's voice held a note of surprise.

"The weather is so nice I thought I'd sit out in the garden for a short time. The leaves are so pretty swirling about. Soon they will be gone." As she herself would, most likely.

"Be sure to put on something warm. You do not want to come down with a cold or a severe chill." Her cousin put on her best "mothering" expression, looking down her short, upturned nose.

"I promise." Maria waved her hand over her shoulder and continued down the steps. Mothering was all well and good, and she'd be sure to wrap up, even though the day looked warm. One never knew when the wind would change.

That was why Maria needed time to herself, to think things out and form a plan. Relying on Jane all her life was no solution. As she stepped onto the floor, she straightened her shoulders. She must think how to begin yet again.

"Tend to Galahad, please Peter." Hugh Granger slid down from atop his roan gelding and tossed the reins to the young groom, who bobbed his head and quickly moved off to walk the horse as he cooled down. The ride had been long and the news at the end of it hadn't been the best. He shouldn't put off telling Lady Kersey, much as he hated to add to her burdens.

The lady who'd arrived at Kersey Hall, almost a year ago now, had had Hugh's sympathy from the moment he'd been introduced to her. Very young she had been then, carefree and seemingly much in love with her husband. Hugh had wished his master and mistress happy, although based on his then only two months' acquaintance with Lord Kersey, he doubted that the lady would remain so infatuated with the earl.

From the moment the old earl had died, the new Lord Kersey's behavior had been less than circumspect. Even while he'd been in mourning for his uncle, Kersey had managed to entertain himself on a regular basis with local women. The man had been generous with his coin, so Hugh had gleaned from the servants downstairs, but he'd had no compunction against taking his pleasure as often as he pleased, with little regard for whether the girl was completely willing or not.

Heading for the front entrance in search of Chambers to discover Lady Kersey's whereabouts, Hugh slowed his brisk strides a trifle. His anger always got the better of him if he didn't pause and reflect. The earl was dead and in his grave these past six months. No further punishment could be levied against him, save that doled out by God in heaven. Or Satan down below. Not that Hugh had any doubts which way the late Lord Kersey had journeyed. Still, he couldn't help the fury that overcame him whenever he thought about the burdens Lady Kersey had had to bear because of the earl's perfidy. Not only the shame of discovering her husband's infidelity, but uncertainty of her future here at Kersey Hall.

He'd been sure the document he'd signed on that fateful day in April had been a will. God knew Lord Kersey had to have known his chances against Lord Remington were long at best. Why hadn't the man provided for his wife and child as any gentleman with means would have done? But, apparently, from the gossip in the servants' hall, Lady Kersey had been left absolutely nothing by her husband. Shaking his head, he knocked on the front door, the funerary hatchment still hanging there, dark and forbidding.

Chambers opened the door and Hugh strode in. "Can you tell me where Lady Kersey is?"

"I believe her ladyship is in the rose garden, Mr. Granger."

Hugh nodded, then did a quick turn and headed back outside, striding across the gravel drive and onto the grass lawn. The garden was located to the rear and east of the house, a large area filled with roses of all description during the summer months, although now only a few blooms still clung to life there. Still, on such a mild day as this had been, the garden would likely prove an oasis for the countess.

Rounding the archway that served as entrance to the garden, Hugh glanced about, but the nearest seating area was empty. She might have ventured deeper into the vast landscape, toward the farthest end of the enclosure. The semicircular courtyard there, paved in white Italian marble, with a three-tiered fountain of the same stone, had been a favorite haunt of the previous earl. The tranquility of the place — the quiet splashing of the waters coupled with the occasional birdsong or gentle sighing breeze — had not been lost on Hugh when he had occasion to visit it in search of his master. Given her circumstances, Lady Kersey certainly had need of such a place.

He topped a slight rise that gave on to a set of steps leading down to the courtyard and spied the lady seated on a bench beside the fountain, exactly where he supposed she might be. But the tableau before him differed from what he'd expected. He stopped on the top step, gazing at the small figure in gray twirling a bright yellow leaf idly in her hand. Something about Lady Kersey had changed.

The neat, dark hair was piled up on her head, charming as always with the stray, unruly curl that had managed to escape its pins. A paisley shawl draped around her slim shoulders, the long black fringe almost brushing the ground, had slipped open in the front, revealing the pale gray of her gown.

Gray gown?

Hugh stopped halfway down the stairs. Lady Kersey had replaced the unrelieved black of full mourning with the dull, but still lighter, colors of half mourning. He'd become so accustomed to seeing her in dark clothing that this change had struck him at first as out of place. Nothing could be further from the truth. The silvery shimmer of the pale cloth gave the lady a vibrancy not present while she'd been garbed in black. A beautiful woman, to be sure.

She raised her head as if she'd heard his thought, and Hugh sucked in a breath at having been caught staring at her. What on earth had he been thinking? Continuing on down the stairs, he nodded to the countess, trying to be as nonchalant as possible, despite the odd beating of his heart.

"Good afternoon, my lady. Chambers said I could find you here."

"Good afternoon, Mr. Granger." She laid the golden leaf in her hand carefully on the bench and smiled up at him, her amber-colored eyes wide and bright. "What brings you to find me today?"

Hugh's words suddenly stuck in his throat. She looked so innocent sitting there, and

48

rather peaceful. He hated like the devil to be the bearer of more bad tidings for her.

She cocked her head. "Mr. Granger?" Her petite brows dipped slightly. "Are you quite well?"

Shaking off his mental misgivings, Hugh nodded and found his tongue. "I am, thank you, my lady. But I have sad news to tell you. I had an urgent summons early this morning to go to the Tates' house at the farthest boundary of our holdings. Mr. Tate apparently fell through the roof he was patching yesterday and broke his leg rather severely."

Lady Kersey flinched, her face twisting in sympathy. "How ghastly. Has the man been tended to?"

"I sent immediately for Mr. Lambert, the surgeon in Wickford, to attend him. While I waited I walked around to inspect the property, which seemed well, except for the now gaping hole in the roof over the kitchen. I've sent several fellows from the home farm out to repair the damage, but Mr. Tate will likely be incapacitated for some months to come." Hugh swallowed hard, the sight of the farmer's broken bones poking through his flesh still fresh in his mind. "He may lose the leg, the surgeon said. Or worse."

"Dear lord." Lady Kersey gasped and her

face paled. She stared at him, blinking back tears. "What can we do for him and his family, Mr. Granger?"

"You are very kind, my lady." That the countess's first thought had been for the family's welfare and not for the possible economic burden to the estate itself made Hugh respect the woman even more. Of course women tended to think more on the personal side of things rather than the business. But then, that's what he was there for. "They are fortunate that the accident occurred after the crops had been gathered in, for there's nothing much left to do in the fields until spring. They have a small garden and some animals for their personal use, but Mrs. Tate and their older children take care of them. I told her that, once the roof is fixed, if she needed any other such work done about the place, to notify me and I'd make any necessary arrangements."

"Very good, Mr. Granger." The lady smiled warmly at him and Hugh's heart thudded painfully. "I will prepare a basket with some things for the family if you can have it taken for me?" Her face darkened. "When will the doctor know about Mr. Tate's fate?"

"When I left he simply said he would have to wait and see. He'd set the bone and dressed the wound and planned to return to the farm in a week to see how the break was healing. If all was well, and there was no infection, he'd be more optimistic about Mr. Tate's outcome."

"And if all was not well?"

"Then he'd have to amputate the leg and hope that saved the man's life."

Lady Kersey winced.

"And in that case, or if Mr. Tate were to die, we would need to make arrangements about the farm itself."

"Arrangements?" She looked at him blankly.

"Yes, my lady. We would need to find a new tenant for it, if Mr. Tate can't work the fields."

"What?" The countess's dismay was tinged with outrage. "We cannot turn the family out to starve."

"We would have no choice, Lady Kersey. You must see that." Hugh hated the way she was now looking at him, as though he'd proved himself the villain in some Drury Lane drama. "The farm has to be worked or the estate gets no value from it."

"Could Mrs. Tate not work it? She and her children?"

"I daresay she knows almost nothing about planting or cultivation of the crops and there's only one child, her eldest who is eleven, who could help at all." He shook his head. "Even if Tate survives, if he loses his leg, we would have to replace him with someone who can make the farm produce."

Even before he finished speaking, the countess shook her head. "No, there must be some other way, Mr. Granger. I cannot countenance a family being treated thusly just because the husband is incapacitated."

"But, my lady . . ." As much as he admired her conviction, Hugh could see that Lady Kersey needed to understand how Mr. Tate's injury had changed his family's circumstances, perhaps forever. He sighed. "Let us wait and see how Mr. Tate gets on. There's no use borrowing trouble. Best wait until you own it."

"I agree, Mr. Granger." The lady smiled at him again, and the afternoon seemed to brighten. "I will pray very hard for Mr. Tate's swift recovery." She went silent for a moment, then took a deep breath as though girding herself for another battle. "Can you tell me if there is a dower house or property on the Kersey estate?"

"A dower house?" It was Hugh's turn to be startled. "Why, yes, my lady. About a quarter of a mile from the main entrance to Kersey Hall. But it's been unused for more than twenty years."

"Oh." She bit her bottom lip, her teeth worrying the tender flesh. "Would it take much work to make it habitable again?"

Hugh had visited the property many times in the years he'd been employed by Lord Kersey, to inspect for damage, the last time almost a year ago. "Last year when I went on the inspection tour of the property after harvest, it had sustained a little damage to one corner of the drawing room due to an oak limb that had fallen and broken out a window. We repaired some minor damage to the floor and walls and replaced the window completely." Hugh raised an eyebrow. Why would the lady have such a sudden interest in the dower house? "The house itself is sound. It might require some minor repairs here and there. The curtains and bedclothes would likely need to be replaced, but other than a thorough cleaning and checking the flues to make sure they draft properly, there is nothing major that needs doing. The house could be ready to be occupied within a week or two."

An eagerness lit Lady Kersey's face and she rose from the stone bench. "That is excellent news, Mr. Granger. Would it be possible for me and Lady John to view the property today?"

"Today, my lady?" He couldn't keep the surprise from his voice. Lady Kersey had never asked about the dower house before. Why this sudden interest? Of course he would never question the lady on the matter, still it seemed most odd . . . unless she'd heard news that the Kersey heir had been located. That would make her questions not only reasonable, but of the utmost importance if she suspected she would no longer be welcome at Kersey Hall. "Why, yes, I can take you there as soon as you can be ready. Shall I have the carriage brought around?"

She wrinkled her brow, an eagerness in her face and an excited tension in her slim body. "Oooh, I would love to ride, but my cousin might prefer the carriage. Let me return to the house and ask her." A gleeful smile spread across her lips and she placed a small hand on his arm. "Thank you so much, Mr. Granger."

Their eyes met and Hugh had the sensation of falling into dark pools that might be fathoms deep. To have made this lovely woman happy seemed now to be his greatest accomplishment. "You are most welcome, my lady."

She picked up her skirts and scampered up the steps, outdistancing him in moments.

Mouth dry and heart beating a painful tattoo in his chest, Hugh let her go. As he had said, he knew better than to borrow trouble, but he knew it when it came knocking at his door. Nothing could come of these unexpectedly tender feelings for Lady Kersey. He was a gentleman, to be sure, but his prospects were as uncertain as the lady's own future, and both dependent on the next Lord Kersey's goodwill. On which neither of them could count to any degree at all. Best to treat this budding *tendre* as nothing more than a fleeting notion that was not to be pursued.

He started for the house, all too aware that what he thought with his head might not make a bit of difference to what had taken up lodging in his heart.

CHAPTER THREE

Although she'd not run this fast in almost a year, Maria sped toward Kersey Hall as though she were attempting to fly. Her spirits had risen so abruptly she suspected she might be able to do just that if she could concentrate on flight for a minute or two. There were too many other exciting things, however, to contemplate instead. Mr. Granger's revelation that there was a dower property with a house in need of only minor repairs had made her heart flutter, the possibility that she might have found a safe haven sending a wave of relief surging through her body. The rush of heat that had poured through her when she'd grasped Mr. Granger's arm, however, had certainly had nothing to do with the safety the dower house might provide.

A tingling warmth had shot up her arm when she'd laid her hand on him, the hard, strong muscle of him evident even through his linen and jacket. They'd been so close — closer than she ever remembered being to him before — the scent of the fresh lemon and rosemary cologne he used had filled her nose with a heady aroma that now seemed to cling to her as well. A clean, yet masculine smell she liked very much. So different from the heavy bergamot with which Alan used to all but drench himself.

Maria slowed as she approached Kersey Hall. She was still in mourning, even if she did not actually mourn her husband's passing very much. Clearly she should not be relishing another man's cologne, nor his very masculine form and presence. And she certainly had appreciated Mr. Granger's imposing figure when he'd topped the rise and started down the steps toward her just now. Nice broad shoulders set up his powerful frame without making him too terribly big. His height, too, was very pleasing as he did not tower over her as most men did. Today he'd been dressed for riding, in a blue jacket and light brown buckskins that had subtly emphasized his narrow waist and hips. Making her wonder what it would be like to be held against that taut, muscular body.

A rush of fire to her face made her clap her hands over her cheeks to hide the telltale red. She should not be thinking such things. Not about anyone, but certainly not about Mr. Granger. He always seemed so serious about his work, it must be uppermost in his mind at all times. Although he'd been deferential toward her, Maria doubted he saw her as anything other than his late employer's wife and probably never would. That thought sent a pang of regret to her heart.

Shaking her head to wipe the image of Mr. Granger from her mind, she started for the house again, slowly. She could not allow her feelings to lead her into yet another disastrous entanglement. What she had allowed to happen with Alan could not be repeated with Mr. Granger. She'd learned a thing or two about the world — and about men — in the past year. A woman needed to be on her guard every moment and keep her heart shielded unless she wanted it broken time and time again. She'd let her passions rule her last year and a dalliance had turned into marriage to a man who had only pretended to love her in order to gain an heir. Such hurt and disappointment she would not countenance again. And of course there was her child to think about now as well. She must put these inappropriate thoughts about the steward out of her mind and concentrate on finding a way to provide for herself and little Jane. That would begin with this tour of the dower house.

Determined to act only in her own and her daughter's best interest from now on, Maria mounted the steps to the house, intent on finding her cousin and persuading her to come chaperone her visit to the dower property. Not that she didn't trust Mr. Granger to act the perfect gentleman. Rather she needed to ensure that she remained the perfect lady.

The carriage rumbled along the short, disused driveway that led to Francis House, the small manor that had served the dowagers of the Garrett family for two centuries. Maria pressed her small nose to the window, drinking in the autumn landscape of orange and gold leaves glittering in the afternoon sun, and sighed. "This is a beautiful prospect, don't you think, Jane?"

"It is indeed." Her cousin peered out the window on the other side. "This could be the perfect place to raise little Jane. Near enough to the Hall for her to know her heritage and far enough from the new earl and his family so that you will have some independence in what you do."

"If he is so generous as to allow us to stay,

and provide for our maintenance." Maria sat back on the leather seat, her worries about the future returning with a sharp jolt. "Remember, I will have no funds to live on, even if we have a roof over our heads."

"Could you apply to your parents for an allowance, do you think?"

Jane's idea was not new to Maria. She'd contemplated such a request ever since Mr. Granger had affirmed the existence of a dower house. Living there quietly with the child would be preferable to imposing on her parents, although they might instead wish for her to return to Oxfordshire to be close to them. "I have considered that, yes. First let us see if the house will suit. If it is too large, that plan may not be feasible."

The carriage came to a halt on the circular driveway before a stately redbrick house, and Mr. Granger appeared to hand them down.

Jane peered at the structure. "I would not describe it as 'too large' at all. Nor terribly inviting."

Perhaps a quarter of the size of Kersey Hall, the two stories of Francis House were set evenly, in a symmetrical box with chimneys at either end. A short flight of steps led to the front door, stone urns on either side that should have held flowers but instead stood overgrown with weeds. Empty windows both upstairs and down gave the house a distant look, as though it were standing back, judging them.

"It hasn't been in use since the old earl's mother died, my lady, in 1795 so I've been told," Mr. Granger said, closing the carriage door. "The house should have been kept up better, perhaps, but his lordship never married, so there was no expectation of its being used for many years. He only asked for a yearly inspection and cleaning, which has been carried out meticulously under my supervision." He led them up the stairs and unlocked the door. "However, when I reported to Lord Kersey that the curtains needed replacing, or the floor in the library was sagging, he always waved it away. So while there are not significant repairs or replacements required, there are many small ones." Opening the door, Mr. Granger waited for them to enter. "Welcome to Francis House, ladies."

The narrow entry hall gave onto a staircase at the far end leading to the first floor. To the right a drawing room yawned, empty save for a large shape under a dust sheet that might be a sofa. Maria poked her head inside. A good-sized room that could become quite cozy with more furniture and a good fire. They continued down the corridor, past the library, music room, and the breakfast room, all mostly empty and a little dusty, but still quite charming. "How many bedrooms are there, Mr. Granger?"

"Six, although two are larger than the others. The dowager's chamber is this way." He led them up the curving staircase to a largish apartment that included a dressing room and bathing chamber. The prospect from the chamber was fine as well, overlooking the gardens and a pond beyond.

"What must the last dowager have had in mind when she installed such an extravagant space in her chamber just for bathing?" Maria could see little of the windowless room, part of the dressing room that had been walled off. To have set aside that much of her apartments to ensure she could bathe in private was luxury indeed.

"Perhaps something to do with creature comforts, my dear." Jane cut her eyes from Maria to Mr. Granger, then smothered a smile. "There is so much that can be done for one in a private bath that one cannot have done in a more public area."

"It holds a central tub and has heated racks for warming the towels." Mr. Granger nodded toward the chamber, but he glanced at Jane then backed away and into the bedroom. "Next time you come I'll bring a light so you can view it properly. If you approve of the property, that is."

Turning toward the window, Maria clasped her hands together. "Oh, who would dislike this charming prospect? Or the wonderful conveniences, such as this bathing chamber? Do you truly think I might be able to live here, Jane?"

Her cousin shrugged. "I see no reason why not. If you settle in before the heir takes residence, such deference in giving way to his position may go far toward him allowing you and little Jane to remain here permanently." Her gaze fixed on the steward. "Don't you think so, Mr. Granger?"

"Quite right, my lady." The man stood, suddenly unsteady on his pins. "If his lordship sees that you are amenable to living here, leaving the main hall for him and his family without any fuss, he may wish to appear magnanimous by allowing you to reside here." Mr. Granger suddenly dispelled the serious nature of his comments, with a boyish grin. "At least that is what many gentlemen prefer to persuade themselves they are doing, rather than turning his distant relations out into the road and being gossiped about afterwards."

"Do you think he will turn us out, Mr.

Granger?" Panic shot a lump into Maria's throat until she could scarcely breathe. That would mean utter disaster for her and her child. "What would Lord Kersey have done?"

The young man's brows furrowed. "Do you mean your husband, my lady? You would know how he would handle such a problem better than I."

"No, no, the old Lord Kersey." She glared at Mr. Granger. "I know only too well what arrangements my husband would have made for a widow over whom he held the slightest advantage."

Jane's strangled expression as she hastily moved to the window made Maria want to hide herself in the darkened bathing chamber, but she refused to do that. What she'd said about Alan, although not fit for mixed company, was nevertheless the truth as she had come to know it. She must pray nightly that the next Lord Kersey would not have such evil proclivities.

Mr. Granger had taken the opportunity to stare intently out the window toward the pond in the distance. "Just so, my lady. I did know his lordship, your husband's uncle, very well indeed. And I can assure you, he would have thought it his duty to the family to make a home for the widow of his relative, whether or not he knew them." Turning to face her, Mr. Granger smiled encouragingly. "I sincerely hope that trait has been passed down to the next Lord Kersey, my lady."

"Th-thank you, Mr. Granger." His kind blue eyes, vivid as crystal gemstones, and the sympathetic words made Maria's heart beat faster. Try as she might, she couldn't look away from the brilliant color that reminded her of the earrings she'd inherited from her grandmother. Blue topaz. The most beautiful color in the world.

"I think we should perhaps return to the house, my dear." Jane's firm hand grasped Maria's arm and compelled her out of the bedchamber. "The sun will be setting all too soon and there are always dangers lurking . . . after dark."

Her cousin's pointed remark snapped Maria out of her reverie. Dear lord, how long had she been gazing at Mr. Granger like a moonstruck schoolgirl? Fire blazed in her cheeks so that the chilly air was a welcome relief when they reached the outdoors. The coachman opened the door and Jane all but shoved her into the carriage, then followed her in and plumped down on the seat beside her.

Neither of them spoke, Maria silent in the

hope Jane would say nothing about her very forward and revealing behavior at the dower house.

"Well, if a lady wished to be obvious about a flirtation, she had best come take lessons from you, my dear." Jane spoke nonchalantly, although her meaning was clear enough.

"I don't know what came over me, Jane." She truly didn't. One moment she'd been thinking that perhaps she might be all right if Lord Kersey was as generous as the previous earl, and the next she couldn't drag her gaze away from Mr. Granger's enthralling eyes. "Do you think he noticed?"

With a snort, Jane sat back in the seat. "The man would have had to have been blind not to. But then" — her cousin's eyes narrowed — "he seemed just as fascinated with staring into your face as you did with him."

"Oh!" Maria resisted the urge to cover her blazing hot cheeks once more. "Did he really?"

Sighing, Jane shook her head. "Babes in the woods, both of you."

"What do you mean?"

"I will grant you Mr. Granger is a very handsome gentleman, with a great deal of good sense and kindness. However" — Jane stared straight into Maria's face, unblinking, until Maria began to squirm on the seat — "you cannot begin to think warmly about someone of such unremarkable prospects."

Maria blinked. She'd been certain Jane was going to scold her for having "warm" thoughts about anyone while in half mourning. "How do you know what his means are?"

"He is a steward, my dear. If his prospects were better, he would be tending to his family estate, not someone else's." Jane sighed. "That is a shame, I'll grant you. He runs the estate efficiently, seems very knowledgeable about all aspects of the business end of things, yet he's got lovely manners and is, I must say, very handsome indeed. But he's likely a second or third son of a noble family, or from the upper gentry, with no expectation of any sort of substantial inheritance. Which makes him ineligible for you."

"I have not said I was setting my cap for him, Jane." Maria smoothed out her pelisse, avoiding her cousin's eyes.

"You might as well have done so publicly just now. It was written plainly on your face. Thank goodness I was the only one there to see it." Her cousin gave a little shudder. "So you must snip any incipient feelings you are fostering for Mr. Granger before they can grow. Prune them now, before they can bloom and land you in yet another unwise marriage."

Opening her mouth to defend her feelings — even if she didn't quite know what those feelings were — Maria drew in a breath, then shut her mouth, her words unspoken. Perhaps Jane was right. She hadn't known Alan at all when she'd allowed him to seduce her and worm his way into her bed. Neither did she know very much about Mr. Granger, although at her innermost core she was certain he was not the cad Alan had been. Still, it would be prudent to wait, to learn more about Mr. Granger, both from him and from others, before allowing herself to even consider any sort of alliance.

Much as she regretted it, she must make Jane's advice about providing for herself and her child of paramount importance when deciding anything to do with her future. Mr. Granger would remain at the estate and Maria could not only observe his behavior, but could engage him in conversation and discover any potential prospects he might have. She wasn't ready to give up on the kind steward so soon. Especially not when he stirred her in a way no one had since she'd married William.

The carriage arrived back in front of Kersey Hall, and Jane and Maria preceded Mr. Granger into the entryway. As two footmen assisted them in removing their outer garments, Chambers hurried forward, a silver salver in his hands.

"My lady, my lady." He bowed to them both. "Mr. Granger, this arrived for you about a half hour ago. I would have sent it out to the dower house, but I wasn't sure how important it was."

Mr. Granger frowned as he gazed at the square of foolscap, folded and sealed, though the latter lay crooked across the paper. "It is from my younger sister. She has written the direction almost illegibly, which is not her usual way." A frown furrowed his brow as he popped the seal off, unfolded the missive and began to read. "I hope all is all right at home."

"Thank you, Chambers." Maria nodded to the butler. "John, Martin, that will be all." The footmen took her and Jane's outer wraps and left. "Please bring a pot of tea to the drawing room, Chambers." She wanted to get the servants out of the entry hall as quickly as possible, for Mr. Granger's face, though it had not so much as twitched as he read the letter, had grown alarmingly pale. "Mr. Granger, will you have some tea with Lady John and me?"

Jane shot her a glance and nodded.

"Mr. Granger." Fearing the worst, Maria carefully placed her hand on his arm. Anyone deserved comfort at a time of such great distress. "Has something happened?"

He looked up at that, his lips drawn into a thin line, his entire body taut as if steeled for a blow. "I beg your pardon, my lady, but I must leave at once."

"Leave?" Maria and Jane echoed the word at once.

"What has happened, Mr. Granger?" Maria gripped his arm, as much for his comfort as to steady herself for whatever blow must have fallen.

His countenance remained immobile, though his lips trembled slightly. "My sister writes that our elder brother with whom she resides has met with a terrible accident." Once more the crystal-blue eyes locked onto hers. "They fear the wound is mortal and . . ." Glancing away, he straightened his shoulders, regained his composure, and stepped away from Maria. "I take my leave of you, Lady Kersey. I regret that I must leave you with the work of the estates at such a time, but I dare not delay even an hour." He tore a slip from his sister's letter and scribbled words upon it. "If you are in dire need, write to me here, at my family home in Lavenham, Suffolk. I will try to advise you from there."

"Thank you, Mr. Granger." Maria raised her chin. She would ease his burden of leaving as best she could. "Do not worry about the estate. With my cousin's help, I can assume much of the day-to-day management. But I will write to you if the new Lord Kersey is found." She grasped his hand again, willing her warmth into his cold flesh. "I will pray each day for your brother's recovery."

With a nod to her and Jane, Mr. Granger withdrew his hand, turned on his heel, and strode back through the entry hall. A moment later the front door boomed and a sudden silence descended on Kersey Hall.

CHAPTER FOUR

The distance between Kersey Hall and Hugh's family's home, some two miles beyond the wool town of Lavenham, was not great. Still, he feared it would be too much to allow him to arrive at The Grange in time to bid his brother goodbye. Despite the gathering shadows of the late afternoon, he urged Galahad to greater speed, the melancholy refrain of "what on earth had happened to Christopher" running through his head.

His sister had written the barest minimum of words before sending the cryptic message, the words seared into his brain.

Hugh, Come home at once. Christopher has been shot. God alone knows if he will live. The doctor has been fetched. I need you now, Brother.

Arabella

Poor Bella. To have been home completely alone, save for the servants, when this tragedy occurred must have been devastating to her. For that, if for nothing else, he blamed himself. He'd been amenable for Bella to have a companion this year, to help dispel some of her painful shyness during the few social occasions she managed to attend. But Kit had insisted that their sister's lady's maid was perfectly capable of seeing her through any party without the need of another mouth to feed.

His brother acted as though their coffers were bare, although that was hardly the case. Hugh had gone over the books with The Grange's steward last quarter and it had been correct down to the last ha'penny. No money was missing and the crops had done well last year, despite the cold summer. This was cause for rejoicing, not for fighting. His first thought had been a hunting accident, which did happen out in the woods from time to time. Then the memory of Lord Kersey had sent Hugh down the pathway leading to a duel as the explanation for the injury. Still, what could have provoked a duel? Certainly not a woman, as had been his lordship's case. Kit had written a month or more ago that he was about to become betrothed to Margaret Westgate, daughter of a prosperous gentleman farmer, much as Kit was himself, but recently come to the neighborhood. He'd been taken with Miss Westgate more than a little, for his letters to Hugh had bordered on the boring as they recounted every moment he'd been in the lady's company. So a jealous husband couldn't be the problem. Had Kit offended someone? That seemed very odd behavior for his mild-mannered brother, but stranger things had happened. Perhaps someone had insulted Miss Westgate and Kit had taken it upon himself to defend her honor.

Hugh shook his head as he and Galahad flashed through the village of Lavenham. Only a couple more miles and his conjectures would be at an end. He leaned forward and spoke in Galahad's ear. "Come on, boy. Give me that last spurt of speed and you'll have oats enough and all the hay you could want."

The horse seemed to understand, for he miraculously picked up the pace to a gallop, leaving the half-timbered Tudor houses behind in a flurry of yellow and brown leaves. In what seemed like moments, they sailed through the stone gateposts, huge figures of wolfhounds guarding the entrance to the estate. Hugh pulled Galahad down to a canter as they neared the circular driveway, and to a trot as they turned onto the crushed gravel. Fred, the head groom, stood waiting for him.

"Praise God you're home, Mr. Granger." The stocky man had Galahad's bridle in his hands before the horse had quite stopped.

"Thank you, Fred." Hugh jumped down from the saddle, tossed the reins to the groom and took the steps two at a time. He came to a full stop at the front door, knowing he must enter, but dreading what he would find just inside. Clenching his jaw, he knocked.

The door jerked open revealing Littles, the family's usually unflappable butler, looking harried for the first time ever and much older than Hugh remembered, with lips drawn in and shoulders stooped.

"So good to have you home, Mr. Granger. Come with me, please. Miss Granger is waiting for you in your brother's bed-chamber." Littles moved quickly toward the stairs.

"Is my brother still alive?"

The butler stopped on the first step and turned toward Hugh. "He was when I came down to await you, sir." He closed his eyes and winced. "I cannot say if he yet lives."

Hugh bounded past the servant, taking the steps two at a time until he reached the landing on the first floor. He raced down the left-hand corridor to the suite of rooms at the far end where he stopped, a sudden dread settling over his heart. When he opened this door he might find his life had changed irrevocably. Grasping the door handle, the polished metal cold on his palm, Hugh sent up a prayer for his brother's life and opened the door.

It took a moment for his eyes to adjust to the dim interior. Someone had drawn the curtains but neglected to light more than one candle. The single flame sat high atop the chest-on-chest to the side of the massive four-poster bed, flickering in some unseen draft and casting lurid shadows throughout the room. In the middle of the bed lay Kit, eyes closed, a stark white bandage wound around his head and jaw.

Holding his breath, Hugh crept forward, trying to divine whether or not his brother still breathed. As he neared the foot of the tall bed, a low, keening sound rose from somewhere to his left.

Hunched over in one of the Queen Anne chairs, Arabella sat with her head pressed to the burgundy spread that covered Kit. Her dark hair had blended into the coverlet in the uncertain light, so he'd not noticed her at first.

"Bella."

With a gasp she darted up. "Kit?" She leaned over the prone figure, searching his face.

"No, Bella." Hugh strode around the bed. "It's me."

She jerked her head around, her face lighting up as recognition dawned. "Hugh!" Launching herself into his arms, she burst into tears. "Hugh. Oh, Hugh, I am so very glad to see you."

"Shhh. I came the very moment I received your letter." He moved her away from him and fished his handkerchief out of his pocket. "Here. Dry your eyes." Dread mounting, he turned his gaze toward the still figure that had not moved despite their sister's outburst. "Is he gone, then?"

Wiping the tears from her cheeks, Bella shook her head. "No. At least I don't think so. Look." She pointed to the covers over Kit's chest, rising ever so slightly, like a bellows that worked badly. "But Mr. Preston said he cannot live much longer." Her tears began again, flowing down her cheeks in shiny streams. "The wound is mortal."

"Dear God." Pulling his sister back to his chest, he wrapped his arms around her slim body, now shaking with grief. His own anguish burned like a roaring fire, sweeping through him until his chest tightened, ready to explode with unshed tears. The older brother he'd always adored lay dying and there was apparently nothing he could do to save him. He swallowed hard against the bile that crept up his throat, forcing it down, keeping the tears at bay. His sister needed him to be strong. He could not fail her in that. Clearing his throat, Hugh breathed deeply, steeling himself. "What happened?"

"Miss Westgate." Bella's sobs muffled her voice.

Hugh's breath caught. Had a duel indeed been the cause of his brother's demise? "What about Miss Westgate?"

Bella raised her head, mopping her streaming eyes with the already sodden handkerchief. "Yesterday morning, Kit rode over to visit the Westgates. He didn't tell me what he was about, but he was all smiles at breakfast. Quite excited. But he was always that way when he visited Margaret." She glanced at the still figure and sighed. "He absolutely adored her, you know? Whenever he came back from a visit he would talk about her for hours."

Hugh nodded. His brother's letters to him, infrequent though they were, had been filled with all kinds of little details about his visits to Miss Westgate.

"She must have known of his deep regard for her. I mean, she's not a stupid person, from what I know of her." Bella's voice had grown cold, making Hugh glance sharply at her.

"What do you mean?"

Frowning, Bella shook him off and stared into his face, her blue eyes rimmed in red and snapping with anger. "She must have known he loved her, Hugh. Anyone could see it. Kit could never mask his feelings about anything."

"Well, that is true enough." Hugh had always teased his brother that he wore his heart upon his sleeve. "So what did he do?"

"He asked her to marry him, of course."

An icy chill raced down Hugh's spine. "And?"

"She refused him." Anger twisted Bella's beautiful face, giving her a grotesque look, like the mythical Gorgon Medusa. Indeed, had Miss Westgate been present she might very well have been turned to stone. "She thanked him and told him, of course, that she understood the honor he bestowed upon her, but that sadly she must decline his offer." Bella's frown deepened even more. "Wretched girl."

"But surely Kit must know he should try again." He glanced at the form on the bed.

"I have been given to understand that a woman may refuse a proposal one day and accept one the next."

"Not Miss Westgate." Bella followed Hugh's gaze to their brother. "When he arrived back home, there was a huge commotion at the front door. I was practicing at the pianoforte but the great noise drew me down the stairs. Kit was shouting, Hugh. Shouting at the servants." She turned back to him, fixing her stare on his face. "Shouting at *Littles* to bring him a bottle of brandy."

Her words staggered him. In his lifetime, Hugh had never heard Kit raise his voice to anyone. That he would do so to his servants, and especially to the butler who had been his staunchest advocate Kit's whole life, was almost beyond belief. The fact that his brother had demanded spirits was also so much out of his normal character as to make Hugh believe Kit had lost his reason. "What happened then?"

"Littles went off to get the brandy and I was so amazed at the scene I'd just witnessed, I stumbled on the steps. He looked up at me and his eyes were so cold, Hugh." Bella hugged herself and shivered. "Then he snapped at me. 'What do you want?' I scarcely knew what to think. It was like a stranger stood before me. I asked what had happened and he told me Miss Westgate had refused his proposal. She said she had come to an understanding with Mr. Fairchild, although only her family had known of it. And she was sorry if his hopes had been raised, but she had tried subtly to make him understand her circumstances."

Hugh raised his gaze to his brother's still form. Poor Kit. Such a betrayal from a woman he'd convinced himself he loved must have been devastating.

"When Littles brought the brandy, Kit locked himself in the library for hours, drinking, I'm sure." Putting a hand over her eyes, Bella sobbed again. "I should have sent for you then, Hugh. You could have talked to him, one man to another. Made him see this was not the end of the world."

"That is not your fault, my dear. He was so distraught I doubt there would have been anything I could do to persuade him. . . ." Hugh frowned, the horrific truth of the situation finally dawning on him. "Dear God. He shot himself, didn't he?"

Nodding and crying, Bella covered her face with the handkerchief.

Dumbfounded, Hugh cringed at the very thought. How could his brother have done such a horrible thing? From childhood they had always gone to church. His brother must have known it was a mortal sin to take his own life. How could his despair have become so egregious? Hugh paced to the end of the bed and back, worries about Bella's future suddenly taking precedence over his grief for his brother.

If Kit actually died of such a wound, it could have profoundly disastrous effects on their sister, and on Hugh himself as well. The former Lord Kersey had confided in Hugh, not long after he'd come to work for the gentleman, that a friend of his, Lord Ainsworth, had hanged himself after losing twenty thousand pounds gaming. Contrary to the usual leniency in such appalling deaths, instead of giving a verdict of lunacy or melancholia, the courts had ruled his demise a true suicide — *felo-de-se* — and the family had, by law, forfeited all their property to the Crown.

Hugh stared at his brother, a chill running through his body. Surely the circumstances of Kit's desperate act would be seen as the work of an unhinged mind. If not, he and Bella stood to lose not only their brother, but their entire way of life. Their home and stables, the money set aside for Bella's dowry, the modest but precious family jewels, indeed all manner of income save

Hugh's salary at Kersey Hall would be taken from them. And there was little Hugh could do to mitigate the circumstances. "Where is Mr. Preston?"

"He was called to the home of a woman in town who has terrible pains in her head."

Hugh needed to speak with the man, the surgeon who served Lavenham and its environs, as soon as possible. "I'll have Littles send to him immediately. I want him to tell me everything about Kit's wound. Perhaps there is some indication that it was an accident."

Shaking her head, Bella picked up her blue shawl that had slipped to the floor beside her chair. "Mr. Preston said Kit had placed the pistol to his head, here" — she indicated her right temple — "and held it there for quite some time. There was a little round indentation there." She drew a shuddering breath. "But Mr. Preston thinks at the last moment the pistol slipped and that's why the bullet entered at his jaw. That's why he lives still. But . . ." Her voice dropped to a whisper. "There was so much blood, Hugh. I ordered the footmen to roll up the carpet and burn it."

"Come here." He opened his arms and she fled to them, her tears drenching his shirt once more. "Shhh. Don't think about it. We will weather this." He stared over her head at their brother. Pray God they could weather it if the worst came to pass.

"Bella. Look at me."

She tilted her head back and raised her eyebrows.

"When did you last eat?"

"I'm not hungry, Hugh." She shrugged away from him.

"You need to eat all the same. If you wish to stay with Kit, you will need to keep your strength up." He was heartened to see the familiar stubborn frown appear on his sister's face. "We can take turns sitting with him, and when we cannot, I'll have one of the footmen here. I promise you, he won't be alone for a moment."

"Oh, very well." She pulled the shawl up over her shoulders. "Come dine with me?"

"Presently. I'll send to Cook to have dinner ready in an hour. Go change and I will meet you in the dining room."

With a look back at Kit, she squeezed Hugh's hand and left.

Hugh strode quickly to the chamber always kept for him in the house. He went directly to the writing table on which always sat a decanter and glasses. With a less than steady hand, he poured a good two-thirds of a tumbler and gulped it down. The long, slow burn of the brandy steadied him and his mind began to tick off what had to be done.

Send for Mr. Preston. Hugh needed to know every possible detail about his brother's injury and what they could expect and when.

Write to the family solicitor and apprise him of his brother's condition. Had Kit made a will? If not, what did that mean for Hugh and Bella? It was always best to know as much as possible in order to prepare for every eventuality.

And he must write to Lady Kersey, informing her that he would not be returning to Kersey Hall. The thought gave him a twinge of pain, for he'd have liked to have seen the lady once more. Not that anything would have come of his growing regard for her. Still, he regretted losing that tenuous connection he'd experienced with her in the garden this afternoon. God, had it just been this afternoon?

He took another sip of the spirits as his conscience smote him. What would she do now without a steward? If the heir continued to be elusive, she might tarry at Kersey Hall for a year or more. She'd need someone who could carry on the work of the primary estate as well as oversee the other properties that belonged to the earldom. Could he abandon her so completely without a backward glance?

Perhaps he could arrange to help her hire someone to replace him. Yes, that would be best. He could ride to the Hall for a day or two to help interview prospective stewards. Between Bella and the servants Kit would be well taken care of and if he did succumb to his wounds, Hugh would only be an hour or two away. If he died . . .

Hugh set his empty glass on the desk and scrubbed at his face with both hands. What was he thinking? If Kit died and the local magistrate did not rule his death due to "melancholy" or "lunacy," he and Bella would be turned out of The Grange with nothing and no place to go. No, Hugh must keep his position at Kersey Hall at all costs. It provided a house and a salary that, with strict budgeting, could supply all their needs. And he would not have to burden Lady Kersey with the task of finding his replacement. He drew a deep breath and some of the gloom that had swirled around his head lifted.

He would need to beg a leave of absence only, in order to set all the affairs here in order. When he took up residence at Kersey again, Bella could come with him, although he understood there would be a disagreement with that on her part. But given time, he could sort it all out. Even having settled that much in his mind lightened his spirits considerably.

And if the idea that he would still be able to see Lady Kersey engendered a large part of that rise to his spirits, he needn't admit that to anyone. Especially not to himself.

CHAPTER FIVE

Late November 1817

Wringing her hands, Maria sat tensely beside Jane on the soft leather seat of the carriage as it made its way slowly past dead grass and sodden leaves toward Kersey Hall, dread of the long-awaited meeting with the new Lord Kersey filling her heart.

A fortnight ago, Mr. Clarke had written her that his senior clerk had finally located and authenticated the claim to the earldom. A Mr. William Garrett, a gentleman owning substantial land in America, had been discovered, via birth records tracing the lineage back to a younger brother of Alan's great-grandfather, to be the late Lord Kersey's heir.

The month of November had thus begun extremely badly, for Mr. Clarke's letter had come just upon the heels of the dreadful announcement of the death of Princess Charlotte of Wales in childbed. Maria had resumed her black mourning clothes and wept for two days, partly for the loss of the princess, who was everyone's darling, but partly because her own future was now to be decided by an absolute stranger and she was as helpless in one tragedy as in the other.

A wave of superstitious fear had consumed her and she'd written hasty letters to her friends, formerly of The Widows' Club — Charlotte, Elizabeth, and Fanny — to assure herself of their continued health after the births of their children in July. Jane had told her she was being foolish, but Maria could not throw off the unsettling feeling of impending doom and had sent the letters anyway. All had replied with glowing reports of the health of themselves and their children and had kindly asked after her own. Still, the feeling of alarm had continued to press upon her until now she trembled as if the carriage took her toward a gallows.

"Stop fidgeting, my dear. I tell you, it will be all right." Jane patted Maria's hands, then cringed as the wind whipped the rain against the glass pane, beating at it in blustery gusts. "I cannot imagine that Lord Kersey will dismiss you out of hand. Surely he will take your circumstances into consideration." She turned back to Maria. "The fact that you have already removed to the dower house amply demonstrates your willingness to be both reasonable and practical."

Upon receipt of Mr. Clarke's letter, Maria had made the bold choice of moving her small household to the newly refurbished dower house. She, Jane, the baby, her lady's maid, an undercook and a footman, hastily elevated to cook and butler, had settled into Francis House, named for the first Dowager Countess Kersey's family, with amazingly little fuss. Some intuition had told Maria she should not be in residence when Lord and Lady Kersey took possession of the estate. Therefore, last week she and Jane had solemnly watched the stream of carts and carriages conveying the new earl's belongings along the main road to the house from the cozy drawing room that faced the driveway. And yesterday she'd received an invitation to tea at Kersey Hall, expected perhaps, but daunting still.

"But are people really swayed by such things, Jane?" When money was involved they often seemed to care about little else. "From what I have gathered from my inquiries to Mr. Clarke and Mr. Granger, Lord Kersey is under no obligation to offer me anything."

Jane's brows rose to an alarming height. "You wrote to Mr. Granger?"

"I did." Maria sat back on the sofa, raising her chin defiantly at her cousin. "I have been in contact with him regarding the running of the estate ever since he left. You knew that. And once Mr. Clarke told me the heir had been found, I of course passed this information along to Mr. Granger as well." She cast her gaze down to her hands clenched in her lap. "And I might have asked his advice as to whether he knew if I was in any way entitled to live at the dower house."

"But you know you do not have a right to it unless the current lord agrees."

"Yes, I know that, but it hurt nothing to inquire. Mr. Granger knows practically everything about the Kersey estate." Maria risked a glance at Jane and regretted it instantly. Her cousin had narrowed her eyes and now glared at her through the slitted lids. "I thought he might have known of some family tradition that would make it a precedent."

"I see."

Hopefully, Jane did not see. Maria had relished the correspondence she'd been able to exchange with the steward these last six weeks. His brother had continued to linger,

91

still unable to either succumb to or recover from his wound. Mr. Granger had promised that as soon as the new earl arrived, he would make arrangements for his brother's care and return to Kersey Hall. That promise had become Maria's one shining hope in the fog of despair she often found herself in these days. With Lord Kersey's appearance here today, she could at least look forward to Mr. Granger's arrival in the very near future.

Why she should do so, she refused to dwell upon. Their encounter at the fountain, the last day Mr. Granger had been in residence, was seared into her memory. That touch of his hand . . . She refused to think of it now, although she'd done so often in the dark nights since his departure. A foolish thing perhaps. But perhaps not.

"We are here." Jane's voice brought Maria out of her reverie regarding Mr. Granger. Shaking off the longing she couldn't quite deny, Maria looked out at the familiar entrance to the house that had until recently been her home.

As the carriage slowed to a halt, Maria drew in a deep breath and looked at Jane. "Are you ready?"

Her cousin nodded. "Are you?"

"I had better be."

Two footmen with umbrellas scurried to convey them to the house. Maria greeted Chambers, who smiled and bowed. "Lady Kersey, Lady John. I'm so pleased to see you again, ladies. The family is gathered in the drawing room."

"Thank you, Chambers." Maria smiled at the butler and they started down the corridor toward the staircase. "Have Lord and Lady Kersey had any trouble settling into the house?"

"There was a bit of confusion about which rooms were to be designated for which of their two sons, my lady. The heir, Lord Wetherby, wished to be placed in the chamber that overlooks the garden, although I informed his lordship that the heir has, in past generations, been housed in the chamber closest to the master's suite of rooms." The elderly servant shook his head as they approached the top of the stairs. "That room, as you know, overlooks the woods."

"And did Lord Kersey instruct his son to follow the tradition?" Jane cut her eyes at Maria, who smothered a smile.

"No, my lady, he did not." The disapproval in Chambers's voice rang loud and clear. "His lordship said he didn't care which room Lord Wetherby chose, he must come to an accord with his younger brother as to how the rooms would be apportioned." The butler's countenance stiffened. "After that pronouncement there ensued quite a row between Lord Wetherby and his brother over possession of the green room."

Jane leaned over to whisper in Maria's ear. "It sounds as if the new earl has two rather unruly children. One can only hope they will be sent off to school *post haste.*"

Maria smothered a giggle, then sobered as they approached the drawing room. Arranging her face into serene lines with a pleasant smile on her lips, she took a deep breath and walked confidently into the room.

The sea of unfamiliar faces froze Maria just inside the room. She'd been expecting only Lord and Lady Kersey, but here were three additional gentlemen she did not . . . She sucked in a breath as her gaze met that of the third gentleman — the deep, brilliant blue of Mr. Granger's eyes.

The pressure of Jane's hand on her arm propelled her farther into the room, her befuddled mind unable to register anything other than Mr. Granger's presence and the wild thought that he was more handsome than before he'd left. But what was he doing here? Of course, she'd written him about Lord Kersey's appearance, but somehow she'd believed he'd let her know that he had returned to Kersey Hall. Then she wouldn't have been so shocked to see him.

Mr. Granger stepped forward, a warm smile on his lips. "Lady Kersey, Lady John, so nice to see you once more." He bowed, then turned to the imposing silver-haired gentleman and willowy lady just behind him. "Lady Kersey, Lord Kersey, may I introduce Maria, the Dowager Lady Kersey and her cousin, Lady John Tarkington?"

Startled anew to be called the dowager countess, Maria dipped a curtsey then raised her face to meet the new owners of Kersey Hall. Lord Kersey had some little resemblance to Alan, his height mostly and the almost sharp, pinched look of his nose. Otherwise, his countenance was rather pleasing, with blue eyes and a pleasant smile. His wife, too, smiled broadly as she stepped forward.

"Lady Kersey and Lady John, the new earl and countess, Lord and Lady Kersey." Mr. Granger bowed and stepped back, but his gaze remained on Maria's face.

"So lovely to meet you, my lady." The countess curtsied, then turned to Jane. "My lady."

Lord Kersey stepped forward and gave a clipped bow. He still smiled at them, although it did not quite reach his eyes. "We

95

have been looking forward to making your acquaintance for some time, ladies. Mr. Clarke has given me all the particulars of the situation with the previous Lord Kersey. May I extend our condolences to you, Lady Kersey?"

"Thank you, my lord." Something in the man's intent stare made Maria uncomfortable and she dropped her gaze. "You are most kind."

After a short, awkward pause, Lady Kersey spoke hastily. "Lady Kersey, Lady John, may I present our sons, Anthony, Lord Wetherby, and James? They are both recently returned from our former home in Virginia."

Both young men smiled and bowed, the elder coming forward slightly to stand in front of Maria. "Delighted to meet you, my lady." He smiled, showing white, even teeth, and a whiff of bergamot wafted over Maria, making her mouth dry instantly. Lord Wetherby's cologne brought Alan instantly to mind, and suddenly highlighted the keen resemblance this young man bore to her late husband. The same curly, golden hair, same height, same deep blue eyes that assessed her with a cool admiration. A chill raced down her spine and she drew her silk shawl more firmly around her shoulders.

"So pleased to meet you." Thankfully, James Garrett seemed to take his looks from his mother, being somewhat shorter than his brother, with light brown hair and eyes and a short, upturned nose.

"Thank you, Mr. Garrett." She smiled at the young man. "I am somewhat over-whelmed meeting so many new people. I have been quite the recluse since April."

"How stupid of me. You must be confused with all the new faces. Please." He indicated a seat on the sofa.

"Thank you." Gratefully, Maria sank onto the cushion and glanced about the room.

Jane still stood, speaking to Lord and Lady Kersey about her late husband, Tark. Mr. Garrett had taken a chair across from her and seemed ready to make polite con-versation. His brother stood over by the fireplace, taking in the whole scene with an appraising little smile on his lips. Pray God the man stayed there.

The sofa cushion beside her dipped and she turned to find Mr. Granger seated there. A wave of warmth rose from her neck to her forehead. He was turned out well, in a suit of steel gray that was excellently cut, although she quite preferred him in his rid-ing clothes. They gave him such a rugged, masculine air.

Lord, she must get hold of herself. Think of the man as an acquaintance, nothing more. "I did not know you had returned, Mr. Granger. Has your brother quite recovered from his injury?"

His lips hardened, but he spoke evenly. "I regret to say, no, my lady. My brother is much as he has been these many weeks. But with the arrival of Lord Kersey, I needed to return to this estate. I have made arrangements for my brother's care while I am absent and will be kept apprised of his condition." He paused, then his countenance lightened. "I have brought my sister to stay with me, however."

"I didn't know you had a sister." She actually had little knowledge of Mr. Granger's life outside the confines of his work on the estate.

"She is not quite out of the schoolroom yet, but under the circumstances I thought it best that she not be left at home now, even with a companion." His blue eyes had a distant look to them. "In case the worst occurs — and I do not see how my brother can cling to life much longer — I believe it best for her to be here with me, rather than alone with him and the servants."

"I am so sorry, Mr. Granger. Might I request the pleasure of meeting Miss Granger when it is convenient for you?" Maria glanced down at her hands, then back to him. "We are not so very far apart in years, she and I, and I have had some experience with grief."

The corners of his mouth rose just perceptively. "That would be an honor for her, my lady. When I have settled us into the house more completely, I will tell her of your wish to be introduced to her."

"Mr. Granger, what a pleasure to see you again." Jane lowered herself into the chair opposite Maria, smiling much too broadly at the steward. Such a facial expression never boded well for the recipient of it. "Does your return mean that —"

Maria grasped her cousin's hand and gave a slight shake of her head. "Mr. Granger's brother has not improved, my dear."

Jane immediately replaced her insincere smile with an expression of sympathy. "I am so sorry to hear that, Mr. Granger."

"You are very kind, Lady John."

Lord and Lady Kersey joined the little group. "Mr. Granger was just telling us the status of the tenant farmers." Lord Kersey helped seat his wife on the sofa beside their son, then proceeded to stand over all of the little group, save for Lord Wetherby, who continued to stand in front of the fireplace.

"The crops have come in well this year, thank goodness. The only bit of bad news being about Tate."

"Mr. Tate?" Maria sat up, sudden alarm bells ringing in her head. She'd been out to the farm to visit Mrs. Tate several times since Mr. Granger had told her of the father's injury and the family's plight. She could have sworn the man had been on the mend.

Mr. Granger's lips firmed. "I'm sorry to tell you, my lady, but Mr. Tate succumbed to his wound."

Maria's stomach dropped, a metallic taste flooding her mouth. "No." Tears pricked her eyes, but she blinked them back. She'd ridden out to check on the Tates almost every week since Mr. Granger had left. "He seemed to be doing so well."

"I stopped by the farm as we journeyed in yesterday. He had apparently died the day before. I inquired, but Mrs. Tate was too grief-stricken to be able to tell me much, other than her husband's leg had suddenly begun to pain him. He'd rubbed the spot where Mr. Lambert had set the bone, trying to ease it when he'd gasped and slumped in the chair."

"Well, I must say, the man has left me in the lurch," Lord Kersey interjected, a perturbed frown on his face. "At least he'd gotten his crops in. You are making inquiries, aren't you, Granger? When you told me yesterday I said we need to find a new tenant quickly, so he can move in before the weather turns."

In the midst of taking a handkerchief out of her reticule, Maria froze, then raised her gaze to the annoyed countenance of Lord Kersey. "You'll turn them out of their home? When the family is devastated by Mr. Tate's death?"

"Maria." Jane pressed her lips together and grasped her hand, giving it a hard squeeze.

The new earl's brows rose. "They should have been removed when the man was injured, once it was clear he'd never walk properly again. Mr. Granger should have seen to it then." Lord Kersey turned to her and his features relaxed. "He did tell me, however, that he was following your orders to let them remain on the farm. A charitable notion, my lady, but scarcely a practical one. Tenant farms must be run by able men or the estate will not survive."

"The Tates' current tenancy still has three years to run, my lord." Mr. Granger spoke up, with a glance at Maria. "I did suggest that Mrs. Tate could run the farm for the next few years until their oldest son will be of age to take it over."

Sending Mr. Granger a grateful glance, Maria wiped her eyes and raised her chin. The steward was an extraordinarily kind man.

"And I said at the time I preferred to have able-bodied men running my farms." Lord Kersey waved the suggestion away and glared at his steward. "You will see to it, won't you, Mr. Granger?"

"Of course, my lord. I will ride to Wickford tomorrow and post an advertisement. Word will spread fast enough that we should receive inquiries within the week." He glanced at Maria, his blue eyes apologetic. "With luck you should have a new tenant by Christmas."

Maria gasped, which brought another, harder squeeze of her hand from Jane. If these attempts to silence her continued, her hand would be sore as the dickens tomorrow.

"Splendid." Lord Kersey was suddenly all smiles. "I expect this Christmas to be one of the merriest my family and I have ever celebrated."

"What will you do, my lord?" Jane smiled brilliantly at the earl. "My husband's family usually gathers to attend church followed by an enormous Christmas dinner."

"We have spent the last few years in Virginia." The countess spoke up for the first time. "The celebrations there were much different than here."

"Much different." Lord Kersey rejoined the conversation, coming to stand beside the sofa. "We were often invited to attend house parties where there was hunting during the day and dancing and gambling in the evenings."

"And an excellent table set the entire time." Lord Wetherby sauntered toward them. "Mr. Morgan at Heart's Ease in Chesterfield always served suckling pig along with roast goose and a delectable cornbread stuffing to which his cook added oysters from the Chesapeake Bay." He eyed Maria. "I can almost taste it now."

Lord Kersey glanced around at the little gathering, his gaze coming to rest on Maria. "This year, in our new home, I propose a similar house party to celebrate the season of goodwill. The invitations will be sent out this week and our guests should arrive around the twentieth of December and remain with us through the New Year."

"Excellent, Father." Mr. Garrett nodded vigorously.

"What a splendid plan, my dear." Lady

Kersey's face lit up. "I shall begin preparations immediately."

"Of course, we shall wish you to join us as well, Lady Kersey. Both you and your cousin will be most welcome to the gathering." His lordship's gaze seemed to burn into Maria's face, as if daring her to refuse.

"That is most kind of you, my lord." Almost biting her tongue at the words, Maria smiled back at him. After the way he proposed to treat the poor Tates, the last thing she wanted to do was take part in some extravagant party with Lord Kersey posing as the beneficent host. However, with her own position almost as precarious as Mrs. Tate's, she could ill afford to risk the enmity of the man who could turn her out as quickly as he did his tenants.

"Yes, very kind indeed, Lord Kersey." Jane nodded her agreement, beaming at the Kerseys. Maria would have to speak to her as soon as they returned to the dower house. Perhaps some illness might be arranged to befall them just as the house party was beginning.

The door opened, admitting the butler carrying the silver tea service.

"Ah, thank you, Chambers." Lady Kersey nodded to the small table in front of her and the servant put the tray down before

104

her. "That will be all." After the man had left, she looked brightly at Maria and Jane. "And how do you take your tea, ladies? There is nothing like a good cup of tea on a chilly day to raise the spirits, don't you think?"

Alone in her chamber at last, Margery, the new Countess of Kersey, sat before the mirror perched on her toilette table, dragging her new silver-backed brush through her dark hair, her arms heavy with exhaustion. If these last weeks were any indication of what she must do to take her place as the lady of Kersey Hall, she would need an additional lady's maid at least to help prepare her for this new role.

The past three months had been a whirlwind that had swept up her family and plunked them down in a strange new world. Her husband, William, had had no idea he'd been in line for the earldom. Their lives had been lived largely in Virginia, in relaxed and gracious if somewhat primitive surroundings. Two years ago they'd returned to England for her father's funeral, to dispose of a parcel of land she'd been left in his will, and enjoy the delights of the London Season before returning to their home in Dinwiddie. The prospect of returning to that life, however, had been irrevocably thwarted when Mr. Clarke had contacted them regarding her husband's lineage.

The brush slipped from her fingers and Margery banged it on the table. Her shoulders sagged. She so longed to return to their sprawling, white clapboard house, Garland, along the banks of the James River in Virginia. Kersey Hall was at least three times the size, with three or maybe even four times the servants. Margery shuddered. She disliked intensely to meet new people, even servants. Their arrival here in Suffolk had proved a nightmare for her, although William and their sons had taken to their new roles in the lap of luxury with shocking ease.

Anthony had garnered quite a reputation as a rake since his father's elevation to the peerage, something she worried about constantly. A young gentleman should sow his wild oats, but Anthony's behavior of late had become excessive. She'd have William speak to him once more, now they were somewhat settled here. James had always been quieter in his tastes, thank goodness, and that had not changed. William had actually begun to consider allowing both sons to take over the Kersey townhouse in London next Season, while he hired the most fashionable address he could find in the most prestigious neighborhood for him and her. She already dreaded the hectic pace she would have to adhere to, and it was at least six months in the future. Her life in Virginia, once so common and ordinary, she now deemed a paradise.

The door to her chamber opened.

"I am already in my gown, Mason." The new maid had begun to make it a habit to check one last time before going to bed, to see if Margery required anything. Usually, as now, there was nothing to do. "You may go."

"I will pass the message along, Lady Kersey, when I see her again." William chuckled as he closed the door.

Margery whirled around and started up. "Oh, I'm sorry. I didn't know you'd be coming to me tonight." In keeping with an apparent longstanding and awkwardly strict Kersey family tradition, the earl and countess slept in separate chambers unless the lord sought an amorous visit. Usually Margery welcomed such attentions from William. Theirs had been an arranged marriage, true; however, over the past twenty-five years they had developed a fondness for one another. Whenever he'd come to bed, a dark green banyan covering his tall frame and a matching nightcap with the tip swinging jauntily over his shoulder, as now, she'd enjoyed his attention thoroughly. Tonight, however . . . tonight she really must plead a headache. If not, she would be so weary she would likely be performing her duties while sound asleep.

William waved her back in her seat. "After our little tea party I thought it best we were of one mind regarding the Dowager Lady Kersey and Anthony."

Lowering herself back onto her chair, Margery cocked her head. "The dowager and Anthony? What on earth do you mean?"

"I didn't think you saw his interest in her this afternoon." William paced over to the high bed and leaned back against it, arms crossed. "You really must pay more attention to what goes on around you now, my dear. Social interactions are everything. A good hostess is always aware of everything happening at her entertainments." He frowned and rubbed the back of his neck. "Anthony did not bother to hide his interest in the dowager. And I can see why he would be interested. She's young, pretty, with a frailty that is becoming in a woman." Her husband eyed her, and smiled. "I can certainly understand that. But now that he is heir to an earldom, we need to look much higher for his bride. Little Maria is totally unacceptable as a prospective wife for him."

"But she seems so sweet, William." Margery had been very taken with the young widow, whose doubly tragic circumstances she'd been apprised of before they'd left London to come to Suffolk. "If she returns his interest I see no reason why they should not marry. She could exert a much needed steadying influence on Anthony."

Her husband waved that argument away as if shooing a fly. "You really must think more in terms of the overall, my dear. Anthony will someday be the Earl of Kersey. As such, he should choose a bride who will bring in a sizeable dowry to help expand the family coffers. The dowager countess, from everything I learned from Mr. Clarke, is a veritable pauper."

"She is?" Margery cocked her head from side to side. "But how can that be? She must have had settlements drawn up when she married the last earl."

"They eloped, my dear." William's grin spread across his face as if someone had handed him a present. "No settlements, no jointure. The lady lives in Francis House solely because I allow her to. Until now she's been drawing money from the estate for her living expenses, but that will have to stop." Tapping his chin with his forefinger, he wandered toward the blazing fireplace. "Yes, she really must be turned out as soon as possible."

"But, William, surely that is not necessary?" Alarmed, Margery rose and hurried toward her husband. She'd hoped she might find a much needed friend in Maria. "Her upkeep cannot be more than a pittance given the wealth of the Kersey estate."

"Oh, her expenses are not the reason she will be turned out." He looked down at her, eyebrows raised in that supercilious way he had that always made her feel stupid. "Anthony's interest in her, my dear. We cannot have her forever tempting him."

"If you warn our son she is not an acceptable bride, he will abide by your decision." Anthony had always obeyed his father, albeit more reluctantly of late. Their elevation in status had made him even more arrogant toward everyone, as if he truly could do whatever he pleased without repercussions.

"Oh, I have no doubt about that. Anthony is nothing if not shrewd about a business deal. No, I don't fear that he will marry her." William scowled, his lips in a twisted snarl. "I fear he will seduce her. He's never had any scruples about who occupied his bed. The more the merrier has been his motto since he was sixteen."

Margery bit her lip, but could say nothing. It was not a charge she could deny. "I understand that, but she is a widow, although not yet quite out of mourning." She shrugged. Hers was not the place to censure what a woman did for her own pleasure. "Still, if she is a willing partner, what would be the harm?"

"Every harm in the world, Margery, if she began to increase." He blew out his breath contemptuously. "Anthony's string of bastards is long enough as it is. Those girls were bought off with trinkets. This one he would have to marry. And our hopes for a strategic marriage would be crushed to dust. No," he said, shaking his head and turning away. "She will go and soon. The question is, should it be before or after the Christmas party? I am afraid news of her dismissal might put a damper on the festivities, but every day she stays she is a temptation for our son."

"Not necessarily, my dear." If Margery had learned anything in her twenty-five years of marriage to this man, it was how to reason with him. "It's not as if the dowager countess were staying under our roof and therefore would be a constant enticement. Anthony might very well not see her again until the party. You know he cannot seek her out nor visit her at the house without my presence. He's not a fool, you know."

"Perhaps." William stood at the door, gazing down at her, massaging his chin as he always did when mulling over something. "It might not become us in Society's eyes to turn her out on the eve of the season of Christian charity."

"I agree wholeheartedly, my dear." If Margery could keep Maria close by for even a short time, perhaps she could confide in her about William's concerns regarding Anthony. Once the widow was on her guard, surely she would avoid him at all costs, if it meant she could remain at Francis House. And in the meantime, Margery could subtly suggest to James that the dowager countess might be a good match for him. If he married Maria, not only would he have gained an excellent wife whom his brother would not dare touch, but she would have gained a daughter-in-law she could cherish as both kinswoman and friend. "I think it best to wait until after the Christmas party is over." Smiling into her husband's face, she took his hand and drew him toward the bed. She always caught more flies with honey. "One never knows what will happen in a new year."

CHAPTER SIX

The next afternoon Maria sat in the cozy downstairs drawing room, bouncing little Jane on her knee, making the baby laugh and coo as she blew bubbles and slobbered all down her chin.

"You will be quite unpresentable, darling, and Nurse will have to come and change you." Maria made a buzzing sound with her lips and the baby shrieked with laughter.

Little Jane had grown so much in the past six months, Maria could scarcely take it in. Her daughter could sit up unassisted, played incessantly with a particular doll she'd had since birth that was therefore quite grubby, and had begun to babble, repeating the "b" sound in short, staccato bursts, then switching to "m." She repeated that sound so often Maria had gotten quite excited several times, believing she'd actually spoken the word "Mama." False hope, but so exciting nevertheless.

The door opened.

"Come see what your namesake is doing now, Jane." Maria laughed as the baby stuck out her tongue and blew, making a sputtering sound that Maria found hysterically funny. She looked up to find Saunders, the butler, standing just inside the room, Mr. Granger in the doorway.

"Mr. Granger, my lady." The servant bowed swiftly, trying valiantly to maintain his decorum, then turned and fled past the steward, who had stepped inside.

"Mr. Granger." Grasping Jane in her arms, Maria struggled to look at his face. Of all people to appear when she was so disheveled, the steward was absolutely the last one she would have wanted. Her hair was straggling around her face where the baby had grabbed it. Her gown was rumpled from where Little Jane had bounced incessantly while they waited. She certainly didn't want to know what she looked like, although Mr. Granger must be getting an eyeful. "I didn't expect to see you here." She glanced around the room, but nothing came to mind save, "Won't you please take a seat?"

Again, the last thing she wanted with her appearance so ragged, but it was out now.

"I didn't mean to intrude, my lady." His

smile was genuinely kind. "I see you have your hands full."

"We are waiting for Lady John for tea. I thought to include the baby would be a welcome surprise."

At that moment little Jane let out a wail, pushing her legs against Maria's leg and leaning precariously as though she would launch herself backwards onto the floor.

"Oh, gracious." Maria tried to grasp her child, but the squirming infant was like so much quicksilver. Any moment she would likely wriggle out of Maria's grasp and fall headfirst onto the Persian carpet. Panic shot through her as her grip on Jane began to loosen.

"Here we go, Lady Jane." Mr. Granger stepped neatly in, seized the little girl around the waist, and carried her harmlessly to rest against his chest.

Wide-eyed, the baby stared at him, the surprise on her face turning Maria's fright into laughter.

"Thank you so much, Mr. Granger." Maria sagged with relief. She needed to find more time to spend with her daughter so she would become accustomed to handling her on her own. Her cousin had frowned on the suggestion, but Maria had stood up to her. She wanted to take care of her child as much as she possibly could.

"Not a'tall. I've always had a good hand with babies." He shifted Jane to his other shoulder, jogging her slightly. It must be working because her wailing and struggling had ceased. She seemed in awe of Mr. Granger. "I've had my share of taking over with them when I've visited tenants." He smiled and Jane burbled in delight. "They seem to like me."

"Well, this one does at least. Will you come to me, darling?" Maria held out her arms and the baby eagerly leaned out and put her arms around her mother's neck. "There we go." Bouncing the child slightly, to hopefully keep her contented, Maria turned her attention to Mr. Granger. "Is there something I can help you with, Mr. Granger?"

"No, my lady." Shifting from one foot to the other, he shook his head. "I came to tell you that I rode out to the Tates' farm this morning."

"Oh." Frowning, some of the joy went out of Maria's heart. Poor Mrs. Tate would be so distraught at having to move from their comfortable home at this time of the year. The weather had held off the past week or so, but when Maria had visited Kersey Hall yesterday she'd been chilled to the bone by the time they'd returned. "I am so sorry for her. How is she faring?"

"As well as can be expected. Timothy, the oldest boy, is trying his best to do as much as possible for his mother. He's only eleven years old, but hereabouts that's considered almost a man. With help he could possibly run the farm come the spring." Mr. Granger stared at her, then looked away. "If they are still there in the spring, that is."

Something in his glance gave her pause and she peered at him more closely. "But Lord Kersey ordered you to replace them with an able-bodied tenant."

"And I told him I would advertise the tenancy in Wickford." His deep blue eyes flashed with a wicked gleam. "However, everyone in Wickford knows that farm was leased to Jonathan Tate. I'll lay a wager with you, my lady, that no one in Wickford inquires about that property. And as I did not suggest sending an advertisement to London, or any other large town, I think it's fairly safe to say that Lord Kersey won't even think about the Tates until the new year." Mr. Granger's grin reminded her of her William's smile as a boy when he had been up to something. "When he finally realizes there have been no inquires, I can plead some confusion about the instructions. If I manage this correctly, young Tate and his mother will have the crops half in the ground by the time Lord Kersey is aware they are still on the farm. Hopefully, by then, we will be able to convince the earl that keeping the Tates on the land will be the best course of action."

Maria beamed at him. Such a truly kind man. One willing to risk his own position to see a wrong righted. If Lord Kersey found out about the subterfuge, he might very well sack Mr. Granger. The new earl had struck her as a gentleman who wanted things according to his orders and would let nothing stand in the way of his getting it. "Thank you, Mr. Granger. From the bottom of my heart."

Despite the intuition that it was a mistake, Maria allowed her eyes to meet his, and fell headlong into the unfathomable blue depths. She clutched Jane closer to her, as if the baby could help keep her steady.

Intense to the point it excluded everything else, his gaze captured her, held her as tightly as he had her child. If they stood any closer he'd be able to hear the hammering of her heart. A yearning she'd not felt since William had left with the army that long-ago morning assailed her now. A longing for a man's arms to hold her tight. For this man's arms to keep her safe from every hurt the world could throw at her.

As if coming up out of a chilly pond, Maria gasped and stepped back, clutching Jane to her so hard the baby squawked in protest.

"Not at all, my lady. I am glad to give the Tates a chance to remain in their home." Mr. Granger now turned toward the window, seemingly absorbed in the blustery day.

"Good afternoon, Mr. Granger."

Both Maria and the steward jumped as Jane's words made her presence known. How long had she been standing in the room? From the narrowed eyes she turned on Maria, she'd witnessed more than Maria cared to have to explain to her cousin.

"Good afternoon, Lady John." He bowed to Jane and his face assumed a pleasant mask. "I had merely come by to inform Lady Kersey about the fate of the Tate family. She's taken an interest in them since the autumn, you see, and I thought she'd like to know that they have been informed of Lord Kersey's decision to change the tenancy."

"Very thoughtful of you, Mr. Granger." Jane's face was pleasant, but her voice held just enough frost to let Maria know that they would be discussing Mr. Granger's visit in detail and for some time to come. "I am certain my cousin is grateful for the most current news about the Kersey tenants."

"Indeed I am, Cousin." Maria jumped to the steward's defense. Jane could give all the looks she liked. She was still grateful for Mr. Granger's intervention on the behalf of the Tates. "I believe I told you that Mrs. Tate had become my special cause?"

Brows raised to a painful height, Jane marched to the sofa and sat. "Perhaps you did mention something about Mrs. Tate." She held out her arms for her namesake. "Do sit down and have tea with us, Mr. Granger. I am certain you can regale us with fascinating tales of all of the tenants."

Maria handed the baby over to her cousin and sighed. Jane was a dear, but she had her own notions about what was and was not correct behavior for Maria. But this time, if it saved the Widow Tate, Maria was going to have a say in things.

"Thank you, Lady John, but I have some business I must attend to that will not wait. I just stopped in to give Lady Kersey word." He turned to Maria. "I will keep you informed, my lady."

"Thank you, Mr. Granger." *Godspeed,* she added silently. "Please do let me know if there are any further developments."

"My lady, my lady." With an elegant bow, he left.

Before Jane could utter a word, Maria rose and rang the bell.

The door opened almost immediately. The butler had obviously been hovering about.

"Tea, please, Saunders."

"Yes, my lady."

When he had gone, Maria strolled back to the sofa and gingerly lowered herself onto it, steeling herself for the blast.

"What do you call yourself doing, Maria Kersey?" Jane hissed, apparently in deference to the baby who was going to sleep in her arms. "Making sheep's eyes at Mr. Granger."

"I was doing no such thing." Oh, goodness. Jane had entered well before Maria had been aware of her presence.

"Do not tell me what I did and did not see. I hesitate to think what kind of scene I would have come upon five minutes later."

Maria had to draw a deep breath to keep herself from denying what her cousin had so obviously witnessed. "I cannot help it if I like the gentleman, Jane. Hearts cannot be ruled."

"As your current circumstances show very clearly." Her cousin shook her head and pressed a kiss to the sleeping baby's cheek.

"I do not see anything wrong with Mr. Granger as a person, my dear. He is a gentleman and very kind and rather handsome into the bargain. But you must always keep this little one in the front of your mind, Maria." She lifted the child in her arms, rocking her gently. "You don't have yourself alone to think of this time. You must do what is best for little Jane."

Maria sighed again, deeper and more heartfelt. Her cousin was right, of course. She could not ally herself with a gentleman who could not provide well for her and her daughter. No matter how relentlessly she was drawn to him.

"This just arrived for you, my lord." Chambers offered the Earl of Kersey a silver salver with a single letter upon it.

Lord Kersey looked up from a book on Nash's architecture, a glass of brandy half full in his hand. He plucked it from the tray and waved a hand of dismissal in the direction of the butler. God, it felt good to have servants to wait upon one hand and foot, as the saying went. He had adjusted to his new life with astonishing speed, although Margery had not taken to being the Countess of Kersey as well as she might. He shrugged and looked at the letter. She'd come around eventually.

Franked in London and sealed with a blob of black wax. The seal was unfamiliar . . . Kersey cocked his head to and fro. He'd seen this seal before, but where? Pausing before he ripped it off, the peculiar-looking crest caught his attention. Three stars pierced by a lance or spear . . . Clarke! It was from the family solicitor, by Jove.

Kersey relaxed back in the chair and popped the seal. He'd met with Mr. Hezekiah Clarke in London some months ago about assuming the Kersey title and estates and had thought that meeting sufficient to get everything in order. Apparently not. He unfolded the letter, winced at the sight of the spidery handwriting, and began to read.

Dear Lord Kersey,

I regret to have to inform you of a piece of gross negligence that has befallen your family's account with Grimes and Clarke, Solicitors. The incident has only just been uncovered by the office, and the clerk responsible has been dealt with.

In order to rectify the situation, I will take care of the matter personally. I plan to arrive at Kersey Hall on Monday, November 24th, with all the necessary documents. If three o'clock is convenient, my lord, I will see you and the Dowager Countess of Kersey at that appointed time.

Yr ob't servant,
Hezekiah Clarke

Kersey cocked his head. Why on earth did the solicitor want to meet with the dowager countess? Had they uncovered an unknown legacy left her by one of the lady's kinsmen? Did the woman indeed have money? He tapped the letter against his hand. Best to see the lay of the land before involving the lady in something that might amount to nothing more than a paltry bequest of pin money.

And something niggled in the back of his mind, urging him to discover what this "gross negligence" was and how it affected him and his family before telling Maria about it. He'd meet with Mr. Clarke alone. If the findings warranted it, he'd have the dowager countess fetched from Francis House, and not a moment before.

CHAPTER SEVEN

Cold November rain sheeted down the windowpane in the downstairs receiving room, the flickering light of the candles casting awkward shadows in the somewhat gloomy room. Lord Kersey raised a cut-crystal glass of Madeira, a prickle of anxiety brushing the hairs at the nape of his neck. Ever since Mr. Clarke's letter arrived, he'd brooded about what the "gross negligence" might have been. Surely nothing he need be overly concerned about.

However, if the matter had been important enough to bring the wizened little Clarke — who could be no younger than seventy years old at the least — out in such wretched weather on a two-day journey, something had to be seriously amiss. Kersey swallowed the last of his wine and allowed the sweetness to soothe him, recalling happy times in Virginia. Whatever the situation with Clarke turned out to be, it could do nothing to upset his elevation to earl. Of that he was certain. Mr. Clarke had confirmed it with him when they met in October. There really was nothing to get upset about.

And yet Kersey's foreboding had grabbed hold of him so firmly that when the mantel clock chimed three, he jumped as if the chimes were a pistol shot. He must get control of himself. He glanced at the sideboard. There was more Madeira there, but he didn't think that would help. He'd also instructed Chambers to supply him with a decanter of cognac, just in case he required stronger spirits. The brandy might steady him, but he didn't wish his senses impaired while listening to Mr. Clarke's revelation. If only he were through this cursed waiting. Where the devil was the man?

Unable to sit still a moment longer, Kersey rose and paced to the sideboard. He set his glass down and stared at the decanter filled with beautiful amber-colored brandy, licking his lips. Perhaps a small taste would calm him sufficiently. He reached for the bell-shaped bottle just as the door opened. He jerked his hand back, raised his chin, and strode forward as Chambers ushered in Mr. Clarke.

"Mr. Hezekiah Clarke, my lord." The butler bowed and withdrew, leaving Kersey to stare at the stooped little man, so thin it seemed he might have been blown to Kersey Hall by the gusting wind.

"Mr. Clarke, so good of you to come. Please have a seat, sir." Kersey indicated the cerulean-blue flowered sofa. "Would you like a drink?"

The little man settled himself on the cushions, his black leather case at his feet, and waved the offer away. "Thank you, no, my lord. I wish to have this business settled as quickly as possible. You cannot know how aggrieved it has made me ever since the negligence came to light. I have scarcely been able to eat or sleep." He stared balefully at Kersey, his eyes enormous behind the lenses of his small oval glasses. "This sort of carelessness has never been tolerated in the firm, as it could irreparably tarnish the otherwise spotless reputation my family worked hard to attain for the past one hundred years."

Truly alarmed now, Kersey sat on the sofa beside the solicitor, fine sweat popping out on his brow. "How serious is the situation, Mr. Clarke? And how the devil did it happen?"

"As to the seriousness of the matter, I will leave that to your estimation when I am done with the explanation." The solicitor's lips thinned to a sharp line. "How this state of affairs came to be is most decidedly due to the inattention of a very inept junior member of my firm who, I will tell you quite frankly, has been sacked with no reference whatsoever."

Kersey sat back, dread trickling coldly through his veins. Whatever had occurred was likely of some monumental consequence for Clarke to speak so disparagingly of his employee — or rather former employee. The decision to forgo the cognac had been a bad one. "What did the man do?"

"It is what he didn't do, my lord." Fishing in his capacious black bag, Mr. Clarke came up with a handful of papers, which he sorted through, muttering to himself as he laid each one aside. At last he plucked up a single sheet of foolscap, creased as if it had been a letter at one time, and refocused his attention on Kersey. "The foolish man in question did not think to put this letter into my hands, nor even to tell me of its existence until last week." His hand shook so that the paper created a slight breeze. "Instead, he filed it — or rather I should say misfiled it — in the folder with the papers for the Kaster estate, a minor client of ours who just last week made a new will.

Which action caused us to open that file and discover Jenkins had put the document intended for the Kersey file into that one by mistake."

Suddenly very curious about the paper Mr. Clarke held before him, Kersey squinted at it, trying to read the uppermost line, but the scrawling handwriting revealed nothing to him. Steeling himself against the catastrophic revelation he now knew would be forthcoming, Kersey swallowed hard and asked, "What was the document your clerk misfiled, may I ask?"

"The previous Lord Kersey's last will and testament."

The slight groan as all his breath left Kersey's lungs might have escaped Mr. Clarke's notice, but Kersey didn't think so from the man's startled expression. Still, it might be all right. No need to panic yet. It could be nothing more than a tempest in a cream pot. The previous earl might have done as Kersey had thought earlier and left his wife pin money or a favorite painting with sentimental value. "What does it say?"

Mr. Clarke blinked, as if coming out of a deep fog. "Where is the Dowager Lady Kersey, my lord?"

Trusting to his instincts, Kersey took a breath and let a lie rise smoothly to his lips.

"Still prostrate with grief over the death of her husband, I'm afraid, Mr. Clarke. She truly is in a very delicate state. The previous Lord Kersey was her second husband. The first one she lost scarcely two years ago in the Battle of Waterloo. The double tragedy has quite devastated her."

"I am so very sorry to hear that." The solicitor did look genuinely sorry for the dowager countess's bad luck with husbands.

"I told her of your intended visit, but she sends her regrets that she cannot receive visitors at this time." Donning what he hoped was a somber expression, Kersey shook his head. "Perhaps it would help if I could convey some of the information to her tomorrow." Now for the *coup de grace.* "If her husband left her something that might make her burden even a little easier to bear — a favorite chair of his, or the carriage that they courted in — I would be happy to pass the information along to her. It might lift her spirits so well she will leave her bedroom for the first time in months."

Mr. Clarke studied Kersey's face, then pursed his lips. "I am afraid that I cannot divulge that information to anyone but the dowager countess, my lord. You may, however, tell her that there is an inheritance for her and her daughter — one with which I believe she will be very pleased." The solicitor's gaze slid away from Kersey's. "I will write to her shortly with instructions regarding it."

Kersey froze, a deep-seated dread appearing from nowhere. Mr. Clarke's guarded manner made him wonder just how much of the earldom's holdings his predecessor had given away. Forcing himself to focus, Kersey cleared his throat. "Are you certain it's not a forgery?"

"One of the first things I investigated, my lord, I assure you. My firm may already be liable for misplacing this document. I did not wish to have the will contested on top of that." Clarke's voice rose an octave. "No, the witnesses have confirmed that this was the will of Alan, Lord Kersey, written on April 22nd, 1817. His lordship sent the will on to me in London and died later that day."

Kersey swallowed hard, then managed to ask calmly, "And you can give me no idea of what this inheritance will take from the earldom's assets?"

"Until I speak with the dowager countess, I am afraid not." Clarke hesitated, then nodded. "I can only say that there will be a significant change to the Kersey resources."

Dear God. Kersey sat back in stunned silence, trying not to show his anguish at this blow. A significant change. That could be anything from the unentailed jewelry to a minor property to one of the five major estates. Thank God Kersey Hall, the largest of the properties, was entailed and therefore safe. His mind whirled feverishly, calculating how much income might be lost to the little dowager countess. He'd pored over the account books as soon as he'd arrived at Kersey Hall, and been gratified to learn how prosperous the earldom was. Change that income by even a small percentage and he might barely be able to scrape by on this estate, much less live a stylish existence in the London townhouse. If indeed that terraced house in Mayfair was part of the entail. In time, the other entailed properties could be made to produce more, but it would be slow going. He and Margery might even have to remain here and eschew Society for the Season. He shuddered at the idea.

His companion's face drooped. "So you can see, my lord, why it will be somewhat more difficult to conduct this business through the mail. But as Grimes and Clarke are responsible for the original error, we will make every attempt to accommodate the dowager countess." Mr. Clarke stood and slipped the papers back into his black leather valise. "Please give the dowager our sincere condolences on the death of her husband once more and inform her that I shall write her as soon as I return to London. At some point, when she is ready, she must journey to London and sign several documents, including her own will."

"Of course." Kersey stood, looking down at Mr. Clarke, thinking furiously about how this catastrophe could be remedied. "I am certain she will be overjoyed to receive this news. Please let me know if there is anything else the earldom can do to facilitate matters."

"You are very good, Lord Kersey." Mr. Clarke grasped the handle to his case, which looked as if it outweighed the gentleman by several pounds, and strode to the door. "Please tell the dowager countess that if she has questions, and I suspect she will have many, she has only to write me."

"I will do that, sir, you have my word." Kersey managed to smile at the older man before the solicitor strode out into the corridor, where Chambers hovered about with Mr. Clarke's coat and scarf, ready to show the gentleman the way to his carriage. "Chambers, after you've assisted Mr. Clarke, please ask Lord Wetherby to attend me here as soon as possible."

"Certainly, my lord." Chambers helped Mr. Clarke with his coat and dark blue knitted scarf before escorting him out.

No sooner had the door closed, than Lord Kersey called to the butler. "Chambers! Bring Wetherby to me now."

Wide-eyed, the butler bowed, then hurried to the front staircase. He paused but a moment, perhaps to catch his breath, then shot straight up the steps.

Cursing low under his breath, Kersey headed back into the receiving room, making a straight line to the cognac. No need for restraint any longer. Disaster had arrived and must be met head-on. He poured a full tumbler then took a deep sip, allowing the mellow burn to trace its way down into his stomach where it created a glow that went some little way toward comforting him. He'd taken another long sip when Anthony rushed in, wearing only breeches and a stained shirt, looking as if he'd just risen from his bed. At three thirty in the afternoon, it was not beyond the realm of possibility.

"What the deuce has happened, Father?" His son yawned, rubbing his eyes with the heel of his palm. "Chambers insisted you needed me immediately." He looked about, a petulant grimace on his face. "I see no disaster to merit being dragged from my bed."

"You'll see it clearly enough presently." Kersey downed the rest of his drink and eyed the decanter. He'd like nothing more than to drain the cut-crystal bottle and make this entire nightmare go away, at least temporarily. At last, however, he set the glass down and turned to his offspring. "I have just been handed a piece of news that could ruin us, and I mean financially in the worst way. Unless we can agree on the one course of action that will save us."

Anthony scrubbed his hands over his face, eyed the decanter, and said thickly, "A hair of the dog wouldn't be amiss right now."

Shaking his head, Kersey poured a generous tot and handed it to his son. "I agree you're going to need this."

Glancing at his father through slitted eyes, Anthony knocked back the cognac with a practiced hand and wiped his mouth on his sleeve. "What's the matter?"

"Mr. Clarke, the solicitor, has just left, and to say he bore bad tidings is a gross understatement." Kersey plucked the empty glass from his son's fingers and set it carefully on the table. "His firm has discovered a last will and testament written by the previous Lord Kersey on the day he died."

Anthony blinked and his jaw tightened, then he relaxed. "How bad can that be? The lands and property are entailed. He cannot have given any of that to anyone else."

"True. But he could and did leave a bequest to his wife and daughter."

With a shrug, Anthony reached for the brandy. "And how much does that amount to?"

"Clarke wouldn't say anything except there would be a *significant* change to the Kersey resources."

The decanter slipped through Anthony's fingers and thumped loudly on the table. "Significant? How significant?"

"We don't know. But you now see our predicament a bit more clearly." Kersey grabbed the brandy and poured sizeable amounts into both their glasses. "There is a good deal of unentailed property thanks to the old earl, including estates, the London townhouse, art, jewelry, and I don't know what else. It sounds as though a substantial portion of it has been settled on the Dowager Lady Kersey. Unless we can do something to return it to the fold, so to speak."

Anthony glanced sharply at his father. "How would you propose to do that? Contest the will?"

"Unfortunately, that is not possible. Mr.

Clarke, blast his thorough heart, has authenticated it with the witnesses. It will undoubtedly stand up in an English court." Swirling the amber liquid, Kersey refrained from looking at his heir. Letting the suggestion come from his son, rather than as his own decree, would help ensure Anthony's wholehearted compliance with the only plan available to them.

"Damn." Anthony took a swallow of the cognac, the wheels of his mind almost visible as he sorted out their options. "Well, there is one thing we could do, although it would be quite distasteful, I'm afraid."

"Yes, I am sure it will be." Kersey relaxed. Praise God the boy was beginning to think like a Garrett. "Still, I don't believe the duty will be as unpleasant as it might be if the lady were less comely. She seems a pleasant armful at least."

His son stared at him as though he were mad. "What does her looks have to do with it?"

Kersey frowned. "Only that marrying a handsome woman would be more enticing than marrying a plain one."

"Marry her?" Anthony's shocked expression puzzled his father greatly.

"Of course. You will need to marry her to return our rightful property to the family's control." Kersey's brows dipped lower. "What did you think I meant?"

"That we need to kill her, of course."

"What?" The tumbler of brandy slipped from Kersey's hand and smashed to the floor, shards of glass and spirits spraying the expensive red and cream Aubusson carpet. "Are you mad?" He stepped away from the mess and grabbed Anthony's arm. "Don't let me hear you speak of such a thing ever again. Killing the woman is wrong, and even if it weren't, if you were caught you'd swing for it."

Anthony jerked his arm away. "I'm joking, of course. It's just that anything would be better than being saddled with a mousy little thing like her." He swallowed the last of his drink, then hurled the glass into the fireplace. Sparks flew as the dregs of the brandy blazed up. "Why can't you leave me out of it? Marry her to James instead. He'd probably jump at the chance to bed a woman regularly that he didn't have to pay for."

Appalled at his son's callous attitude — although they'd never been close, he'd not seen this sort of behavior in Anthony before — Kersey nevertheless tried to make him see reason. "James's marrying her won't do. It would bring the assets back to the family, but not to the Kersey estate. As he doesn't stand to inherit, unless something untoward befalls you, he'd be a fool to simply deed it back to the earldom. He'd more likely decide he'd be better off retaining the property to create his own little empire."

"I won't do it, Father. She'd be an agreeable tumble once or twice, nothing more. I'll not tie myself to her for all eternity." Anthony crossed his arms and leaned back, like a recalcitrant horse balking at a difficult jump.

"So keep her in the country and carouse to your heart's content in Town. You won't be the first gentleman to do such a thing for money." Kersey shook his head. He'd believed Anthony would have seen the necessity of this plan as quickly as he had. So now he needed an inducement to sweeten the pot. "Marry the girl and get her with child as quickly as you can. That may solve all your problems. Childbirth is a chancy thing. Look at what happened to Princess Charlotte, and she had the best doctors available." He turned away from his son, letting the words sink in, and raised the decanter. "Care for another drink?"

Silence echoed in the still chamber until his son's footfalls scuffed the parquet floor. "Fill the damn glass."

Repressing a smile, Kersey did exactly

that, then handed the almost dripping tumbler to Anthony. "I thought you would see reason. There's simply no other way to secure these assets."

"You don't even know what she stands to inherit. It could be next to nothing — something left to shame her, like all her husband's small clothes or the oldest horse in the stable. I might be throwing away my prospects for a collection of chamber pots."

"The solicitor said the change to our coffers would be significant. We cannot afford the risk."

Anthony took a substantial sip, then tipped the glass toward his father. "I'm telling you, a widow who's lost two husbands in such a short space of time must be out of her mind with grief. Easiest thing in the world for her to take poison, or walk out into a lake and drown herself." He glared at his father. "Trust me, no one would suspect a thing."

"Do you also intend to commit infanticide while you're disposing of the mother?" Exasperated by his son's bloodthirsty streak, Kersey poured himself another as well. "The solicitor said the will benefitted both mother and child. If something happened to the dowager, do you think for a moment you'd be able to get closer than a stone's throw from that baby? No." He inhaled the cognac's sweet fragrance. It seemed to have a calming effect on him. "Trust me on this, Anthony. Seduce the little widow — child's play for you, I'm sure."

His son shrugged, but a hint of a smile ghosted across his lips.

"Marry her, assume her inheritance, whatever it is, and then carry on with your life as you normally would. Your mother seems rather taken with the young widow. She can likely keep her entertained here at the Hall while you amuse yourself more handily elsewhere."

Scowling, Anthony took a long sip of the brandy. "I suppose I will have to do it, won't I?"

"You are the only one who can."

"It's rather difficult being the family savior."

"Yes." Kersey nodded. If such a title smoothed the young puppy's way to performing the deed, then let him think so. And God help the dowager if her inheritance proved to be inadequate. He might be hard pressed to restrain his son's more violent proclivities.

CHAPTER EIGHT

Early Tuesday morning, Maria came downstairs to find Jane already at breakfast, busily cracking a soft-boiled egg. She hit the shell a precise blow that neatly severed the slightly pointed top from the rest of the rotund body. Scooping out the tiny bit of egg, she topped it with a small pat of butter and popped it into her mouth, smiling as she savored the morsel. "Will you join me for eggs and toast, Cousin?"

"How did you know I was behind you?" Maria came forward into the room, her head cocked.

"You must blame Saunders, I assume." Jane discarded the empty sliver of shell onto her plate and began on the larger portion of egg. "He is so enamored with his elevation to butler he has taken to polishing the silverware once a week. This smooth strip around the teapot" — her cousin tapped it with a fingernail — "is as reflective as a mirror. I saw you quite distinctly as you came to the doorway."

"So I suppose you do not have eyes in the back of your head, although I for one would not lay a wager on it." Maria sat across from Jane and laid her napkin in her lap. "Another pot of tea, Saunders, with a boiled egg, toast, and jam."

"You know you could have your breakfast delivered to you in bed." Jane raised her head from the egg cup. "Although you are widowed, I am certain that much of an alteration can be claimed if you wish to laze about in the mornings."

"I could say the same thing to you, Cousin. You could take your rest as well until later in the day." Maria smiled with an archness to her voice.

"Indeed, I could. But I would then miss all the to-do which will likely break out at any moment."

"What do you mean, 'to-do'?" Anxious for some distraction, Maria grabbed a cold piece of Jane's toast and began to slather it with the creamy butter.

"It has been four whole days since we met the Kerseys." Sprinkling salt onto her bite of egg, Jane proceeded then to the pepper before eyeing her breakfast with pure joy. "I will wager that the earl will either send for you or put in an appearance himself so he can watch your face crumple when he tells you to pack your bags, he is throwing you out."

"Throwing us out?" The knife in Maria's hand hovered above the piece of bread, butter perched on the tip of the utensil. "He indicated no such thing the other day, Jane." She grabbed Jane's hand and squeezed. "Have you heard something?"

"Not a word. Really, Maria, unhand me." Her cousin pulled her hand from Maria's death grip and shook it. "My handwriting will never be the same. You will not recognize a letter from me when I finally have occasion to write you again. As it is, I must send to Kinellan once more, postponing my visit."

Jane gave her eggshell a final scrape and, finding nothing on the spoon, then set it on her plate. "I am promising him, however, on my oath of honor, that I will attend his party this Christmas. If you do not wish to be alone with just Saunders and Cook, you might ask to visit your parents. Surely they could make room for you and the baby for a short stay." Jane paused. "I seem to have come very far afield from the point I was making . . . Oh, yes, will Lord Kersey come by today to send you packing from Francis

House."

"Really, Jane, must you be so dramatic? The next time I see you, you will be on the stage in Drury Lane."

"If I'd had no prospects of a good marriage I might well have gone on the stage, despite its scandalous reputation." Folding her napkin precisely, Jane gave the linen a parting crease with her fingers. "I believe I would have had much more fun than I have had, even with Tark."

"Jane!" Maria's cheeks heated. Everyone knew that actresses were no better than they should be. To have her cousin admit that she would have indulged in . . . such doings with gentlemen other than her husband was quite shocking. Of course, Maria had found out her cousin had a wild streak she never would have guessed a year ago.

"Oh, I wouldn't do it now, mind you. Although I have managed my share of discreet liaisons since coming out of mourning." The far-off look in her cousin's eyes was accompanied by a totally sly smile. "One must protect one's reputation even in widowhood."

"Jane, for goodness' sake. You were speaking about Lord Kersey forcing me to leave."

"Oh, yes. Well" — Jane rose and laid her folded napkin on her plate — "the earl has likely been able to give the matter some thought since our meeting on Friday and has come to the conclusion that it will be much more convenient for him if he does not have to pay the upkeep of a woman and her dependents to whom he is not really related at all. Therefore, expect a letter" — Jane pretended she was receiving a letter and unfolded the invisible document — "telling you that after further consideration he wishes you to pack your things and return to from where you came." With a sweeping gesture, Jane pointed her finger at the door.

Which at that precise moment opened, and Saunders walked through the entryway and right into Jane's finger.

"Ooof." The butler staggered back as Jane snatched her finger away from him. "I beg your pardon, my lady." He straightened his vest with one hand, and brought the other from behind his back, holding a silver tray with a letter on it out toward Maria.

She gave one wild, stricken look at Jane. Surely her cousin hadn't conjured this missive with her remarks of a few minutes ago. That would be absurd. Hesitantly, Maria took the letter, looking from Saunders to Jane, not quite knowing what to do.

After an awkward moment of silence, the

butler bowed and withdrew, leaving Maria and Jane staring at the sheet of creamy stationery.

"Perhaps it is not from Lord Kersey." For once Jane seemed taken totally aback. She bit her lips, and kept clenching and opening her hands.

Dutifully, Maria turned the letter over, revealing the melted red wax wafer and the imprint of the Kersey crest. A fit of choked laughter bubbled up in Maria's throat. This couldn't be happening, yet what Jane had just suggested seemed to be coming to pass.

"Don't be silly, my dear." Her cousin must have caught her panicked air, for Jane pressed her hands stiffly to her sides. "It is likely a simple invitation to dine this evening."

About as likely as an invitation to take tea with the Prince Regent. She stroked the heavy, smooth paper, turning it over and over. Nothing to do but open it and face whatever was to come. Straightening her back, Maria ripped off the wafer and unfolded the letter.

Dear Maria,
    Given our somewhat formal meeting last week, I did not have time to discuss

147

with you the situation the estate finds itself in at present.

An icy chill trickled down her spine, the cold fingers of doom touching every part of her as it made its way down to her toes. Read it. She must read the rest of it. Maria closed her eyes, breathed deeply, then opened them and read on.

As she read further, the ice spreading through her veins stopped. She lifted her gaze from the letter to Jane's face, her slack jaw making her mouth drop open.

"Maria?" Jane was beside her, her hand supporting her arm as though she thought Maria might swoon. "What has happened?"

"Lord Kersey has asked me to leave Francis House and return to Kersey Hall." She could scarcely believe the words as she said them. Hadn't understood them the first time she'd read them.

Jane stepped back, her face a study of confusion. "He's asked you to go to Kersey Hall and live with him and his family — like one of the family?"

Nodding, Maria held the paper out to her cousin. "Read for yourself." Excitement built in her as Jane pored over the document.

"He gives no true explanation as to why

he's making this request." Jane finally put the letter down on the dining table, her brows still furrowed.

"Does that truly matter, Cousin?" The relief that she finally allowed herself to embrace almost made Maria giddy. "Perhaps Lord Kersey consulted with Mr. Granger about the expenses of having the dower house running as a separate household versus having everyone under one roof." She wanted to whirl around the room as if dancing a waltz. "The most important thing is that little Jane and I will have a home from now on, until she marries."

"Or you do."

Maria met Jane's gaze, but her cousin looked innocent enough. "Well, I suppose that is true."

"If you decide to marry again you will, of course, leave Kersey Hall, unless there is no need." There was no mistaking the mischievousness in Jane's voice now.

"I have no idea what you mean."

"If you don't, allow me to enlighten you." Jane made sure the door was closed, then returned to Maria. "Soon you will be living in the same house with two very handsome, very eligible gentlemen, one of whom is heir to an earldom. Suffice it to say that any woman with uncertain circumstances such as yours, would deem it prudent to make herself receptive to either of the gentlemen with an eye toward bringing one or the other of them up to scratch."

"Actually, I'll be living on the same property as three gentlemen, my dear." Oddly enough, when she'd read the offer from Lord Kersey, the first thing that had popped into her mind — other than utter relief — had been that now she might see Mr. Granger more often. "Mr. Granger's house is not far from Kersey Hall, if you recall."

A look of profound stubbornness that included chin, jaw, lips, and nose, transformed Jane's pleasant features into those of a gargoyle atop a French cathedral. "If you will be guided by me, Maria, you will forget about Mr. Granger's existence completely. I am sorry if you have developed some sort of *tendre* for him. I do understand he is a good man, but he has no prospects that would be of any use to you and little Jane. Nothing good can come of an attraction between you and him."

"Who said I was attracted to him?" The shrill voice that denied the very thing she desperately wanted to hide from Jane. From everyone. Most of all from Mr. Granger.

"I would wager on it, Maria. So if you do have any feelings for him, my dear, you need

150

to nip them immediately, like a sudden frost kills the late roses. Be ruthless in order to be fair to yourself."

Jane could be so vexing sometimes. "I do not plan to marry *anyone* else at this juncture in my life, my dear, so I hope you don't intend to harp on this subject until the Second Coming." Maria sat down at the table and picked up Lord Kersey's letter once more. A miracle indeed. "Would you ring for Saunders and order a pot of tea, please, Jane? We can discuss the move and lay out what we must do to make it as easy as possible."

She needed a bit of rest and reflection before the flurry of packing began once more. Hopefully for the very last time.

Shifting uneasily from one foot to the other, Hugh knocked upon the door to Francis House. Lord Kersey had asked him to oversee the Dowager Lady Kersey's move from the dower house back to Kersey Hall, a request that filled him with both eagerness and unease. The move itself puzzled him. Lord Kersey had given no explanation as to why the widow was returning to the main house, not that he needed to give Hugh any explanations. Still, given the recent visit by Mr. Clarke, Hugh wondered if this move had something to do with the will he had signed in April.

Mr. Clarke had arrived at Wingate at an ungodly early hour on Monday morning to show him the page with his and Chambers's signatures and asking if it was, to his knowledge, the same paper he had signed in April. In addition, he asked for the particulars of Hugh's encounter with the late Lord Kersey on that morning. Hugh had obliged him and given a truthful account, including his subsequent journey to London and visit to Mr. Clarke's establishment to deliver the letter.

"Could you have found no one else, Mr. Granger, to whom you could have given this document? You must have understood its import given your employer's circumstances." The scrawny little man had admonished him both with word and disparaging look.

"Am I given to believe, Mr. Clarke, that you are in the habit of employing clerks who are so incompetent that they cannot file important documents correctly?" That single question had deflated the solicitor's supercilious air. "Whoever the man was whom I spoke with gave me to believe he had the authority to act on your behalf when you were from the office. Otherwise I would never have surrendered that letter to him."

Mr. Clarke's pinched face had drawn in even further, as though he'd bitten into the sourest lemon in Christendom. "Just so, Mr. Granger." He cocked his head, his pale blue eyes suddenly piercing. "Did Lord Kersey inform you of the contents of the will?"

Hugh shook his head. He'd wondered mightily for months what Kersey had written, especially after it became apparent that Lady Kersey and her child had received nothing in the way of financial maintenance. All along he'd assumed the earl had wanted to provide for his wife and coming child and thus the last-minute document. Of course, he'd had no idea the will had been misplaced and now hoped fervently that her husband had left Lady Kersey a means by which she could live comfortably and raise their child without worries. With the revelation that the will had now been found, Hugh's hopes for the lady had been raised once more.

The cold wind whistled past Hugh's head, making him shiver as Saunders opened the door to Francis House and he hurried in. Perhaps this move had something to do with the provisions of Lord Kersey's will. In any case, it meant that, since the dowager would now be residing at Kersey Hall, he would likely see her more often. A blatantly foolish hope on his part, but one that occurred to him as soon as the words instructing him to oversee the move had left Lord Kersey's mouth. "May I have a word with Lady Kersey, Saunders?"

"Her ladyship and Lady John are upstairs overseeing the packing, Mr. Granger." Saunders's sullen demeanor did not go as far as insolence, but Hugh understood how grievously the man would resent being demoted back to footman.

"I do not wish to deter them from their occupation; however, Lord Kersey has sent me to oversee their return to the Hall. I will not trespass upon much of her ladyship's time, but I do need to speak with her." Another steward might have gotten the man sacked for such an attitude, but Hugh had great patience. He'd discovered early on in his career that disgruntled servants quite often had their uses.

"If you will wait in the reception room, sir, I will tell the lady you are here." Saunders executed a crisp turn and hurried away.

Hugh wandered to the front window, but the blustery wind sounded cold against the glass pane and he retreated to the fire that smoldered on the hearth. Nothing remained in the room save the large pieces of furniture and the curtains, which would be left to molder as they had before Lady Kersey had come to give them warmth and purpose. Although the lady's presence again in the great house would be welcome, it saddened him to think of this cozy house becoming an empty shell once more.

"Mr. Granger."

Hugh whirled and caught his breath. He'd not seen Lady Kersey for more than a week, so the sight of her, cheeks pink, blue eyes sparkling, attired in a deep lavender day dress with black trim, rendered him speechless. Aware of the deep silence in the room, he coughed and forced himself to speak. "My lady. Thank you for receiving me. Saunders informed me that you are overseeing your packing. I would not disturb you, but as I am to manage the actual event, I wanted to make certain you understood when everything needs to be ready."

"Please have a seat, Mr. Granger." She indicated the sofa to him, then sat in the chair opposite. "Of course, I will be happy to meet with you anytime you wish . . ." The lady came to a halt, her previously pink cheeks now almost scarlet. "To discuss the move, I mean."

"Naturally, Lady Kersey." The image of

155

them meeting . . . alone together as now, but in his home . . . in his bedchamber . . . Heat poured through him. Had the fire blazed up? Suddenly his cravat seemed to cut off his air supply.

"So when would you like me to be ready for you . . . for the move?" More flustered than he'd ever seen her, Lady Kersey avoided his eyes. She clasped her hands in her lap, twisting them helplessly.

"Would tomorrow be too soon? Only your belongings and Lady John's need go at this time. The rest of the furnishings can be returned to storage at any time."

"Yes, tomorrow will be fine." She managed to smile at him. "We are almost done now."

"Do you require any assistance?" Hugh tried to keep the eagerness out of his voice, but it was impossible. All he had to do was set eyes on the woman and he couldn't control himself.

"Oh, no." Her gaze darted away again. "We shall be fine, I'm sure. What, um, what time will you want to fetch us?"

"It needn't be early. What time would be convenient for you?" Merely sitting here talking to her was creating a riot in his breeches. If he didn't leave soon his proclivities would be exposed for the lady to see in the form of tented pants.

"Will eleven o'clock be acceptable to you?" The clear topaz blue of her eyes, deepened by the near-blue hue of her gown, sought his — pools he would love to drown in.

"That will suit excellently, my lady." Keenly aware of his body's incipient mutiny, Hugh shot out of his seat. "I will make sure the carriage is readied for you as well as the cart for the luggage."

"That is very kind of you, Mr. Granger." She rose and stepped toward him.

Hugh took a step back toward the door. If the lady put so much as a hand on his arm, he'd commit a breach of impropriety the likes of which Francis House had likely never seen before. He'd never lost control with a woman before, but this one . . . Her presence acted as the strongest of spirits, but to his very soul as well as his body. He had to get out of the house now. "Not a'tall, my lady. Good day."

With the briefest of bows, Hugh turned and fled. But not before catching a glimpse of Lady Kersey's startled and somewhat sad countenance.

The chill wind was welcome as Hugh stepped into the carriage and rapped for the driver to take him back to Kersey Hall. As he settled back on the seat, Hugh breathed a sigh at his escape without mishap. If the lady was going to have this effect on him merely by being in the same room as him, he would have to be much more circumspect about when he met with her. His still unruly flesh twitched anew when his thoughts strayed back to the sight of her in the rich lavender gown that accentuated her full, round breasts.

He groaned as his cock thumped insistently against his small clothes. This *tendre* would be the death of him yet. Folly of the worst kind as there was no hope of it being returned. The woman was titled, the widow of an earl. His family was eminently respectable, well landed and well monied. At least he would have been, had he been the first son. And now, with his brother barely clinging to life these many weeks, the very real possibility existed that Hugh would soon have nothing with which to provide for even his sister, much less a lady and her child.

Shaking his head to drum some sense into it, Hugh forced himself to face the stark reality. Maria, the Dowager Lady Kersey, was well above his touch, at least at present. If Kit recovered and no lasting scandal ensued, Hugh might speak to his brother about being set up in one of the family estates. If he had a sum of money to live off of while he put the property on a paying basis, then perhaps . . . just perhaps, he could make his affections for the lady known and offer her a life beyond Kersey Hall.

Those were a lot of ifs to have to overcome, but if he felt this strongly about Lady Kersey, he owed it to himself to at least try to give her the option of saying yes. If she instead said no, at least Hugh wouldn't resort to the disastrous path Kit had tried to take. He'd merely drown his sorrows if not himself, in his employer's best cognac. If one was going out in a blaze of glory, one might as well do it up right.

CHAPTER NINE

Dinner the next night was rather more festive than Maria had expected, even though her reception throughout the day had been abnormally cordial.

When she and Jane had arrived, late in the afternoon, they had been greeted warmly by both Lord and Lady Kersey and shown to the rooms they'd occupied previously. Maria's room, however, seemed to have undergone a hasty renovation. A new Turkish carpet, beautifully made of red and black wool with a design of intertwining rosettes, leafy tendrils, and a palmette border, took the place of the previous plain green rug. The bed hangings too were new; a thick, rich burgundy cloth with matching coverlet had replaced the green and yellow flowered hangings. The deep color soothed her, whereas the previous, somewhat faded green ensemble had made her feel bilious at times. A final addition of an elaborate folding screen, black and gold, painted in a design detailing several Chinese couples greeting one another, surprised her most — even to her untutored eye the piece looked extremely costly.

Why Lord and Lady Kersey would have spent so much money to refurbish an already serviceable room for a poor relation, there only by their good graces, was quite a puzzlement. Maria intended to consult Jane after dinner, to see if her room had been likewise redecorated and speculate on the reasons behind it.

Now at dinner, although Maria found the food as delicious as before, it was much more elaborately prepared than Cook had done when Maria was mistress at Kersey Hall. She had usually requested two or three simple dishes for her and Jane. Tonight she had counted six courses, and they had not yet come to the end of the meal. Were the Kerseys trying to flaunt their wealth before her eyes in an attempt to cow her? Well, they were beginning to succeed.

She lifted her wineglass to her lips and caught the eye of Lord Wetherby. He smiled across the table and raised his glass to her, his gaze intent on her mouth. Flustered by the obvious interest of this very sensual man, Maria took only a sip of the excellent wine, afraid she might choke and draw attention to herself. Turning to her dinner companion, Mr. James Garrett, she smiled and asked, "How do you find Kersey Hall, Mr. Garrett? It must be very different from your home in America."

The gentleman wiped his lips on his napkin, and returned her smile. "Indeed it is, Lady Kersey. Our house in Virginia was much smaller, although I must confess I preferred the vista the plantation afforded from the front porch." His deep brown eyes took on a nostalgic shine. "Sitting out on that porch of an evening, watching the sun set across the rolling lawn that led down to a picturesque creek, well" — he leaned toward her and whispered — "I confess I'd take it over the woods and formal gardens here at Kersey Hall without a thought."

"You miss your home, then?" Of all the family she'd met, Mr. Garrett had made the most favorable impression upon her. He seemed a truly genuine soul, unawed by the titles his family now boasted. Of course, as the second son, he had no title, but it seemed not to bother him at all.

"I do. If Father can find no occupation for me here, I will be happy to sail back to Virginia and take over the running of Bellevue."

"Named for the view you spoke of, I assume?"

"I like to think so, although I have no idea really." Mr. Garrett shrugged. "Neither Father nor Mother has ever spoken about the origins of the estate."

"Perhaps if you return there you can search it out," Maria said, as the footman set a plate of small, light cakes in front of her along with a white, frothy syllabub. "Oh, this looks delicious." She took up her spoon. "And festive. It has been a wonderfully festive dinner altogether."

"Indeed it has, Lady Kersey." Somehow the earl, all the way down at the far end of the table, had heard her remark. "You may take that as a compliment to you, my dear. We are feasting in style to celebrate your return to the house." He glanced at Jane, whose brows had arched delicately over her wide blue eyes. "And you as well, Lady John. The family is happy to be once again under one roof."

"Thank you, my lord." Hesitant to say more, Maria almost let her comment end there. The excellent wine she'd just imbibed, however, had sufficiently loosened her tongue to allow her to continue. "Although I will say, I do wonder at it. I left before your arrival at Kersey Hall because I did not wish to trespass on your family's privacy."

"Nor would you have done had you stayed in the first place. You are family, my dear." Lord Kersey raised his glass and beamed at her. "Distant though the connection may be, you are part of the Garrett line now. You and your daughter. Lady Jane must be raised to understand her place both in Society and within the family itself. And what better place for that to occur than her ancestral home?"

"You are very kind, I'm sure, my lord." Putting a spoonful of the sweet concoction into her mouth assured no more talking for the moment. She still could not fathom why his lordship would want her back in the house. Perhaps it did have something to do with the Garrett family connection. Still, she was a poor relation. Why rejoice in that?

"Yes, Lord Kersey, I dare to say Maria and I were both stunned at your generous offer to return to Kersey Hall." Jane's soft, mannered voice hid an intellect that few men could rival. Kersey had best be on his guard or else her cousin would make him look a fool with few words and no wasted motions. "As you pointed out, it is right for Jane to take her place in the household, albeit she will not do so for more than sixteen years. I wonder that you would incur such an expense for her maintenance for all those years to come, when you might as well have turned her and her mother out into the hedgerows."

"Not into the hedgerows, Lady John." Lady Kersey spoke up, her voice scandalized. "Lord Kersey would never turn a defenseless woman and child out with no place to go, although I am certain there are those who would do it."

"I beg your pardon, my lady, my lord, if I seemed to suggest you were a common rogue who would do such a thing." Jane glanced at Maria sharply, employing their private signal to meet after dinner to discuss whatever turn of events had given her pause. Apparently Jane's sensibilities had not been convinced regarding Lord Kersey's altruistic nature. "I can see you are far from common."

Maria bit her spoon to keep from spewing syllabub all over the table. Jane would be the death of her yet.

Dinner ended at last and the gentlemen rose while the ladies made their way out of the room. Jane sidled up to Maria and whispered, "We must talk. Retire as soon as the gentlemen appear in the drawing room."

Nodding, Maria followed behind them

down the corridor whose walls were resplendent with paintings and artworks in the current fashion, although some done by master artists of previous centuries. It had been her pleasure each evening to walk the hall and stop to gaze at the various paintings. She would have done so again this evening, but Lady Kersey kept them at a fast pace all along the way to the blue and green drawing room.

Jane went directly to the fireplace, Lady Kersey to her bellpull and gave it a vigorous tug. Bringing up the rear, Maria had a moment to discern Jane's summons likely had to do with further speculation about their change in fortune, and drifted toward her cousin, her hands outstretched to the cozy blaze.

"I think the weather is growing colder, don't you, my dear?" Maria glanced at Lady Kersey, who had seated herself in the room's largest chair, a dark blue figured pattern that drew the eye. "Is it something pressing?" Maria whispered.

"No, I don't think so, but come to me as soon as you retire." Rubbing her hands together briskly, Jane shuddered. "I do believe it may snow again in the next day or two, don't you, Lady Kersey? One can always tell by how early the leaves of the chestnut tree fall."

The topic of weather was thoroughly discussed, but the gentlemen still did not make an appearance, although the tea did. With a sigh, Jane moved to the sofa and settled herself in to wait. Having no other recourse, Maria followed after her, then sat beside her cousin, casting her mind about for some other acceptable topic.

"I have not yet discussed this with my cousin, Lady Kersey, but as Maria now has such an excellent companion in yourself, I am hoping she may be able to spare me to accomplish a long promised visit to the north in Scotland." Jane sounded eager as she accepted a cup from the countess. Almost too eager. Did she have something in mind that didn't actually involve her leaving? Or did she truly plan to leave Maria here with the strangers who were supposedly her family?

Once the notion had been spoken, Maria found she did not want to think of Jane leaving her side. Her cousin had been her staunchest supporter, via correspondence, all during the awful time when Alan was being unfaithful, and she had come from London immediately after Alan had died, remaining with Maria despite her own wants and desires. Well, perhaps it was time to let her cousin go and find her own kind of happiness. Lord knew she deserved to finally see the Scottish marquess she'd kept waiting for over half a year.

Steeling herself for the blow, Maria grasped her cousin's hands and squeezed them. "Although I am loath to let you go, Jane, as you must fully know, I do believe you have kept Lord Kinellan waiting for far too long." She patted Jane's hand. "Will you go to him for Christmas, then?"

"I received an invitation to a Christmas house party at his estate in the Highlands just yesterday. I was going to send my regrets, but now I am leaning toward making the long and arduous journey." Jane's eyes sparkled, the excitement in them evident. "I would, however, need to leave here quickly. As you say, the weather seems ready to change, and any significant snowfall will make the journey impossible. Therefore" — Jane grasped Maria's hand — "since you are well taken care of here, Maria, I believe I will take advantage of having already packed my bags and take my leave of both you and Lady Kersey in the morning."

Maria's brows rose almost to her hairline. "Had you already planned this, my dear?"

"I have been thinking about it ever since

we learned you were to return to Kersey Hall. If you do not need me as a companion, I truly would like to go to Scotland."

Clenching her jaw, Maria took up her cup, tepid by now, and continued to smile. Jane deserved this, deserved to find happiness with Lord Kinellan. That would only be possible if she went to him now. "I shall miss you very much, my dear. But you will regale me with stories about a true Scottish Christmas and I will do the same with the Kersey's house party here."

"It will only be a small gathering, Lady Kersey." The countess leaned toward her eagerly. "But I hope it will suffice to make the season merry, despite the sorrow of all these deaths this year." She shook her head, seeming genuinely concerned. "I think you are very brave, my lady. Your husband has been gone only a short amount of time, yet you are carrying on, meeting new people, managing new skills. I fear I could never do such things if my husband had died. I should be prostrate with grief."

"I have found everyone grieves in their own fashion, Lady Kersey." Jane smoothly took up the conversation. "Maria has been widowed before. We both lost husbands in the Battle of Waterloo. After the initial shock, one comes to accept it. If your family did right by you at your marriage, then you will have your settlements or a jointure to see you and your children through the most trying time. Afterward there are other options."

"Such as remarriage?" Lady Kersey sat forward eagerly. "Do you plan to remarry after your mourning has passed, my lady?"

"Please do call me Maria. As we are to be the closest of friends and family, that ought to be the right thing to do." Somehow, though, it didn't *seem* right. But as they were both called Lady Kersey, it would be the easiest method of address in the long run.

"Thank you, my dear. And I beg you to call me Margery." The lady's delight showed all over. Her eyes brightened, she sat straighter in her chair, and her mouth broke into a wide, pleasant smile. "It will be lovely having a friend in a house full of men." She turned eagerly to Jane. "Two friends, if you will call me Margery as well. Even though you will be leaving us so soon, you must return to us, Lady John. Especially if dear Maria does indeed remarry."

"I am honored, Margery. You must call me Jane as well." Her cousin's demeanor had softened toward the countess. "Of course, I would be delighted to attend Maria's wedding, especially as I was unable to do so the first two times she married. Are you looking for another husband, my dear?" Mouth twitching with suppressed laughter, Jane flashed Maria an "I told you so" glance.

"I fear I am not, Cousin." Much as she might be attracted to Mr. Granger, this was hardly the time to speak of such a thing. "I am, of course, still in mourning for the late Lord Kersey. But even after that time, I have no plans to remarry." She looked at her hands clenched in her lap. "I seem to not have much luck with marriage at all. And of course there is the scandal of my late husband's duel and the cause for it." Maria shot a pensive look at Margery, but the lady's expression showed only interest, not censure. Perhaps she had not heard of Alan's perfidy. "My cousin has had word from Town that the tale still lives. While it does, I dare not show my face."

"I suspect that now the new Lord Kersey has taken up his title, some of that speculation will die down." Jane's words soothed her, but only a little. At this point, Maria would simply prefer to remain in the country and avoid the tongues that would certainly wag as soon as she showed her face in Town.

"Oh, my dear." Margery grasped Maria's

hands. "I do understand that you would be hesitant to go back into Society too soon. But what if you come to feel some affection for another gentleman? Not before your mourning is finished, of course, as that would not be seemly. However, you cannot say if your affections might not be engaged with someone eventually. Would you like more tea, ladies?"

Maria nodded and handed her hostess her cup, although Jane shook her head.

Margery poured more tea, added sugar and milk, and passed it back to Maria. "I couldn't help but notice how well you and James seemed to get on at dinner, Maria." Smiling, she attended to her own cup. "He is quite a good man, I must tell you. Steady, you know. Always so attentive to me. And he has a knack for the running of a property. He helped his father a good deal with the management of our estate in Virginia."

"He spoke of your home in Dinwiddie, I think it is, quite fondly." Wary at all the praise Margery heaped on her child, Maria sent a quick glance to Jane. Was their hostess suggesting an alliance with her second son? "I enjoyed our conversation."

"Yes, James has always loved Bellevue. I daresay he may eventually make it his home, as my husband and Anthony will likely make their home here at Kersey." The countess picked up her cup. "Have you ever wished to see America, Maria?"

The lukewarm tea in her mouth suddenly refused to be swallowed. Caught between the choices of being utterly rude and spewing tea all over her hostess or drowning in it, Maria opted to force the beverage down her throat. Tears came to her eyes as the painful swallow progressed. At last it passed, and she gasped for breath.

"I don't believe my cousin has ever expressed a wish to visit the former colonies, my lady." Dear Jane, ever to the rescue. "Did you find your life there as enjoyable as your son did?"

"Oh, yes." The lady smiled warmly and set her cup on a side table. "I loved it quite as much as James. We were there for ten years, long enough for me to make friends. Good friends." Her eyes brightened. "However, I fear I shall never see them again."

"You do not think Lord Kersey will ever return to the property? Not even if your son takes up residence there?" Jane's expression showed only an interested regard. Maria suspected some underlying reason for the query.

"I suppose he might return one day." She looked off toward the fire, her face a study in dismay. "I would very much like to visit it once more, especially if James had taken up residence there."

"Then I pray the earl does decide to journey back to Virginia, Margery." The wistfulness in the lady's face touched Maria's heart. "I think you were happy there."

Continuing to stare into the fire, Margery nodded.

"I fear I will not be happy anyplace but England." Maria spoke forcefully, and from her heart. "I have never been one who enjoys traveling overmuch. If I can remain here at Kersey Hall, I am certain I shall be very happy to do so. Another reason why I do not think I shall marry again. If I stay here I am not likely to have many prospects."

At that, Margery turned back to her. "I think you may be wrong there, my dear. With your Kersey connections and your own charming manner, I believe you may have any number of gentlemen vying for your hand."

"Then too, I have learned my lesson, my dear. If I marry again, it must be for love alone." This revelation had come to her not long ago, when she had been speaking to Mr. Granger. If he was indeed the one with whom her affections lay, then she must remain a widow if she was to care properly for her daughter. "Not duty, not expectation, not infatuation. But truly for love of the gentleman."

"A wise decision, my dear." Jane gave her hand a squeeze. "I know nothing other than a deep and abiding love could ever induce me to marry again."

"And you may be surprised, Maria, with whom you do fall in love." Margery gave her a knowing look as she reached for her tea. "Love can take you unawares, when you least expect it. So do not make too hasty a decision about what you will and won't do. When love commands, a woman can do nothing but follow it."

At that cryptic and somewhat alarming statement, Maria and Jane exchanged a glance. They would meet later to confer on Lady Kersey's words and what they seemed to imply for Maria.

CHAPTER TEN

"Twenty-five, twenty-six, twenty-seven." Maria kept count as Hatley, her lady's maid, pulled the silver-backed brush through her long sable hair. The ritual hair brushing every evening before bedtime soothed Maria, though not so much as it had when she herself did the brushing. Before she'd become Lady Kersey. Now, the maid had informed her almost a year ago when she'd first come to Kersey, she should do as little as possible as befit her new station. So now she always had someone assist her to bathe, to dress, to brush her hair. She often thought that if it were humanly possible, the maids would eat for her as well.

A knock sounded on the door and Hatley left off at stroke twenty-eight, put the brush down, and went to answer it.

Maria snatched up the brush and pulled it through her hair. Twenty-nine, thirty.

"My lady!"

Guiltily, Maria held the brush out to the maid.

"Your cousin, Lady John, is here." With a stern look, Hatley took the implement and retreated to the dressing room.

"Oh, Jane. Explain to me why I cannot brush my hair myself." Maria rose from the chair and crawled up on the tall bed. She patted the fresh burgundy cover beside her. "If someone was seeing me do it, I would understand why a maid would perform the service. The upper classes are supposed to eschew manual labor of any sort. But no one sees me brush my hair but me." She poked her lips out in a pout. "I daresay everyone would believe my maid brushes my hair whether she does or not. So why can't I brush it instead? No one will ever know."

Jane laughed, wrapped her shawl around her firmly, and climbed the short two steps then flopped onto the bed. "Well, I assume your husbands saw you doing it. At least William would have."

Fire touched Maria's cheeks. Her few nights with her first husband, her childhood friend, had been frightening and embarrassing. She remembered lying in bed, upstairs in her father's house, with the covers pulled up to her chin the first night of her marriage. That image, and the long minutes after William had crawled in beside her, were the only memories she had of her first marriage. He'd left two days later for the army, and had never returned. "Actually, he didn't. I was . . . It was a confusing time for me. Everything happened so quickly. We were only together for two nights and . . ."

"You were so very young, my dear. Sixteen, isn't that right? Not even properly out of the schoolroom."

"Yes. We wanted to wait, wanted to be married when we were older. But William felt his duty to country keenly. So our parents allowed us to marry in case . . . in case he didn't come home." Maria bit her lips. There was something about her marriage she'd not told a soul. "When William's parents saw that he was so set on going into battle, they talked to Mother and Father and pushed them hard to agree to the marriage. They wanted us to marry in the hopes that there would be a child, you see."

"In case William didn't come home, yes. I'm so sorry, my dear."

Brushing at a tear that had trickled down her cheek, Maria sniffed and hugged her knees to her. "It seems so unfair that I should have had Alan's child so quickly after we . . . were together. Why couldn't it have happened that way with William? I'd likely have stayed at home with my parents and raised his child there, where everything was familiar. I would not be here, in the huge house with all these strangers. William's parents would have loved a grandchild so much. Now I have Alan's daughter, but there's no one else to share her with."

"I'm so sorry, Maria." Jane slid over and wrapped her arms around her. "Are you dreadfully unhappy here?"

"Not dreadfully, no. But I do miss my life at home. I just don't think about it very often, because it makes me sad. But tonight, Mr. Garrett spoke of his longing for home and it made me think about my home as well."

"I think Lady Kersey is a fair way toward making a match between you and her son. Her second son, thank God." Unwinding her arms from Maria, Jane leaned back, her elbows on the bed. "The oldest one, the heir, is trouble in no uncertain terms. I was watching him tonight at dinner."

"Oh, you were?" Banishing her melancholy, Maria stretched out on the bed, her head propped up on her hand, so she faced Jane. "Do you have hopes of snaring him for a tryst now?"

"Heaven forbid." Jane's head thumped

back on the bed. "Didn't I just say the gentleman was trouble? No, I was watching him watch you and his brother."

"He was watching *me*?" Maria bounded up, her hair swirling around her. "Why?"

"You are a beautiful woman with a sweet disposition. Why would he not be interested in you?"

"Because I have no fortune. Indeed, no means of keeping myself without the good-will of his family. Women like that can be had in any village and indeed on every street in London." She'd noticed Lord Wetherby's interest, but much preferred his brother's conversation.

"Oh, I didn't say he'd be interested in marrying you." Chuckling, Jane sat up. "Lord Wetherby is destined for a grand marriage to the daughter of a duke — or at the least a marquess. His father will see to that. But in the meantime, he must amuse himself somehow in the country. What better way than a dalliance with a pretty woman, especially one so close to hand?"

"Jane!" Maria stared at her cousin, a chill running down her arms. "You don't think Lord Kersey brought me back to live at the Hall so I could dally with his son, do you?"

"That would be a touch Machiavellian, wouldn't it?"

"What?"

"Never mind." Jane sighed and shook her head. "The point is, if you did choose to dally with Wetherby, and you began to increase, he would have to marry you, or the scandal would ruin the whole family. You are here under the protection of Lord and Lady Kersey."

"I have no plans to dally with anyone, including Lord Wetherby." That was not strictly true, of course. If the occasion arose, she might indulge in a dalliance with Mr. Granger. But Lord Wetherby was out of the question.

"It would answer the question of what is to become of you." Abruptly, Jane slid to the floor. "Married to the heir, you would eventually become Lady Kersey once more."

"I am Lady Kersey now." Much good the title had ever done her.

"You know what I mean."

"I do, and I mean it when I tell you I will not marry again unless I am in love with the gentleman." Gathering her nightgown around her, Maria stood on the stool close to the bed and marched down the two steps. "I look at the love matches Charlotte and Elizabeth and Fanny have made, how happy they are, and I can't help wanting that for myself." She stared at Jane, her heart sinking. Perhaps her cousin didn't believe in marriage for love. "Don't you want that with Lord Kinellan?"

Wrapping herself with her silk shawl, as if girding herself for battle, Jane fixed her with a defiant stare. "I am not in love with Lord Kinellan. I have a fondness for him, that is true. And he is an excellent lover, but we are not in love."

Stunned, Maria's brows rose sharply. She'd often wondered about the extent of her cousin's liaison with the handsome Scottish lord. Now she knew. Not that she blamed Jane. Maria had met him the once, when he had escorted Jane to Kersey Hall after Alan's death. Even in her shock and grief, Maria had admitted Kinellan was a splendid figure of a man.

Of course, she was a naïve young woman, who didn't know much at all about love and passion. That was how Alan had managed to seduce her. He'd convinced her that he loved her and had then used that in turn to further convince her, as he had wanted all along, that she loved him. Had she not believed that, she would never have gone to his bed. Well, not after the first time. That had been for the sheer excitement of having an attractive man be attracted to her. Perhaps for some people, that thrill was enough. But she didn't think that was true of her. "I'm sorry, Jane. I should not have asked you that."

Her cousin sighed and held out her arms. "Think nothing of it, my dear."

Maria hurried into Jane's embrace. Lord, she would miss her when she left, but if her cousin was to be happy, she needed to go. "When will you leave?"

"I had thought tomorrow, but I would not be able to travel on Sunday." Jane released her and walked toward the door. "That means I would be detained at some inn to the north of us for an entire day, when I could just as easily set off on Monday morning and travel straight through the week."

"And thereby remain here with me another two days." How sweet of Jane. Her cousin understood how much her departure would affect Maria's spirits and was trying to ease her into the acceptance of it.

"As you say." Jane's smile trembled. "I will miss you as well, Cousin."

It was on the tip of Maria's tongue to beg Jane to stay, but she kept silent. Her cousin deserved her happiness, in whatever form it came. "We shall write to one another every day."

"The expense of franking my letters will likely pauper Kinellan's purse."

They laughed together and Jane left on a happy note. Maria would simply have to make the best of the situation. Without Jane to confide in, she would need to foster a closer relationship with Margery. That idea was fraught with dangers, especially if the lady continued to make overtures toward Maria regarding her younger son. Not that she abhorred Mr. Garrett. Far from it. Still, she could not think of developing an attachment to him when her heart seemed firmly fixed on Mr. Granger.

Perhaps she simply needed more information about the man. If she could glean that he did indeed have prospects, no matter how slight, might that not prove reason enough to consider him eligible? Such information might well be obtained from his sister. So tomorrow she would seek out Mr. Granger and beg the introduction to Miss Granger that he had promised. Who knew where such a meeting might lead?

"Margery?" Lord Kersey slipped into his wife's darkened bedchamber well after two o'clock in the morning, clad only in his banyan and swaying in an effort to remain upright. The fire had burned low and nothing stirred behind the drawn bed hangings. His lady was likely asleep by now.

He'd spent more time than usual after dinner drinking with Anthony and James, trying to ascertain what his younger son had been talking so avidly about to the young widow while simultaneously attempting to keep his elder son from blurting out the scheme for Anthony to marry the Dowager Lady Kersey. Not that he thought James would try to stand in his brother's way, but any man faced with the prospect of marrying an heiress or letting another man do so would most likely elect to wed her himself.

He crept to the bed and pulled the curtains aside, then slid his hand over the covers until he hit a large lump. "Margery?" God, he hoped so. He hadn't stumbled into the wrong room, had he? He'd put away several bottles of wine and several more glasses of brandy. He gave the lump a hard poke. "Margery!"

"What?" The lump sat up in the bed, and shrank away from him. "Who is that?"

" 'S me, Margery. Your husband. William, Earl of Kersey." His complete name sounded so impressive. Too bad he couldn't be called that all the time.

"Good lord, William." There was the rasp of the curtain rings being pulled, then the room flared into brightness.

Kersey blinked at the sudden light. His

wife sat up, her hand on the lamp, her nightgown pulled askew, revealing one plump, enticing breast. Usually such a prospect would incite his cock to leap into action. Tonight, however, it remained soft and uninterested. Too much drink for sure. "I wanted to speak to you about James and young Maria." He leaned heavily against the bed. "Were you able to find out what she and James were talking about so avidly at dinner?"

"Is that why you've woken me up in the middle of the night?"

The irritation evident in his wife's voice was new and a little disturbing. She'd never before said so much as "boo" when spoken to, and now this insolence? What spell was this house casting on his family? First Anthony defying him about marrying little Maria. Then James insisting on returning to Virginia. Now his wife talking back to him and in the bedroom, of all places. "I need to discuss something of monumental importance to the family. Are you quite awake and sober?"

"Of course, I am. You just awakened me. And I am not the one who spent most of the night drinking." Margery adjusted her clothing tying the neck of her gown and removing the sight of temptation. "Now what is it that you wish to discuss?"

"Maria and James. They sat at dinner together and appeared to be having a spirited conversation at one point. We need to make certain that Anthony is put forward to her as the prospective bridegroom. Not James."

"But Maria and James would suit so much better together, my dear."

His wife must have lost her mind. Did she think that such things mattered at all when their livelihood was at stake? "You have not been speaking to Maria about the merits of James, have you, Margery?" He seized her arm in a vicious grasp.

"Aww, William. You're hurting me."

He shook himself and released her arm. All women were a dammed nuisance. "What did you say to her after dinner?"

"Nothing of any consequence, it turns out." Margery rubbed her arm and glared at him. "She and James spoke about Bellevue and his desire to return there. Maria, on the other hand, wants nothing to do with journeying to Virginia. She is perfectly content to reside here, at least for now, and swears she has no interest in marrying again." Margery shrugged. "I assume that puts an end to our hopes of reuniting the Kersey properties."

"On the contrary, my dear. It gives me more hope than ever." Kersey climbed up on the bed and flopped down on the pillows, his head spinning.

"It does?" Margery slid over next to him. "Why? I thought your whole idea was that Maria would agree to marry Anthony."

"And she will, my dear, she will. If Anthony has one virtue, it is tenacity. Once he sets his sights on something, then he will move heaven and earth to make it happen." After more explanation than it should have taken, he'd finally convinced his son of the absolute necessity of marriage to the Dowager Lady Kersey. "And one impediment has just been removed."

"What impediment?"

"James." Kersey opened his eyes to try to stop the room from spinning.

"How was James an impediment?" His wife's puzzled voice grated loudly in his already throbbing head.

"As you said, Maria and James suit one another much better than she and Anthony. So James might have easily persuaded her to fall in love with him and whisked her back to Virginia, along with the control of all her properties." Now the room spun in the opposite direction, making his stomach queasy. "But since she does not wish to travel, and actually wishes to settle down here at Kersey Hall, then James will have the devil's own time getting her to agree to marry him. Which leaves ample opportunity in the coming weeks for Anthony to seduce her into his bed and get her pregnant. Then we can force her to marry him or risk complete ruin for the entire family."

"William. That is a horrible scheme." Margery's voice sounded as sharp as an ice pick in his head.

"Margery, lower your voice or I shall cast up my accounts all over your bedcovers." Kersey pressed his hands against his eyes, trying to keep his brains from leaking out his eyeballs.

"I'll fetch the lavender concoction. My mother swore by it all her life." She paused in the act of getting out of the bed. "Unless you'd like the vinegar instead?"

The mere mention of vinegar almost ensured that Kersey would lose the battle with his stomach. But a deep breath settled him again. "The lavender water, please, Margery."

The pattering of her bare feet on the carpet as she retreated to the door to her dressing room where such potions were stored, made him relax onto the mattress. Anthony could take the plan from here and make certain Maria would land in his bed sooner rather than later. Kersey wanted the girl bound to his heir before the Christmas party welcomed its first guest. He had ample faith in Anthony's reputation with ladies. Now that his son had picked up the gauntlet, so to speak, he'd lay odds little Maria would be warming his bed before the month was out. Sooner, once Lady John took her leave. With no one else to run to or discourage her, Maria would fall easily into Anthony's arms. It was only a matter of time.

CHAPTER ELEVEN

Totaling up the figures on the renovations to the dower house — which had been used approximately two weeks when all was said and done — gave Hugh an unexpected delight. Not that the repairs had been an unnecessary expense, but now the house would likely fall back into disrepair before it could be used by the next Dowager Lady Kersey. The thought of so much time and effort now going to waste should have had him grumbling at everyone he came into contact with this morning. But the effect was actually quite the opposite.

The money had actually been well spent — Francis House was as right as rain now — if only the house would be put to some good use. Of course, Lady Kersey had had the use of it for a couple of weeks, which had given the lady pleasure, and so him. But now his primary job would be to visit it each year and hope to keep the property from becoming run-down again.

He might suggest to his lordship that they rent the house and its park until such time as it was needed for a dower house or as the primary residence of Lord Wetherby, perhaps upon his marriage. Not that that would come to pass for some time to come. Wetherby's reputation had been whispered about all over London, so that even one who visited the city infrequently had heard of the newly titled lord's exploits in gambling and whoring. Such a wild buck would not be settling down anytime soon.

Still, Hugh couldn't help but be delighted by the way things had turned out for the Dowager Lady Kersey. With her return to Kersey Hall, Hugh always walked in the front door with the expectation that at some point during the day, he would get to see the lady. A sight that made the dreariest of days shine like midsummer.

Not that it wasn't torture to see the woman almost on a daily basis, although he spoke to her much more infrequently than he saw her. He managed to discover when she liked to walk or when she came down for tea in the breakfast room. Then he would station himself somewhere nearby, out of sight, and watch as she walked down the corridor or entered a room. Something told him such conduct was unseemly, but he couldn't help himself. He wanted to see her, to talk with her as he'd done that day out by the fountain.

The weather now prevented such meetings outside, but he could perhaps arrange an outing for Lady Kersey and Bella. He'd promised them both an introduction and now seemed as good a time as any. A good one also because it might help distract the lady from the loss of her cousin on Monday.

That settled it. He'd arrange the introduction for tomorrow afternoon, after church. The ladies at the Hall did not attend, but he and Bella went faithfully. After luncheon he would suggest Lady Kersey and Lady John accompany him over to the farmhouse where he and his sister resided, with several servants, for tea.

A knock sounded on the office door.

Hugh turned from his column of figures and barely stopped his jaw from dropping open. There before him stood the Dowager Lady Kersey, splendidly dressed, as always, this time in a deep purple gown with a square neckline that accentuated the curve of her bosom to a sinful degree. He blinked and quickly raised his gaze to her face.

"Good morning, Mr. Granger." The exquisite creature smiled at him, taking

Hugh's breath away.

"Good morning, Lady Kersey," he managed at last. He must not stare at the lady, but it was so hard not to when all he wanted to do was gaze his fill. "How may I help you?"

Lady Kersey smiled, a quirking up of her pink lips that incited a riot in Hugh's nether regions. "I had realized this morning that with my removal to Francis House and then the flurry of the return, I had not had a chance to ask you about the Tates."

"Ah, yes." Hopes dashed that her visit pertained to something more personal, Hugh nevertheless returned her smile and motioned to the nearby sofa. "Won't you have a seat, my lady?" As she complied he closed the door all but a crack and sat on a leather-backed chair opposite her. "I do have something to report on that front."

"Oh, good." She smoothed out her gown and raised her face to his. "How is Mrs. Tate faring? It has been some weeks since I had any news of her."

"I believe her first grief at her husband's loss has passed. Her children seem to be a great comfort to her." He lowered his voice, mindful of the cracked door. "The family is still on the tenant farm. No one has applied to take it over so far, as expected."

"That is excellent, Mr. Granger." Her tones were hushed as well. "It was so good of you to come up with this scheme to help them."

"Unfortunately, it will not work forever. We know that if Lord Kersey finds out there will be the devil to pay."

"He will evict them out of hand, you mean?" Her brows knit over her petite nose in a most charming way.

"That would be the logical assumption." He didn't want to mention that he would also quite likely be sacked for insubordination. "And even if he doesn't discover our little subterfuge, word does get around the counties, about tenants' deaths, you know. Any day, a worker could show up and ask if the tenancy has been filled."

"What can we do to help them if the worst comes to pass?" The lady stared earnestly into his face, her absolute faith in his ability to solve the problem evident in her eyes.

"I . . . haven't quite been able to work that out yet. If the son were older there would be an argument that he could take over for his father. If a prospective tenant happens to apply, I can express to his lordship once more that Mrs. Tate is willing and able to take it over, but I doubt he will be any more amenable about that than he was before."

Lady Kersey sighed. "I am sorry I am not able to provide another solution to their situation either. If only little Jane had been a son, this would not be a problem at all." Her eyes widened, making them an even more startling blue. "Do not think I mean I don't love my daughter, Mr. Granger. I do, most fiercely. It's only that now I have no control over a decision that otherwise would have been mine to make."

"Of course, my lady. I would never think such a thing." One of his most precious memories of her was the afternoon he came upon her playing with her daughter at Francis House. Her love for her child had shone with absolute clarity. "How is Lady Jane?"

"She is well, thank you. Still growing at an incredible rate." Lady Kersey relaxed and smiled. "Every time I see her she seems to have grown an inch." Her smile became tinged with sadness. "But I fear I will not be able to see her every day as I have been used to doing. Since I am returned to Kersey Hall, I expect I shall have to conform to the more traditional ideas about child-rearing and see her only occasionally. My cousin had stressed this to me after the baby was born, but I would not listen. She was all I had, and I wanted to be with her . . ." The lady trailed off, then brushed at her eyes with the back of her hand. "Forgive me, Mr. Granger, if I have become too personal in my conversation."

"Not at all, my lady." He fumbled for his handkerchief and finally presented it to her. "You have not had an easy year yourself, though some might not see it that way. Perhaps you can rebel a little, when no one is noticing, and find your way to the nursery more frequently than others might do."

She wiped her eyes, then clutched the square of linen, kneading it between her fingers. "I have never thought myself a rebel, but perhaps you are right." She smiled up at him, her gaze warm. "For Jane I may well have to become one."

"I think you may not find it difficult at all, when your reason for rebelling is someone dear to your heart." He meant the words to be encouraging, but they had a rather startling effect.

Her luscious lips thinned into a straight line and she sat straighter on the sofa before leaning over to place her small hand on his. "Please tell me how your brother is doing, Mr. Granger. I do not know the particulars about his injury, but I wondered if the circumstances had changed in any way."

At her touch, Hugh became so distracted he could scarcely comprehend what she was saying. All he wished to think about was the warmth that seeped into him from that one spot, as though nothing else had ever brought him this much joy. After a stunned moment, he managed to steady himself enough to compose an answer. "Thank you for your interest, my lady. I am sorry to say that my brother's condition has not changed since the . . . accident. He lies in bed, unable to do more than breathe and take a little nourishment the servants feed him."

"I am so very sorry to hear that. I know this has been an especially distressing time for you and your sister." She squeezed his fingers, but did not remove her hand. "Can the doctors do nothing else for him? He has clung so tenaciously to life, I would think they would be encouraged that he might yet recover."

"Sadly, no, my lady." Hugh sat back in his chair and she did as well, breaking their tenuous contact. "They are, in fact, greatly puzzled that he lives still. According to the surgeon who has attended him from the first, he should have died of his wound shortly after he . . ." God, but he hated to confess Kit's transgression to this woman. But if he wished to pursue any sort of courtship with her at some point in the future, he must trust that his honesty would stand him in good stead with her.

"What did he do, Mr. Granger?" The soft question seemed to echo in the still room.

"He shot himself, my lady. In the head, after the woman he had hoped to make his wife refused his proposal."

"Dear God." Her face paled and her hand flew up to her mouth, as if to take back his words instead of hers. "I am so terribly sorry, Mr. Granger. I had no idea."

"We have not put it about generally, save that he was wounded by a pistol in the hopes people will think it was an accidental shooting. Mr. Lambert, the surgeon, has been discreet, but if Kit does indeed die, Mr. Lambert will be called to testify about the nature of the wound."

"What do you mean?"

"Suicide is a crime, Lady Kersey. If his death is ruled as such, our family will lose everything — land, personal property, money — to the Crown." He'd thought about the inevitability so much he now stated it matter-of-factly. "There is also the dreadful shame that my brother's body will not be allowed to be buried in consecrated ground."

The lady stared at him, her mouth working, though no words came out.

Perhaps honesty had not been the best option. Still, he would rather have the situation laid out for her. It would be her choice how to respond now. "I know this is quite a shock, but I wanted you to know, my lady. You have been so kindly interested in Kit's — that is to say my brother Christopher Granger's — health, I felt I should now tell you the particulars, despite their unsavory nature."

Lady Kersey shook her head, sadness in her face once again. "I thank you for trusting me with this information, Mr. Granger. I know how painful it must have been to disclose it. But I can assure you I will speak of this to no one unless given your leave." She rose, bringing Hugh instantly to his feet in front of her. "If there is anything I can do to help you or your family in any way, please do not hesitate to ask."

"Thank you, my lady." And now he would find out if his forthrightness had been for nothing. "There is one thing you might do, not for my brother, who I fear is simply in God's hands, but for my sister."

"Yes, Miss Granger." Her face lit up and Hugh's heart stuttered. "You were to arrange an introduction between us. I hope that will be possible sooner rather than later."

"That is the very boon I was about to request, my lady." A tightness in his chest made Hugh pause. "Would you and Lady John come to tea with me and my sister tomorrow afternoon at Wingate?"

"Your residence, if I remember correctly?"

"Yes. A small manor house about a mile from Kersey Hall, in the opposite direction from Francis House."

"I would be delighted to meet Miss Granger. I shall ask my cousin, but I am certain she will wish to make the acquaintance as well." Her eyes sparkled with true joy, making Hugh almost giddy with relief.

"Thank you, my lady." She was so close, so temptingly close. Her face tilted up to him brought her mouth only inches from his lips. If he swayed slightly toward her —

She rose up and brushed her lips against his in a fleeting kiss that seemed to last far longer than the few seconds it surely took. Still, he savored the warmth of her mouth, the sweetness of her breath, the closeness of her face next to his. Not a sensual kiss, but one so comforting he could forget the worries for his family completely for those few blissful moments. Heaven in several different ways.

Then she was gone, slipped out the door with only the swish of her purple skirts lingering on the air.

Hugh gazed about the room, not entirely certain what had just happened had been real. And if it had been — and he hoped like the devil it had been — then he must figure out what Lady Kersey had meant by kissing him, and how they could go on from here.

CHAPTER TWELVE

"What did I do? What did I do?" Running lightly down the corridor from the steward's office at the rear of the house, Maria could scarcely believe she had kissed Mr. Granger. How could she have acted so scandalously?

Well, because the poor man had been in need of comfort. Not that such a fleeting kiss could be truly comforting, but at least she hoped it told him she understood his troubles and would be a friend to him. More than a friend, really, if truth be told. If he wished her to be.

She turned a corner and slowed down to a fast walk. If anyone saw her now they would have no idea she'd been in Mr. Granger's office. Had she been caught there alone with the steward, both of them might have been censured. Mr. Granger would have quite likely lost his position. Or worse, they might have been forced to marry. Not that that would be a bad thing as far as she was concerned. She liked Mr. Granger more each time she spoke with him. Not only was he handsome, but a genuinely kind man who cared deeply about his family. He was excellent with children — he'd taken to Jane and her to him in mere moments. And compassionate toward the Tates and his brother.

Yes, if she wished to marry a man with integrity and a clear moral code, Mr. Granger — She turned a corner and smacked into a tall, hard body. Rebounding off the solid torso, she staggered backward, the scent of bergamot filling her nose as she raised her gaze to the equally startled face of Lord Wetherby.

"Lady Kersey, are you quite all right?" He grasped her arm, even though she was standing perfectly still by the time he had done so.

"Yes, my lord. Thank you." She waited for him to release her, but he kept his hand where it was, squeezing her upper arm lightly.

"You must be more careful, my lady. You could have taken a nasty spill." He removed his hand, only to take her arm and twine it through his. "Let me escort you to avoid further mishaps."

Smiling, although she actually wanted to grimace, Maria nodded and adjusted her hand so it lay in the crook of his elbow, touching him as little as possible. "How good of you, my lord. I was going to my cousin's room to help her with her packing."

"That should make for a lengthy journey if we walk sedately, Cousin Maria." He glanced down at her and smiled, showing very white teeth. "You do not mind if I call you that, do you? We are related, of course."

Permission to use such a familiar name with a gentleman she did not know well at all should properly be refused. In Maria's circumstances, however, it might be in her best interest to agree. True, the connection was tenuous at best, but Lord Wetherby's father ruled whether Maria had a home or not. If his son wished to claim a familial tie, she should probably acquiesce so he could tell his father that she was being cordial. "Of course, Lord Wetherby. I would be pleased to be known to you as Cousin Maria."

"And you then must call me Anthony, Cousin." A glimmer of humor shone in his eyes. He was pressing his advantage to the hilt when he knew it was improper.

"Cousin Anthony, then." Lord, but he did

remind her uncannily of Alan, especially when she'd first met him. Dashing, handsome, charming, and so very good at using all those attributes to get what he wanted. No doubt Cousin Anthony was cut from the same cloth.

"What brought you to the rear part of the house, Cousin? Surely there's nothing of interest there save some empty rooms." His dark eyes searched hers, as if ferreting out a secret.

"I had gone to see Mr. Granger." Jane had always said, the best way to tell a lie was to make it as close to the truth as possible. "I had a favor to ask of him."

"Indeed." That seemed to take Cousin Anthony aback. "What *favor* could you want from Granger?"

His implication was clear — a tryst between her and Mr. Granger would naturally be the first thing a rogue such as Anthony would expect. A sudden eager speculation in his face with raised eyebrows and a subtle licking of his lips confirmed it.

"Yes, I wanted to ask him if he would introduce me to his sister, Miss Granger. She is currently residing with him, as you may know. As we are somewhat of an age, I thought she might be good company for me when Lady John leaves on Monday." She beamed up at his fallen face. "I was just hurrying to tell my cousin that we are invited to tea tomorrow afternoon."

"How charming." His tone said otherwise. "I had hopes you might ride out with me tomorrow afternoon. We have not had a chance to get to know one another properly. Dinner conversation can only go so far and we have had precious little of that. I do wish to get to know you better, my dear Cousin Maria."

They stopped at the bottom of the front staircase. Anthony took both her hands in his and squeezed them in an extremely strong grip that came close to being painful. If she ever had to fend this man off, or escape from him, she would be hard-pressed to do so.

"A ride about the property sounds like a lovely outing, Cousin, if the weather will cooperate." Best lay the groundwork for this refusal as thoroughly as possible. For she did not wish to spend any time alone with Lord Wetherby. Despite Jane's advice, to do so would be to invite disaster back into her life. The gentleman might have all kinds of sterling qualities, though she'd heard of none since she'd met him, but he reminded her of Alan, from his coloring to his cologne, and that was enough to ward her off of him for good. "I am engaged tomorrow, and on Monday Lady John takes her leave — I am certain I shall need to rest after the ordeal of telling her farewell — so we may be able to schedule a ride on Tuesday. If the weather permits." And by Tuesday she would have come up with another excuse to put him off. Unless Cousin Anthony was completely bird-witted, he'd realize quickly she did not wish to ride with him any day.

"I shall await Tuesday's dawning with a keen eye." He raised her hands, placed a kiss on the back of each, then released her.

Resisting the urge to wipe her hands on her skirts, Maria nodded to him. "My lord."

"Cousin." The admonishment was half teasing, half serious.

"Cousin." Maria turned and mounted the stairs, keeping her pace slow and even, despite the gooseflesh crawling up her back. If she looked back she'd certainly see Anthony watching her ascend the stairs. When she finally reached the first-floor landing, she risked a look back, but Cousin Anthony had gone.

Blowing out the breath she'd been holding, Maria picked up her skirts and fled toward Jane's room. Never had she wanted anything so badly as to beg her true cousin to stay with her. Anthony's attentions could

208

mean one of several things, and none of them necessarily good for Maria. Still, she must let her cousin go, and learn to cope with the difficulties life had a tendency to throw at her. One way or the other, Maria would learn to be on her own.

Pasting a pleasant smile on his face, Anthony followed Maria's progress up the stairs. Just in case she should glance back, he wanted her to know that he was watching her, to think that he was interested in her. When she reached the top step, with no backward glance, he whirled on his heel and strode quickly down the corridor toward the main study, in urgent need of his father.

He'd been keeping an eye out for the little widow for a couple of days, but the lady had either been spending her days in her room or actively avoiding him. He didn't think the latter — she had no reason to think ill of him yet — so perhaps she tended to be retiring. She did not put herself forward at all, if her behavior at dinner could be an indication.

When the family gathered before being called in, she'd been talking to either his mother or her cousin. He had tried to engage her in conversation both before and after dinner, but she seemed more elusive than a nightjar. At dinner his chances were worse, as his seat necessarily put him at his father's side. Maria sat to his mother's right and her cousin, Lady John, between her and him. He'd speak to Mother about changing the seating — to hell with protocol — if she wanted him to be able to woo Maria.

So today's encounter had been a spot of good luck. He'd been out riding this morning, as was his custom, and had just returned and was heading to his room to change when he stopped to admire the backside of one of the maids, bent over stoking the fire in the library. He'd been debating approaching her — it had been far too long since his last bit of skirt in London — when he'd heard the patter of running feet and moved away from the library door before Lady Kersey had almost barreled him over.

She had seemed distracted, too distracted to have simply been requesting a meeting with Granger's sister. What had she actually been up to? An assignation was obviously his first thought. Widows were generally a wanton bunch in his experience. Once given a taste of bed pleasures, they were in dire need of a replacement after their husbands had cocked up their toes. He suspected little Maria was no different. And the only two gentlemen, other than himself, she might have chosen to lie with were James and Granger. James she hardly knew and was therefore the less likely candidate. Granger, however, he could see perfectly as the widow's paramour.

His long strides had carried him to the small study near the front of the house that his father had taken over as his office. The door stood open and Anthony strode in and went directly to the sideboard. "We may have a problem."

His father's head jerked up from the letter he was reading. "What? What the devil are you talking about?"

"The Dowager Lady Kersey may have taken Granger as her lover."

His father dropped the letter on the desk in front of him. "Good God. Did you catch them together?"

"No." Anthony poured a hefty libation into a sizeable tumbler. "I said 'may have.' I didn't see them, but I did run into the widow on her way back from Granger's office. She gave some flimsy excuse about arranging a meeting with his sister, but I suspect it's more than that."

"You are suspicious of any woman who doesn't fall immediately into bed with you." Father rose and headed toward him.

"But then she put off my suggestion of riding out with me tomorrow. I think she's avoiding me because she's being satisfied elsewhere." Any woman with the prospect of being wooed by the heir to an earldom would be daft to turn it down. "What other explanation could there be?"

"That she really did wish to meet with Miss Granger." His father poured himself a tot of brandy and moved back to his chair. "You are too used to the ways of light-skirts and the ladies in Society. Unlike them, Maria is young and, despite being widowed twice, still rather naïve, according to your mother, who has spoken with her at length after dinner. You cannot judge her by the behavior of the more experienced women with whom you are familiar."

Disgruntled by his father's words, Anthony sauntered over to the leather chair by the fireplace and flopped down. "Are you certain James cannot marry her with the same result? She's not to my taste at all."

"Then change your taste or swallow it until you have made her Lady Wetherby or you'll live to see the estate ruined." Glaring at him, Father sipped his brandy and sat back in his chair. "Are you telling me you cannot seduce this little wench? And here I'd believed your reputation as a rake. Was I wrong to do so?"

"No, you were not. I can get her in my bed." That had never been a problem before. "It's just that she seems not to be attracted to me for some reason." He gazed evenly at his father. "I may, however, need to use other means than charm in order to do so."

After a moment's pause, his father shrugged and nodded. "Whatever it takes, Anthony. She must become your wife by fair means or foul."

Leaning back in his chair, Anthony relaxed against the cushion. He would need to plan a little more carefully if he were to do this properly. Maria had been elusive and often in the company of her cousin. That would change shortly and she would have no one to keep company with, save his mother and, occasionally perhaps, Miss Granger. Plenty of opportunity then to get her alone and compromise her thoroughly so that marriage to him would be her only option.

He sighed. Not the way he'd have preferred the scheme to go, but then beggars could not be choosers. If he didn't want to end up on the rocks, he'd have to seduce his little "cousin," whether she wanted seducing or not.

CHAPTER THIRTEEN

The Sunday afternoon sunshine was thin, but the air around Maria and Jane was crisp, not cold. They had elected to walk to Mr. Granger's because of the temperate day. Jane had been less sanguine about it, but Maria had convinced her by citing Jane's coming journey, cooped up in a carriage for days on end before she arrived in Scotland. "You should get as much exercise and fresh air as you can before you begin your journey," she'd announced to Jane as they stood in the entryway donning their pelisses.

"I have always believed fresh air and exercise are good for children, dogs, and horses, but not for me." Her cousin had pulled on her gloves, then glanced at Maria and sighed. "Very well. I shall suffer the walk for your sake, my dear."

Now they could just see the outline of the little manor house, set back from the road in a clearing ringed by tall trees. As they approached, Maria made out a wildflower garden in front, trailing vines creeping up the end wall, and an arch of roses, the blooms all but gone, over the entryway. Even with the scarcity of flowers, the house was completely charming.

"How lovely." Maria hurried her steps forward. "It's like the houses one reads of in fairy tales."

"As long as it is not the one from *Hansel and Gretel,*" Jane murmured.

"What is that?"

"A German fairy tale Tark read to me not long after we married."

"And it has a cottage in it like this one?"

Jane nodded. "But made of gingerbread."

"How sweet." Maria grinned as she hurried toward the charming little house.

"Actually not." Jane spoke low, to herself.

"Whatever are you talking about, Jane?" At the door, Maria raised her hand to the brass knocker.

"Nothing that concerns you now. I will explain it when you are older."

Maria frowned at her cousin. Jane could be very mysterious when she chose to be. She rapped smartly on the door, which was instantly opened by a tall, thin man, presumably the butler.

"Lady Kersey and Lady John Tarkington."

Maria glanced nervously at Jane. She'd managed to keep from telling her cousin about kissing Mr. Granger, but only because she'd been so intent on telling her about the unexpected meeting with Lord Wetherby. Now, when she saw Mr. Granger again, she very much feared her secret — or at least her emotions — would be written on her face.

They followed the butler into a small entry hall, then down a short corridor to a large drawing room, decorated in warm colors. The pale beige walls brightened the dim light coming through the large windows overlooking a rustic patch of autumn flowers. A Turkish carpet in reds and golds added elegance to the room, as did the tall escritoire and the graceful table and chairs, set for tea with delicate china.

Mr. Granger stood ready as they entered, his sister at his side. She favored him in the squareness of her jaw and the color of her hair and eyes, though not in his height.

"Lady Kersey, Lady John, it is an honor to have you here today." He bowed solemnly, his manner rather more staid than yesterday.

Maria bit her lip, but smiled and curtsied. She could not dwell on that interlude or she would certainly come to grief. Instead she stepped forward to the young lady, who seemed all atremble. "I believe you must be Miss Granger?"

"Yes, my lady." She curtsied, then looked to her brother. "Hugh?"

Mr. Granger stepped forward, now standing a mere foot or so from Maria. "Lady Kersey, Lady John Tarkington, may I present my sister, Miss Arabella Granger? My sister is staying with me while our brother is indisposed. Arabella, Lady Kersey and her cousin are now living at Kersey Hall, although I believe Lady John will be leaving us shortly."

"Very shortly indeed, Mr. Granger." Jane smiled at them both. "Tomorrow morning, in fact. How do you do, Miss Granger?"

"I am very well, my lady." The young lady's cheeks pinkened, and she turned to Maria. "Did you enjoy your walk to Wingate? I like walking very much when I can crunch leaves beneath my half-boots."

"That is fun, isn't it?" Maria laughed, suddenly very light-spirited. Miss Granger seemed a sweet lady, much in temperament like her brother if she didn't miss her guess. "Perhaps we can take a turn outside later and enjoy the fallen leaves together."

"I would like that, my lady." Miss Granger shot a look at her brother, who nodded to the table. "Ladies, would you please be seated?" She then grasped the bellpull and tugged on it twice. "Tea should be here shortly."

Maria and Jane seated themselves opposite one another, which allowed each of them to sit beside Miss Granger. It also allowed them Mr. Granger as their other partner, a circumstance that had Maria's heart thumping loudly in her chest. This was quite the nearest she'd been to Mr. Granger, except for when she had —

Her cheeks scorched, as if she'd stood too near the fire, which in one sense she had. A surreptitious glance at Mr. Granger showed a tinge of pink in his cheeks as well.

Oh, dear. This would never do. She focused her attention on Miss Granger, praying Jane had missed that little exchange with the girl's brother. "How are you finding life here at Wingate, Miss Granger?"

The young lady smiled pleasantly. "Very well indeed, my lady. The house is quite snug and the property is lovely. My chief concern is that I have little to do here." She glanced at her brother and pursed her lips.

He grinned back at her.

"Mr. Granger will take everything about the running of the household on himself, leaving me with only my two favorite pastimes, reading and gardening, to while away my hours." She sighed. "And with the weather getting colder, there is little enough to do in the garden."

"Well, what you have accomplished in such a short time is quite lovely." Maria nodded to Miss Granger, though her gaze strayed momentarily to her brother. That gentleman looked very handsome in a blue superfine coat and breeches, with a waistcoat done in blue and green florals and his cravat tied in a smart mathematical knot.

"I confess I have been able to do little in the garden in the way of planting. Hu— Mr. Granger had already sent instructions about the winter plants by the time I arrived here, although I have been able to take some cuttings and create arrangements for the public rooms." She pointed to a spectacular floral array in a simple white bowl on the mantelpiece. Golden late-blooming roses mingled with a dark wine-colored spray of leaves, sprigs of various berries mixed all about with a fan of greenery at the back.

"You are very talented, my dear." Jane's voice held sincere appreciation. She took great pride in her own flower arrangement, so her words were praise indeed.

Miss Granger beamed. "Thank you, my

lady. I have always taken much joy in flowers, especially at home, where I had the keeping of the garden myself."

The door opened and the butler brought in the tea tray.

"Thank you, Carstairs." Miss Granger took up the teapot, and soon they were all enjoying the hot, fragrant tea and delicious little cardamom cakes.

"Do you leave for home in the morning, Lady John?" Miss Granger had offered a second round of cakes. Maria and her brother had taken more, but Jane had declined.

"No, I am for Scotland, to visit a dear friend who I have had to put off for several months. I have been with Lady Kersey while she was settling into life here at Kersey Hall. But now she has her place amongst the new family, I think it is time for me to journey north."

"Lady John has been terribly kind to me." Maria set her cup into its saucer and sent a thankful look to Jane. "I don't know what I would have done without her these past months. I know I shall miss her terribly."

"But now you have made Miss Granger's acquaintance and that of the current Lady Kersey, you will not be alone at all, my dear." Jane patted her hand. Maria would miss her regardless of her new friends. "Miss Granger, might we take that walk now? I think I must stretch my legs after eating those lovely little cakes." She eyed the floral arrangement above the fireplace. "Could you show me where you found those wine-colored leaves? They are an exquisite color for arranging this time of year."

"Of course, my lady." The young lady rose instantly and addressed her brother. "Will you and Lady Kersey accompany us?"

Maria started, glancing at Mr. Granger and catching his eye. The warmth she found there sent heat streaming to her cheeks until she thought they must be on fire.

"I believe Lady Kersey and I will also avail ourselves of the crisp air, if you are amenable, my lady?" He turned his gaze full on her and Maria's stomach dropped.

"Yes . . . yes, of course," she finally stuttered out. "That would be lovely."

Carstairs assisted them with their coats and Miss Granger led the way out the front door and around the side to the little wilderness they had seen from the drawing room. She and Jane walked together, their avid conversation about the local flora becoming more and more animated as Miss Granger pointed out various plants. That left Maria to stroll next to the silent Mr. Granger, who stared straight ahead as they wound down the path.

The silence lengthened until Maria wished heartily for something to say. However, all she could think of was their meeting yesterday, and her completely inappropriate kiss. Her cheeks stung, although not with the cold. Her behavior had been too forward. Likely Mr. Granger wished never to speak to her again but had been too polite to renege on his invitation to tea.

Still, the memory of that moment lingered, even if the kiss itself had not. He'd obviously been startled — she'd been startled as well, not having planned it at all but had just done it — but he hadn't backed away. So had he enjoyed the kiss? His lips had been firm, his breath sweet with wine. She had the recollection of her hand meeting his hard chest, but she'd been focused, for those fleeting moments, on his mouth, on his nearness, on the fire that erupted in the pit of her stomach and shot downward to her nether regions. She'd not felt that way since . . .

"Please allow me, Lady Kersey, to heartily apologize for yesterday's inappropriate behavior on my part." Mr. Granger continued to avoid her direct gaze, though he seemed to glance her way every second or two.

"I do not see why you feel the need to apologize, Mr. Granger, for actions that were not of your doing. I was the one who kissed you, if you remember." No sooner were the words out than Maria clapped her hand over her mouth. Oh, lord, how had that slipped out? She had not kept herself in check very well the past two days.

"Yes, Lady Kersey." He turned and pinned her with his bright blue gaze. "I do remember that, very well indeed."

Maria's heart thumped in her chest, loudly enough to be heard, she'd wager. "If you do, then you should know you do not need to ask forgiveness for something you did not do."

"Ah, but I was a willing party to it, my lady." His eyes bore into hers until she slowed to a stop, unable to breathe. "A partner in crime."

She struggled to take in a breath to ask, "What crime?"

"Larceny."

Frowning, Maria just stared at him, utterly confused. "What did you steal?"

"I did not steal it, but allowed it to be stolen." He kept his gaze trained on her until she swallowed hard.

"What . . . what?" She could scarcely get the word out.

"My heart, my lady."

Her mouth went dry. Could she be understanding him rightly?

He glanced ahead at his sister and her cousin, but they were deep in conversation, bent over a bed of purple flowers. Gently, he took her hand. "I have no right to even dream of such a boon, but when you kissed me yesterday, I began to hope that perhaps the honor of deepening our friendship might be within the sphere of possibility."

The very words she had wanted to hear from this man, although perhaps they could be deemed a bit hasty on his part, given that she was not out of mourning yet. Still, she had to admit her own wishes toward deepening their friendship were the same as his. What a truly glorious afternoon this had turned into. But they must be cautious. "Oh, Mr. Granger."

She too took a quick look at Miss Granger and Jane, who had just stood up and were turning back toward them. Jane could not know of this or Maria would get the scolding of a lifetime. Slipping her hand from Mr. Granger's, Maria stepped back from him and whispered, "They are coming. We must wait to talk."

He nodded briefly, then abruptly began speaking about a cluster of red flowers ringing a large boulder to the right of the path. "These are *Cyclamen hederifolium,* my lady. The color is lovely and lasts all the way into spring, despite the cold and snow. Quite a hardy plant."

Jane was approaching them, her gimlet eyes fixed on Maria.

"I certainly hope it is, Mr. Granger." She lowered her voice and smiled at him. "I think we are in for a blow. Hello, my dear." She turned her smile on her cousin. "What were you and Miss Granger examining? You looked terribly engrossed with it."

"A particularly hardy species of crocus, Lady Kersey." Miss Granger spoke up brightly. "According to my brother, it has weathered the cold and snow hereabouts ever since he came to Kersey Hall some six or seven years ago, isn't that right, Hugh?"

"It is, my dear. I planted it with my own hands just after the old earl hired me." Mr. Granger's expression remained pleasant, despite a tightening of his jaw. "They are, perhaps, my favorite flower for the winter." His gaze strayed back to Maria's face. "I have loved them for a long time. They can thrive despite adverse conditions" — he chuckled — "and are beautiful into the bargain."

Heart melting, Maria tried to look away, but how could one turn one's eyes from a gentleman declaring his love? Never mind that she couldn't quite tell if it was for the flowers or herself, but she'd wager it was for both of them.

"Yes, I see." Jane's clipped words broke the spell Mr. Granger had been weaving. "They are pretty and rugged when pitted against the elements, but are they truly happy in such harsh conditions? Should they not, perhaps, be more sheltered from the cruel world so they may live and be admired for a longer time to come?"

"But they like the cold weather, my lady." The puzzled voice of Miss Granger broke in. The young lady's brows had drawn down in a slight frown. "The more the elements throw at them, the more they seem to thrive. Like they enjoy the challenge, I think."

"Perhaps they do, Miss Granger." With a sniff, Jane cut her gaze directly at Maria. "Perhaps they do."

After returning to the house, during which march Jane stayed stubbornly by Maria's side, Maria and Jane made their goodbyes and Maria promised to invite Miss Granger to Kersey Hall within the week. Maria and

Jane took their leave and ambled out the front door and onto the crushedshell driveway.

Determined not to have the conversation — or scolding rather — she feared would ensue as soon as they lost sight of Wingate, Maria launched into cheerful chatter about the cyclamens and crocuses. Surely the flowers she was always so enthusiastic about would distract Jane from anything else on her mind.

"Maria, for the love of all that is holy, please tell me you have not been in Mr. Granger's bed."

Stopped mid-stride, Maria gaped at her cousin, appalled that she would think such a thing of her. "I most certainly have not! I barely know the gentleman. Why on earth would you think I had done such a thing?"

Fury in her eye, Jane rounded on her. "Because if you remember, this is exactly the way you acted with Alan Garrett a year ago last August. And you apparently had only known him some hours before he found his way to your bed."

Opening her mouth to deny that accusation, Maria stopped herself before she could say a word. She'd been a scared, grieving girl of seventeen, wide-eyed and totally unprepared for a house party where gentlemen and rogues mingled freely. Alan had been one such rogue. They had conversed a bit, though he'd done most of the talking, then they had danced, after which he'd taken her outside for a breath of fresh air after all the heat of the party. On the veranda he'd kissed her, declared her young and lovely, and talked his way into her bed before she quite knew how he'd come to be there. So yes, she grudgingly had to admit, Jane was within her rights to ask her that.

"I assure you, Cousin, I have not allowed Mr. Granger, nor any other man, in my bed since Alan died." Whether she'd wanted one there was another question. Pray Jane did not ask that one.

"Then why were you and Mr. Granger flirting like a courting couple? It really was quite distasteful, Maria. I only hope Miss Granger, who is a sweet and innocent young lady, did not understand what you two were doing. 'I have loved them for a long time' and 'They are beautiful into the bargain.' " She shook her head vehemently. "A schoolgirl would know better than to act so in public."

"Please settle yourself, Cousin. We were hardly in a public place."

"You were carrying on in front of his sister and me. That is more than public enough."

"We have been very discreet." Maria continued on her way down the path. "No one was in the room when I kissed him." Despite the storm about to descend because of that revelation, the relief Maria experienced by not having to keep it from her cousin was enormous.

"You kissed him?" Jane stopped dead, forcing Maria to turn back to her. "What were you thinking?"

"That he was a sad and lonely man and I wanted to comfort him as best I could. Was that so wrong?"

"Maria." Taking Maria's arm, Jane looped her arm through it and they continued toward Kersey Hall. "I understand that Mr. Granger is concerned about his brother, but you cannot let that cloud your judgment. We have talked about this before. You must marry well if you intend to provide for your daughter and yourself. Mr. Granger is not the sort of man who will be able to do so."

"I have found out a bit more about Mr. Granger." Maria paused to gather her thoughts. She'd promised him that she would not reveal the particulars about his brother's situation, but she still needed to convey to Jane that Mr. Granger would be an excellent and eligible *parti,* without breaking her confidence. "His father was apparently a prosperous landowner, and as Mr. Granger has an older brother, the land and property was passed down to him. However" — she slowed, speaking deliberately — "as you remember, his brother met with a terrible accident and has been in a state of decline ever since. That is why Miss Granger now resides with her brother here, rather than with the invalid who is so incapacitated he cannot act as a proper chaperone to her." In a final attempt to make her cousin understand, Maria grasped Jane's arm. "It is not anticipated that he will survive much longer. At which time the younger Mr. Granger will inherit a very sizeable property."

Her face set in lines of concerned determination, Jane patted Maria's arm. "I am sorry for the Granger family for their grievous trouble; however, if the elder Mr. Granger lingers, or recovers completely, the younger Mr. Granger will have no means of support except as the steward of the property you at one time owned. Can you not see the disaster approaching on the horizon, my dear?"

"I know you are only looking out for my welfare and that of little Jane, but I cannot help but think that I should give Mr. Granger every opportunity to prove himself capable of providing for us." Slowly, Maria spoke the words Jane would be loath to hear. "He has declared himself to me and I have given him to understand I am agreeable to deepening our friendship to the point of . . . something more."

Closing her eyes, Jane sighed. "I feared this would happen, but you are determined as God made you." She began walking with short, quick strides so that Maria had to almost run to catch up with her. "When we arrive at Kersey Hall I will have to write to Kinellan and explain that I once again must put off my visit to his home."

"But why, Jane?" Her cousin must be terribly upset to make her postpone her long-anticipated trip again. "I assure you, I can take care of myself perfectly well."

"I believed that last year, and you ended up married to a most unsuitable man. I will not have such a thing happen to you once more while you are under my charge." With head held high, Jane continued down the pathway, her mind, apparently, irrevocably made up. "Mark my words, you will not make another disastrous marriage, if I have to remain at Kersey Hall until my namesake is ready to make her come out."

CHAPTER FOURTEEN

When Maria and Jane came down to breakfast early one morning several days later, Maria was surprised to find the room unusually full. She and Jane almost always breakfasted alone. Lady Kersey was wont to have a tray in her room, her husband broke his fast very early, and their two sons apparently did not eat breakfast, or ate much later in the morning, for they were never in evidence. Today, however, all the family were gathered around the table, with the startling addition of Mr. Ganger and his sister.

Heat raced into Maria's cheeks. She had not seen Mr. Granger for almost a week. Ever since their tea the previous Sunday, Jane had watched her like a hungry hawk circling a field mouse. Therefore, Maria had had no chance to seek out Mr. Granger, to talk about his declaration and assure him of her interest as well. Now her mouth was so dry she probably couldn't speak a word if she got the opportunity.

An insistent nudging in her back turned out to be Jane pushing her to continue into the breakfast chamber.

"Good morning, all." Jane breezed by her, making for the nearest place, next to Lady Kersey and Miss Granger.

"Good morning, everyone." Putting on a bright smile, Maria went forward, toward the one seat left — between Mr. Granger and Lord Wetherby

"Good morning, my dears." Lord Kersey stopped eating his eggs to beam at her. "So splendid you are down at last."

Murmuring a polite "good morning" to the men on either side of her, Maria slid into her seat and took up her napkin with shaking hands. This assembly had been the last thing she'd expected when she'd come down this morning. Her place between the two gentlemen both a dream and a nightmare.

Lord Wetherby glanced down at her, a knowing smile on his face. He'd tried to get her alone several times during the week, but Jane's almost constant presence had deterred his success. Now he exuded a confidence that gave Maria cause to dread the meal.

On her right, Mr. Granger ate sausages and ham while conversing with his sister. He turned to greet her, smiled briefly, then went back to his other partner.

A footman placed a plate before her and she swallowed hard. Given her current situation, food would likely choke her. Slowly she adjusted her napkin in her lap, lifted her cup of tea and stirred it.

"Did you forget something, Cousin Maria?"

She jumped at Lord Wetherby's silky voice so close to her ear. "Forget what, my lord?"

"The sugar." He nodded to her still stirring hand, although she'd not put either milk or sugar into the cup yet.

"I suppose I did not. Thank you," she added as he handed her the sugar basin. His finger brushed hers in the process and she gasped at the contact of his bare skin on hers. Hastily she fished out the smallest lump she could find and dropped it in her cup.

"Milk as well?" His eyebrow rose, likely in anticipation of another touch of her hand.

Eyeing the milk pitcher, which sat closer to Lord Wetherby than to her, she demurred. "No, thank you, my lord. Not this morning."

She enjoyed tea better with milk, but not

at the expense of further contact with his lordship.

"Good morning, again, ladies and gentlemen." Lord Kersey spoke up over the chatter of the breakfasters. "I know for several of you this morning's summons was a surprise" — he looked directly first at Lord Wetherby and then at James Garrett — "but you really should not have been, given that today is December sixth."

December sixth? Maria looked blankly around the table. Jane's face showed the same confusion that must be on her own face. However, Mr. and Miss Granger were now smiling as well as the Garretts, obviously understanding the importance of the date.

Naturally, Jane would be the one to speak up first. "I'm sorry, my lord, but what is the significance of December sixth?"

"It is Saint Nicholas Day, my dear," Lady Kersey answered, her eyes lit with excitement. "A holiday we enjoyed celebrating in Virginia very much."

"Oh, yes, in my flurry of unpacking" — Jane sent an arch look toward Maria — "I quite forgot the day." Sipping her tea nonchalantly, Jane laughed softly. "I have not truly celebrated it since my children were small."

"Does it have something to do with Advent?" Maria cocked her head. She'd heard the day spoken of, but as the beginning of the Christmas season.

Carefully setting down his cup, Mr. Granger smiled at her indulgently. "If I may, my lord?"

Nodding, Lord Kersey raised his cup in a salute. "Thank you, Mr. Granger."

"It isn't directly connected to Advent, Lady Kersey." Suddenly all Mr. Granger's attention was focused on her, making her want to shrink back in her chair.

All eyes seemed to be on her.

Mr. Granger smiled kindly and continued. "It is, however, a Christian feast day and a celebration of the good works of Saint Nicholas of Myra, who was known for secretly giving gifts to children."

"I remember getting small gifts in my stockings when I was young." That had been fun. How had she forgotten all about that? She would have to begin doing that with Jane next year. "How is it celebrated now?"

"The same way you have said. The evening before, all the children put out their shoes or stockings, and the good saint is supposed to come by in the night and fill them with candy or gold coins." Mr. Granger exchanged a glance with his sister. "You remember that, don't you, Bella?" He turned back to Maria, making tingles of excitement speed through her. "It also unofficially begins the Christmas season."

"I must say, there is nothing whatsoever wrong with the giving of gold coins." James Garrett spoke up for the first time. "When Anthony and I were small, December sixth was our favorite day of the year. We were always in pocket for the rest of the year."

"But the stockings and coins sound like something that should have been done last night, my lord." Cocking her head, Maria reluctantly turned her attention to Lord Kersey. "So how do you plan to celebrate this year?"

"Anthony came up with a grand idea."

A chill sliced down Maria's spine, making her shiver. Anything Lord Wetherby came up with probably forwarded his own aims.

"Usually we gather our greenery on Christmas Eve morning and decorate the house during the afternoon. This year, because we are expecting guests to begin arriving early next week for the house party, Anthony suggested we use Saint Nicholas Day to go gather evergreens so the house will be festive and fragrant for the party." A twinkle in Lord Kersey's eye told her he wasn't quite through. "When we all return to the Hall, perhaps the good saint will have left presents for those who have been good this year."

An excited chattering broke out around the room. Now might be a good time to ask Mr. Granger to arrange a time for them to talk.

Before she could engage him, however, Lord Wetherby leaned over her, making her jump, and whispered in her ear. "I think a day out in the fresh air will be rather stimulating, don't you, Cousin?"

"The crisp air will certainly make for a pleasant walk in the woods, if we don't tarry too long." Maria rose, her breakfast untouched. "We wouldn't want to contract a severe chill, would we?" She hurried to her room, bent on dressing more warmly. The outing did sound like fun, and since Mr. Granger apparently was to be a part of the festivities, she could likely manage to steal some time with him. She wanted badly to talk to him, to assure him of her interest. If they could wander away from the others, perhaps they could do more than just talk.

That was bad of her. She was technically still in mourning for her husband, and here she was looking forward to seeing another man. Well, it served Alan right. He'd seen other women — seen them and more — and while they were married too. He was now dead and so it was time for Maria to make up her own mind about men such as Mr. Granger.

Maria laced up her sturdy half-boots, little worn and very stylish. She added a warmer gown of dark brown merino wool, serviceable but elegant, and a pair of mittens. With her winter-weight pelisse, she should be quite warm enough. She ran down the stairs to the entry hall to find Miss Granger talking with Lady Kersey.

"Look, Lady Kersey." So excited she could not stand still, Miss Granger danced on her tiptoes as she gazed around the room, her face a study in joy. She pointed to a line of stockings, all different sizes and colors, hanging from the fireplace mantel at the end of the hall. A tag with a person's name was pinned to each stocking. "When we return from the woods, Lady Kersey swears there may be presents in these stockings."

"In the spirit of Saint Nicholas's feast day, I suggested the stockings as part of the fun today." Lady Kersey smiled at Maria. She always seemed to genuinely wish to be of service to anyone in need. "It was always such fun to watch the boys digging through their stockings, looking for sweets and coins."

"Oh, but it does sound like a tremendous amount of fun." Squeezing the strings of her reticule, Miss Granger looked about the largish entry. Likely looking for her brother.

Where was Mr. Granger? Surreptitiously, Maria tried to spy him, but his handsome face and broad-shouldered frame were nowhere to be seen.

The front door opened and Mr. Granger strode in. "Ladies, gentlemen, your carriage awaits." He laughed and ushered them out to the circle driveway where a shooting brake stood.

"Surely we could have taken the carriage, my dear." Frowning, Lady Kersey confronted her husband.

"Part of the adventure, my lady," he said as he escorted his wife and handed her into the rustic cart meant to take gentlemen out to the field for shooting.

Mr. James Garrett handed Jane and Miss Granger up and into the open cart. Maria then faced a terrible dilemma. She stood at the rear of the brake, Mr. Granger on one side, Lord Wetherby on the other. Both held hands out to assist her. Of course she wished to put her hand in Mr. Granger's, but to snub his lordship would hardly be either considerate or canny if she wanted to keep her attraction to Mr. Granger a secret. In the end, she placed one hand in either of theirs and clambered aboard to sit by Jane. The gentlemen followed her quickly and the horses started.

"You are a regular Solomon, my dear," Jane whispered. "Still, your preference is showing, if ever so slightly. Learn to school your eyes and you will be fine."

That was a true criticism. Maria had always had a difficult time trying to shield her thoughts from showing on her face, one reason she was such a wretched card player. Anyone who paid a modicum of attention to her, knew her thoughts as well as if they could read them in a book.

"You must instruct me, my dear," she whispered back. "No one conceals their thoughts better than you do. How do you do it?"

Her cousin chuckled. "An old trick, but not easy to accomplish. You must be able to spin gold out of nothing and do so with so much sincerity that people wish to believe what you say is true so much they refuse to accept the truth even when you tell it to them."

"That does sound difficult." Maria sighed. "What is the next best way?"

"Tell the truth." Jane made the statement glibly, but there was enough gravity to it that Maria could tell the advice was not lightly given. "You will always find that to be the safest and truest path."

"And often the most difficult one, if I don't miss my guess."

Jane nodded. "I concede that point, but still you will find, honesty is the virtue that will stand you in good stead in the end."

"What are you two ladies talking about that has made you gloomy?" Lord Wetherby stood and maneuvered himself over beside Maria.

Like a ball out of a pistol, Maria shot back, "The virtue of telling the truth before lies, my lord."

"Good God, no wonder you are Friday-faced." He raised his hands in mock horror. "I beg of you, turn your conversation to something merrier and in keeping with the season, or you shall both turn into a Krampus and punish us all."

"Especially you, my lord?" Jane's voice dropped to a sultry drawl. "Will you need to be punished more than anyone else?"

Lord Wetherby stared at Jane, his tongue coming out to wet his lips. "I have not been an angel this year, but I can be awfully good when I want to be."

"I suspect you are, my lord." The coquettish sound in Jane's voice had the man almost salivating.

This was Jane in her element, always flirtatious and witty. A sensual woman with an appetite, so their other widow friends had told her, that put all the rest of them — even Fanny — to shame. Had she gotten bored waiting around to go to Kinellan in Scotland and now set her cap at Lord Wetherby? Not to marry, of course, but simply for a dalliance?

Well, if it distracted his lordship from her, Maria would be ever so grateful. She hoped to meander off with Mr. Granger for a time at least. If Lord Wetherby was occupied elsewhere, that would make her own flirtation that much easier to begin.

The brake pulled into a clearing, not far, as the crow flies, from Francis House. The trees had changed to evergreen, with pine, fir, and holly scattered in a ring around the natural clearing. The gentlemen jumped out, then assisted the ladies until everyone was in a circle around Lord Kersey, looking to him eagerly for instruction.

"The greenery we like to use in the house is fir, holly, rosemary, and yew if you can find it. These plants tend to be very pungent, so the house will be fresh and lovely for our guests. Oh." He chuckled softly. "We will also need to bring home several mistletoe balls, to make kissing boughs out of." His grin grew broader. "We cannot have Christmas without a bit of kissing now, can we?"

The gentlemen sent up a roar of approval while the ladies fell silent or laughed nervously. Maria did not join in the laughter. She was too busy trying to keep her eye on Mr. Granger, who stood next to his sister and Mr. Garrett. Good. Now if Jane would pair off with Lord Wetherby, she could join the Granger party and perhaps pair off with the man she sought.

"If everyone will gather closer, I will give the signal and you must scatter and bring back as much greenery as you can. Remember, Saint Nicholas is watching! If you want to have something good in your stocking when we return, you must bring back as much of the fragrant boughs as possible." Lord Kersey held his arm up and dropped it. "Begin!"

With a great shout, people began grabbing partners' hands and pulling them off into the woods without further ado.

A strong hand grasped Maria's gloved hand and she turned smiling into the also grinning face of Lord Wetherby.

CHAPTER FIFTEEN

Drat it. Maria's face froze, a pleasant smile plastered across it, even though the disappointment was almost a physical blow. Why did Lord Wetherby have to choose her? Why hadn't Jane's seduction taken him to her instead? At least, that's what she thought would have happened. She glanced around for her cousin, and found her standing with Mr. Garrett, Mr. Granger, and Miss Granger. Mr. Granger was turned away, pointing toward a stand of evergreens to the east.

Abruptly, Lord Wetherby pulled her to him and they started off into the woods to the right of the brake, dodging around trees left and right, forcing her to run until her side ached.

Enough. She gave a mighty tug and her hand slipped free of his. Winded, she stood panting as Lord Wetherby continued on a few feet until he realized he no longer held her hand.

"My . . . lord!" Goodness, but she was out of breath. "I believe we have gone far enough. If we find sufficient quantities of the greenery we seek, we will be unable to carry it all back to the brake."

"We can pile it up here and let the footmen carry it back for us." He had walked back to her and now stood close, so close that his bergamot scent warred with the fresh smell of the firs all around them.

"Then we had best get to it, shall we?" With that Maria stalked off to the right, heading for a large stand of holly bushes that should be easy to collect, praying he would not follow her. The clean scent of the holly brushed the lingering traces of the spicy bergamot away, and she began tearing off small twigs with the bright red berries, avoiding the sharp points of the distinctive leaves.

Mentally bewailing the fact that they had brought no basket to collect the greenery in, Maria lay the torn branches carefully in her arm, going methodically from bush to bush, trying not to strip an entire plant, but leave something of it intact to grow and seed for next year.

A basket and scissors certainly would have been very useful to this endeavor. Maria's hands became scratched, even through the protection of her gloves. Perhaps she should have gone after the fir branches instead. Gathering up an armful of small pieces, she judged she had enough and turned toward the growing pile of branches on the ground. As she tossed them on the heap, one of the holly leaves caught her index finger, jabbing deep through the material of her glove and into the tender flesh of the pad.

"Ouch!" Maria dropped the branches she carried and peeled off her glove. A red indentation showed the location of the wound and she squeezed the finger to see if it still seeped. As she grasped the finger a bright bead of blood welled up on the pad. "Drat."

"What happened?" Lord Wetherby came trotting over, took one look at how she held her finger, and grabbed her hand.

"I just poked one of the holly leaves into my finger. I'm certain it's all right."

"Nonsense." He took his handkerchief from an inner pocket and gently rubbed the place where the blood had come, although most of it had been wiped away. Another gentle squeeze of her finger had produced nothing in the way of her life's blood. Time to move on.

"Thank you, my lord, but the bleeding seems to have stopped now. It was less than a scratch. We can go on with our gathering." Maria tried to pull her hand away from him, but he held her fast in his grip.

"Best let me make sure the cut's not too deep." He held her hand up close to his eyes. A sultry glance at her and he kissed her finger.

"My lord." Desperately, Maria tried to pull her hand away from his lips, but to no avail. As she had noted during her first encounter with him in the corridor at Kersey Hall, the gentleman had strength much greater than hers. And she was here, all alone with him. "I tell you my hand is fine."

"Indeed it is, Maria." He kissed her finger once more before moving on to her open palm. "As is all of you. Exquisite as a porcelain figurine and just as cold." The softness of his mouth caressed her flesh, sending a frisson of warmth to her core. "I suspect you are not always so icy." His lips seared her palm again. "I'll wager I can spread a warmth through you like nothing you have ever known before."

Face hot as fire, both from mortification at his attentions and the heat he was generating in her nether regions, Maria tried to slip her hand out of his grasp. She must protest or else he would think she welcomed his advances. And despite her traitorous body's reactions, she did not want this man's addresses. "My lord, this is most unseemly. Do you not remember I am still in mourning for a husband not yet a year in his grave?"

He raised his head from where his lips had grazed her palm, his eyes coal black, his breath coming in hard pants. "So if you were no longer in mourning, you would not object, Cousin? Perhaps we can find a way to have your bereavement cut short." He snaked his arm around her waist and pushed her against his hard body. "So you may pay your respects to the living instead."

Stricken, Maria began to struggle in earnest. A hard ridge ground into the lower part of her stomach, unmistakably the very large bulge of his erection. If she could not get away from him, Lord Wetherby would surely push her to the ground and take her right here. She remembered well the heat and urgency Alan had shown when they had been here, at Kersey Hall, dallying before they were married. She and Jane had visited Lord Sinclaire's estate, not far from the Hall, and she and Alan had met almost daily. The memory of how, once he had become aroused, it had been impossible to deny him anything came back sharply to her now. Now his kinsman, with a similar reputation as a rogue, seemed very like that as well.

Panic shot through her and she struggled in earnest against him, twisting to and fro. Her right hand he had immobilized, but her other was free. She slapped him on the back, though it was like hitting a wall, impervious to the blow. "Lord Wetherby, let me go!"

Ignoring her, he loosened her wounded hand and grabbed her around the waist. "I have been trying to catch you for weeks, sweet cousin. Why ever would I let you go now?"

"Stop this, my lord." She pushed against him, but it was like trying to move a large boulder. The man was hard as granite. "Let me go!"

"Shhh, they'll hear you."

Scream. She could bring rescue with a simple shout. Gasping for breath, Maria filled her lungs and opened her mouth, only to have his plastered onto her before she could make a sound. His tongue shot into her mouth, thrusting in and out, making her almost gag as he delved deeper and deeper. She pushed again on his shoulders but couldn't find a purchase on his jacket, so the heels of her hands slid harmlessly upward and off the garment. What could she do?

He'd bent her backward over his arm, pressing her so far she could see the sky directly above them. In a flash of intuition, she lifted both her legs off the ground. He'd tipped them so far off balance that they crashed to the ground. His arms had released her as he struggled to regain his footing, so Maria managed to fling herself away from him as they hit the ground. Unfortunately, the fall knocked the wind out of her and she lay staring at the sky once more, struggling to draw breath back into her lungs. Groaning and cursing from close by told her Lord Wetherby had not suffered any grievous harm. An eternity passed as she lay hitching in little gulps of air, praying that she would recover before Lord Wetherby could rouse himself and attack her again.

With a huge effort, she rolled to her side and struggled to her feet. Lord Wetherby had landed face-first on the ground, his head apparently coming down on a rock. He bled, though not copiously, from a gash on his forehead.

"What the devil is going on here?"

Maria whirled around to find Mr. Granger, face darkened with rage, speeding toward them. Right behind him were Jane, Miss Granger, and James Garrett.

Jane darted forward and pulled Maria into her arms. "Are you all right, my dear?"

Although still shaken, Maria nodded. Best for them all if she said nothing about what had just occurred. At least not publicly. "I am fine. There was a . . . little accident. Lord Wetherby took the worst of it I believe."

"Anthony." James Garrett dashed forward to assist his brother to rise, the latter groaning and clutching his head.

"Lady Kersey, tell me what happened." Mr. Granger had come to her side, although he still sent deadly glances at Lord Wetherby.

Sighing, Maria cut her gaze briefly to Jane. Her cousin would understand and forgive the lie she was about to tell. Hopefully convincing enough that Mr. Granger would accept her word, or want to believe her enough to do so. "One of those freakish accidents you read about in *The Times,* Mr. Granger. Rather stupid really."

Lord Wetherby was on his feet now, glaring at her while pressing his handkerchief to his forehead. He'd likely agree with the tale she was about to tell, as it would not paint him as the villain he actually was.

His gaze darting suspiciously between her and Lord Wetherby, Mr. Granger nodded. "Go on."

Keeping Jane's admonition to keep to the truth as much as possible, Maria launched into her tale with what she hoped was believable excitement. "I was gathering holly boughs and one of the thorny leaves pricked my finger rather deeply. I took off my glove and looked at it, but it was bleeding more heavily than it should have done. Lord Wetherby came to look at it and produced his handkerchief to bind it. As we were standing there, very close together, a huge bird swooped down as if to attack us."

"A bird?" Mr. Granger's brows lowered. "What kind of bird?"

"A very large bird. With brown feathers is all I recall. I'm afraid I have no idea what kind of bird it was." Carefully keeping her gaze away from Mr. Granger's, Maria continued. "I think it believed we had some kind of food in our hands, because it dove at us out of the blue."

Mr. Granger narrowed his eyes and peered at her. "Lady Kersey, I hardly think —"

"I believe it was a kestrel, Granger." Everyone turned to Lord Wetherby, still holding his handkerchief to his head. "It wasn't especially large, although it probably startled the lady enough that she believed it to be enormous."

His face a dark study, Mr. Granger folded his arms across his chest and shook his head. "You expect me to believe you were attacked by a kestrel?"

"Kestrels are indigenous to this area, Mr. Granger." Fishing in his pocket, Mr. Garrett drew out a clean handkerchief and passed it to his brother. "I am devoted to the study of birds, so when I was informed we would be removing to Suffolk, I made a study of the birds that inhabit the environs." Peering at the wound when the bloody linen was removed, he shook his head dispassionately. "No, it's still bleeding, Anthony. Keep this pressed against it." He assisted Lord Wetherby calmly and efficiently, seemingly a good man to have in a crisis.

Pity he wasn't the heir. Maria might possibly have persuaded herself to marry such a man as James Garrett. If there had been no Mr. Granger. The thought drew her attention to the steward, standing there, his attention riveted on her. Their gazes met and her heart raced like a filly on a dry track.

"So what happened when the bird attacked you, Lady Kersey?" The intensity of Mr. Granger's scrutiny set her stomach to

254

churning. "I did not hear a scream or a shriek, yet the bird was upon you suddenly. Weren't you startled?"

"I . . . I was so surprised I didn't have time to scream, Mr. Granger. It all happened so quickly. We were standing here, then we were on the ground." She stared keenly at Lord Wetherby. A little corroboration would undoubtedly help allay Mr. Granger's suspicions. "It was . . . sudden."

"Indeed, it was, Granger." Lord Wetherby puffed out his chest, as if enjoying the attention or the drama of the scene. "I was looking at the lady's thumb when out of nowhere the bird attacked me. Hit my forehead. I staggered, but managed to push the lady out of danger before I fell to the ground."

"You pushed her out of danger?" If Mr. Granger's face got any redder, he might have an apoplexy.

"Yes." Maria hung her head. More than anything she hated lying to this man. But it had to be done. For both their sakes. "He did." She turned to face Lord Wetherby. The weasel smiled at her, beneficent and self-sacrificing, and more than a touch self-satisfied. Gritting her teeth, she paused while summoning the strength to finish the task. "Thank you, Lord Wetherby, for saving me."

A groan went up from Granger while Wetherby beamed at her. "Not a'tall, my dear. You must know I'd do it anytime you are in danger."

Mr. Granger looked as if he'd eaten toads. "Then let us pray very hard that she need not call upon you for such services again, my lord. Lady Kersey, I suggest you return to the brake with your cousin, my sister, and Mr. Garrett." The harried steward then addressed the latter gentleman. "Will you be so good as to direct the brake to come to this clearing to pick us up. Lord Wetherby is in no condition to walk so far."

"I am completely capable of walking, Granger." Lord Wetherby brushed past the steward, removing the handkerchief he'd been pressing to the wound. The cut welled with blood, so suddenly it dripped down Lord Wetherby's brow and onto his cheek. The man's face drained of color, his eyes grew wide until the whites shone all around the two dots of blue. He staggered to a halt.

Hugh leaped forward and grabbed Wetherby before his knees buckled. "Go now, Mr. Garrett!"

Torn between wishing to stay with his brother and fetching the conveyance, Garrett threw them a stricken look, then took off at a sprint, crashing through the trees and underbrush. Jane and Miss Granger exchanged a look of their own, then began to pick their way along the path, back the way they had come. Maria leaned heavily on her cousin with her head on her shoulder, quite exhausted from all the excitement. She was so glad this miserable *tête-à-tête* was over, although she had not yet begun to pay the piper for this tune to which she must now dance a jig.

As the ladies and Mr. Garrett vanished into the trees, Hugh returned his attention to Lord Wetherby, well aware that Lady Kersey had just given him a Banbury story for certain. The next question he wished to have answered was why.

Knowing Wetherby's ilk, and the lady's charms, Hugh was pretty sure the heir had assaulted her in some way. When he'd come into the clearing, both of them had been on the ground, the lady getting warily to her feet, her attention fixed on Wetherby, who had been slower to arise. Neither of them had looked to the sky as if fearing the "bird" might return to renew the attack. No, Lady Kersey's sole focus had been making certain she stayed as far as possible from Wetherby.

So if she was protecting him from retribution at his father's or, more likely, Hugh's hands, she must have a reason for doing so. He'd get that from the lady herself later.

"Perhaps you should sit down until the brake arrives, my lord. You don't want your wound to bleed again." Hugh would dearly love to plant the blackguard a facer, give him something to moan about other than the little scrape on his forehead.

"You may be right, Granger." Wetherby sauntered to an outcropping of rock a foot or two away and sat down gingerly. "I cannot risk my life doing such heroic deeds anymore. I must think of the family's future rather than the paltry, outdated attempts at chivalry required by Polite Society. It is ridiculous that all gentlemen must adhere to the strictures of this ancient code."

"And yet adhere they must, or be labeled no gentleman at all." Pacing around the clearing in an attempt to restrain himself from throttling the man, Hugh did his best not to picture his hands around Wetherby's throat. The temptation at this moment might be too great. "Lady Kersey was very grateful for your defense of her during the 'attack.'"

With a slow turn of his neck, Wetherby's gaze came to rest on Hugh, his mouth drawn into an insolent smile. "You think the lady was lying, don't you?"

"A gentleman does not accuse a lady of telling falsehoods, no matter the reason." There must have been a good one to make Lady Kersey defend this wretched man. Hugh had made inquiries about William Garrett and his family to friends of his and his late father's in Town when Lady Kersey had first written him that the earl had been found. The information he'd obtained had been heavily concentrated on Anthony, the eldest son. All of it had been unsavory to say the least. And Hugh's observations of the man firsthand had confirmed his opinion of Anthony, Lord Wetherby to be correct. A bounder and a rake who gambled to excess and did not take losing with good grace, Lord Wetherby had the kind of reputation that would give mothers nightmares. His looks had allowed him to prey upon a variety of women — his position as heir to an earldom would likely entice more to be drawn to him and subsequently ruined.

"Perhaps she did not wish her reputation ruined over a bit of a romp in the woods." The smug face, lips turned up in a cruel smile, made Hugh itch to wipe it off with a yelp of pain.

"If that were the case, I can understand the lady's reluctance to confess such activity. However, I highly doubt that was the truth of the matter." If, by some unimaginable quirk it had been, then Hugh would very quietly relinquish any interest in the lady whatsoever, her preference in men therefore losing her his respect.

"You seem to take a keen interest in the lady's private doings, Granger." Wetherby stretched his legs out before him in a languid pose. "Am I detecting an odor of sour grapes?"

Clenching his fists until his fingernails bit deeply into his palms, Hugh set his jaw and made no reply. Surely if he gave in to his deepest desire and pummeled this popinjay senseless, the earl would sack him and perhaps bring him up on charges. That thought, as well as a superior amount of self-control, prevented him from throttling the miscreant before him. The man's words also may have hit rather too close to home.

The fact that Lady Kersey had not declared herself to him after that kiss in his office last week had preyed on his mind from time to time. Had he misjudged her actions and interest? He didn't think so, but in light of today's events, he would arrange to meet with her as soon as possible and discover once and for all where her interests lay. "The only smell here, my lord, is that of fear. Whether it was the lady's or yours, I don't quite know — yet."

The rumbling of the brake creaking through the underbrush saved Hugh from any further conversation or temptation to plant Wetherby a facer. That time was sure to come, and the sooner the better as far as he was concerned. He'd not mind getting the sack at all if it came on the heels of pummeling that self-satisfied smirk off Wetherby's face. It all depended on what he could get Lady Kersey to confess to him, and when.

CHAPTER SIXTEEN

Lying in her bed, dreading going down to dinner, Maria sighed and turned her face to the wall, wishing for the oblivion of sleep to claim her. No such luck. Her mind kept circling back to the moment when she'd had to lie about what had happened to her and Lord Wetherby, to the enraged look on Mr. Granger's face when she'd thanked the scoundrel for rescuing her. Without a doubt Mr. Granger knew she was not telling the truth. The problem was to let him know why without inciting him to do bodily harm to Lord Wetherby.

When they'd returned to the Hall, Maria had pled a headache, due to the morning's excitement. Lord Kersey had been preoccupied with tending to his son, sending to Cook for hot water, bandages, and broth. He'd subsequently declared that the decorating of the Hall would be postponed for a day or two to give Anthony time to recover, but still before the first expected guests would arrive on Wednesday. Perhaps by then she would have found time to speak with Mr. Granger and straighten everything out.

The door clicked open and Maria turned over. Her maid stood at the end of the bed.

"I was asked to give you this, my lady." She held out a folded piece of foolscap with no name on it.

Maria scrambled to sit up. Two possibilities crossed her mind as to the writer of the note. "Who gave it to you, Hatley?"

"Mr. Saunders, my lady."

Her late butler, now returned to footman. "Did you ask who he had it from?"

"Yes, but he wouldn't say."

Taking the square of paper, Maria waved the woman away. "Thank you, Hatley."

Once the maid had gone, Maria slowly unfolded the missive, dreading to discover the letter writer. Jane would have come to her if she had something to say, lord knows she had said quite enough already about the wretched events of this morning. Either Miss Granger or Lord or Lady Kersey could have written, to check on her welfare, but she somehow doubted it. No, most likely this letter in her hand was from either Mr. Granger or Lord Wetherby. A deep, sinking sensation flared in the pit of her stomach when she thought what each of them might have written to her. She stared at the paper, turned it over in her hands, then simply unfolded it and read the single sentence and signature.

Please meet me in the blue receiving room in half an hour.

Hugh Granger

Relief poured through her like melted snow, cooling her heightened senses. She slumped back onto the bed and pulled the covers around her, a smile stealing over her face. At last she might be able to explain to Mr. Granger both what had happened this morning and what her feelings were toward him. That both explanations were somewhat entwined might make the telling difficult, but she would make him see that she had to act as she had this morning because of her affection for him.

The mantel clock chimed four. Good heavens, he'd only given her half an hour to meet him. That was barely enough time to dress. "Hatley!"

Her maid reappeared and assisted with a hasty toilette. Inwardly, Maria bemoaned for the first time that she could not wear anything brighter than the lavender afternoon gown with gold medallions scattered over it she had now donned. Blue had always been her best color, but this would have to do for propriety's sake. Admittedly, it was her most becoming ensemble, with matching silk slippers and gold locket.

Taking a moment to calm herself, Maria sent up a prayer that everything would come right with this meeting. If Mr. Granger accepted her explanation and her declaration, then they could hopefully move forward to an understanding that would be divulged to the world as soon as her mourning period had ended. Jane would be sorely disappointed that her cousin hadn't made a better match, but Maria had decided she would not think about anyone's wishes but her own. Jane could make decisions for her own life, not for Maria's, especially since they apparently had very different ideas about love and marriage. In the end, Jane would wish her happy, and that was all that mattered.

Hurrying down the main staircase, Maria automatically scanned the area at the bottom for sight of Lord Wetherby. She fervently hoped that gentleman was firmly ensconced in his bed with a handkerchief tied over his wounded face. At any rate, he did not seem to be haunting this part of the house, so she continued down the corridor toward the front of the house. The blue receiving room was located immediately to the right of the entryway and used only for visitors. As no one was expected until Wednesday, the room would be perfect for their need for privacy in this interview.

The door was ajar. Maria put a tentative hand on the latch and pushed it lightly, then stuck her head around the dark paneled door. A fire burned brightly, casting a glow in the room where daylight was fading. Mr. Granger leaned against the mantelpiece, staring intently into the fire, every line of his lean figure a study in elegance. He'd changed into a dark gray jacket, cut excellently to accentuate his broad chest and narrow waist. At the creak of the door, he turned, his waistcoat, blue and gray striped, catching the light, brightening his blue eyes almost to azure. He straightened, his gaze riveted to her face.

Maria's heart thumped loudly and her hands grew damp. She continued into the room, then closed the door all but about two inches. That should serve for propriety's sake. With measured steps more sedate than usual, she headed toward him, thrilled to meet him alone for the first time in a week.

"Thank you for seeing me, my lady." His

voice sounded so pleasantly on the ear. Who would not wish to listen to him speak at every opportunity?

"I am very pleased to do so, Mr. Granger." How to begin her confession? Unsure now that she was before him, she shifted from one foot to the other.

"Won't you be seated, my lady?" He motioned to the small blue jacquard sofa in the center of the room.

"Of course." Self-conscious of his scrutiny, she shuffled to the couch, unable to pick up her feet properly. This would never do. She lowered herself onto the cushion at one end, and put her hands in her lap.

"I trust you have recovered from your ordeal this morning?" He seated himself on the opposite end of the sofa.

An even tone, no touch of derision or smugness. That made her way easier. "Yes, I have, thank you. And I wanted to explain to you what actually happened, Mr. Granger. There were some things that were . . . left out of my story when we were in the woods."

"I suspected as much at the time, my lady." His gaze slipped to his hands, fisted in his lap. "I assume you wish to tell me now that there was no bird involved."

"No, no bird of any kind." A stupid story, but it had served in the spur of the moment.

"I did prick my finger on a holly leaf. That much is true. Lord Wetherby gave me his handkerchief and helped wipe the blood from it." The memory of his lips on her hand made her shudder.

A moment later his hand grasped hers. "What did he do, Maria?"

The use of her Christian name startled her, for she'd not given him permission to use it. Not that she objected at all. But was he trying to take advantage of her, or put her at ease? She'd not be easy about the situation until he knew everything. The tale must be finished, despite the consequences. "He kissed my finger, my palm, then my mouth."

His grip on her hand tightened and his mouth grew taut. "And you allowed this advance?"

"Of course I didn't allow it." Appalled, she snatched her hand away. Did he truly think she had welcomed such liberties from Lord Wetherby? The numbskull. "I told him to stop, but in case you haven't seen his lordship recently, he's a big, strong man. I tried to push him away several times, but I might as well have been pushing away that wall for all the good it did me."

"I beg your pardon, my lady." Mr. Granger's face had gone from pale white to red.

"I do not mean to infer that you would do such a thing, unless you had some affection for Lord Wetherby, then I would assume —"

"Why would you even think that?" What *did* Mr. Granger think of her, after all? "If you remember, last week I was kissing you in your office." She drew herself up, and peered at him. "Do you believe me to be a woman who goes around kissing men indiscriminately?"

"Good lord, no." He scrubbed his hand down his face, drawing a deep breath. "I sincerely apologize, my lady. I just needed to make sure that Lord Wetherby wasn't under the impression that you reciprocated his interest."

Somewhat placated, Maria settled back on the sofa. "No, there was no chance he would have thought that."

Mr. Granger nodded gravely, then cocked his head. "So how did you manage to escape him? Not a bird to the rescue, I believe."

Shaking her head, Maria grinned at him. "No, I simply used his body against him."

"I beg your pardon?" A frown instantly formed on Mr. Granger's face.

"He had me bent over his arm so far that the only thing keeping us upright were my feet on the ground. So I lifted them up and down we went." One of the few times in her life that her wits had served her so well, Maria was rather proud of her solution to the situation.

"Bravo, my lady." His frown turned into a grin to rival her own. "Very neatly done."

"Thank you." Now she wished he would take her hand again.

"So why didn't you tell us this at the time?"

With a sigh, she squeezed her hands together, put her feet firmly on the floor, and launched into the explanation he should have figured out for himself by now. "Had I told you this, in front of the others and Lord Wetherby, I was very much afraid you would have done something rash, such as pummel his lordship senseless." She laid her hand on his and squeezed it. "I know you are dancing close enough to scandal as it is. You need to keep your position here until the situation with your brother is resolved, one way or the other. Beating Lord Wetherby to death would surely get you the sack and worse."

Mr. Granger chuckled and lay his hand over hers. "Thank you for that kindness. In the heat of that moment, I might very well have done something rash."

"Also, to have had such an encounter spoken of might have served as compromising enough that I could be forced to marry Lord Wetherby, although I suspect he would have denied the whole thing. Still, my reputation, which is not as sterling as it could be, given the circumstances of my late husband's death, could have suffered another blow from which it might not have recovered. Which in turn means my daughter might not be received nor be able to make a good marriage when the time comes." Maria shrugged. "So I opted to tell a little white lie which would serve to scotch any scandal and smooth things over within the family."

"I am overjoyed that you have such a good head on your shoulders." Gazing into her eyes, he took her hands in his. "I am terribly sorry if I have hurt you in any way over this incident. That was never my intention."

The warmth from his hands rivaled the heat from the blazing fire. "I never thought it was."

"I just keep thinking about . . ."

"I can't stop thinking about . . ."

They spoke at the same time and stopped, laughing together.

"What were you saying?" Eyes bright in the flickering light, Mr. Granger seemed to be holding his breath.

Suddenly shy, Maria glanced away from

his hot gaze. "I have not stopped thinking about the kiss last week."

"I have not forgotten it either. Unfortunately, at the time, I was not able to make known to you my hopes for a closer acquaintance with you." His voice had lowered to a sultry baritone, sending a sharp wave of desire through her. "I have no right to do so, as you well know my situation with regard to my brother. There is the very real possibility that, in the very near future, I will have no home save the steward's house here. Therefore, I cannot offer for your hand as I would very much like to do."

Blowing out the breath she had been holding, Maria gripped his hands, her thoughts racing. Everything he had said was true. His circumstances were as precarious as hers in some respects, as Jane would certainly point out quickly. And still, the thrill of hearing the words, that he wanted to make her an offer of marriage, could not be denied.

"Mr. Granger, I am aware of both your circumstances and of the great honor you have alluded to, in even considering asking for my hand." She glanced down at their intertwined hands, his much larger and stronger than hers. A strong man with whom she could make a life, who could protect and love her and her daughter.

"However, I am not quite certain you are aware of my feelings toward you." She raised her head to find his eyes trained on her, his mouth a straight, thin line.

Abruptly her hands were empty, and Mr. Granger had risen and strode across the room. "I see, my lady."

She rose and stalked after him. "Apparently, you do not, Hugh."

He whirled toward her. "Why did you call me that?"

"You called me by my first name earlier, to startle me into telling you what you wanted to know. I did it to get your attention."

Hands tucked quickly behind his back, he looked even taller and more imposing. As he so rightly knew he would. "You have it, Lady Kersey."

"Tsk, tsk. Will you call me Lady Kersey when we are married?"

He blinked. "When we are married?"

"Because I should actually be called Lady Maria Granger." She had worked that out days ago, when thinking about that first kiss. "You were trying to propose to me just now, were you not?" Stepping toward him, Maria stopped when she stood toe-to-toe with him.

"I was telling you I couldn't propose to

you, my lady." For once Hugh looked uncertain.

"What you said was that you wanted to ask for my hand in marriage, but you thought your circumstances prevented it." Taking his hand, Maria laced their fingers together. "I don't agree, although I understand your reservations."

"If you do, then you must see that to marry now would be impossible." Yet he raised her hand to press a kiss upon the back, with lips that were warmer than the summer sun.

"Imprudent, perhaps. Especially as I am still in mourning." Although if she put her mind to it, they might be able to marry before the year was up. She would have to ask Jane if that was the law or merely a custom. "Even so, we could, discreetly, contract a betrothal."

"My lady —"

"Maria, if you please." She gazed up at him, reveling at the joy that now shone in his eyes. "You did begin it, and I rather prefer that mode of address, Mr. Granger."

"Hugh, please, Maria." He cupped her face in his hand, running his thumb down her cheek, his touch silky, like a butterfly's wing. "I am honored and grateful and humbled that you would agree to make me the happiest man in the world, but we cannot forget the storm that is brewing. Every day my brother's hold on life must grow weaker. That he has lived thus long is nothing short of a miracle. But one that will not last. When he dies, my family name may be embroiled in a scandal to which I would not want you linked."

"Does it matter that I would not care? Let me be at your side, as a wife should be, for better or for worse." She'd given her pledge to do that twice before. With William there had not been time for either. And in her marriage to Alan, the worst had been a burden she had to bear alone. She'd never had the chance to stand together with the man she loved and face down whatever adversity Fate had deigned to throw at them. "Ask me so that I may be able to say yes."

"My dearest one, if I have any conscience at all, I cannot do so."

"What?" Tears pricked Maria's eyes.

"At least I cannot ask you now." He wrapped his arms around her, pulling her close to him. "I am sorry, but I will not ensnare you into circumstances from which you will not easily be able to extricate yourself should you wish to."

"But I will not wish to." His jacket muffled

her voice, but her position allowed her to revel in his closeness. Despite the ache in her heart.

"Even if you believe that, it will do us no harm to wait to announce our intentions. As you say, your mourning period will not be over for some months. By that time my brother's situation will likely be resolved one way or the other." He kissed the top of her head. "And we shall know then what we face."

Maria sighed. She would much rather have this all settled now, but she was coming to realize that Hugh had a stubborn streak. Not the worst trait for a man to have, but one she would need to get used to. "Compromise" would likely be a watchword for their marriage. And it now seemed more likely that their marriage would take place, she could relax and get to know Hugh better. "I think we should seal this with a kiss."

"You do, my lady?" Smiling, he stepped back from her.

"Isn't that customary?" She knew very well it was not, but if she couldn't be formally betrothed, she could at least have a little fun until they could be married.

"Not that I'm aware of."

"Then let it be our custom." She reached

up on tiptoe to slide her arms around his neck.

"I have no objection to that, my dear." He bent his head and pressed his lips to hers.

No danger of this kiss being a fleeting touch. Without doubt Hugh Granger had definitely taken the helm, controlling what she suspected would be a thorough exploration of her mouth. He tilted their heads slightly so their lips molded together, making everything suddenly so much easier. His gentle pressure encouraged her to press back, hoping he would ask for more still. One thing Maria had to admit, she had enjoyed kissing Alan. He'd also taught her quite a lot. If she missed anything about him, it was his kisses. Now here was a man who also knew what he was about when kissing a woman. She just hoped he intended to show her.

As if sensing her thoughts, Hugh slid his hands up to cup her head, cradling it in them, angling her mouth as his tongue sought entry to her. Oh, so willingly, she opened her lips, allowing him to deepen the kiss. His slow exploration set her pulse, already racing, to a speed so high she felt light-headed. Still, she'd rather swoon in his arms than have him stop.

The sudden creaking of the door froze

them, neither breathing, but listening. Maria hoped against hope that the door had simply caught a draft and blew inward on its own.

The subtle clearing of a throat told her that no, not a draft but a footman had discovered her and Hugh in a very compromising position.

Hugh carefully withdrew, set her neatly on her feet, and they turned to meet the stricken face of Saunders and a tall, imposing gentleman whose hat and coat had not yet been taken. The gentleman's scowl was as dark as the night, his whole countenance glowering at them.

"Lord Kinellan is here to see Lady John, my lady," Saunders announced, then scurried from the room, leaving the three of them in the deathly silence.

CHAPTER SEVENTEEN

"Lady Kersey." Lord Kinellan bowed and glared at Hugh. "You are the grieving widow Lady John has been chaperoning, I believe. I see now why she wrote to me that she must remain as your companion for an unknown period of time."

Her cheeks aflame, Maria had to ignore her own discomfort in order to keep a check on Hugh. That belligerent look from this morning's disaster was back on his face. She placed a restraining hand on his. "One moment, Mr. Granger. Allow me to introduce you before you begin to cudgel one another."

Forcing a smile, she stared into Lord Kinellan's cold eyes. "My lord, may I present Mr. Hugh Granger, the steward for the Kersey properties and . . ." She risked a glance at Hugh, who shook his head slightly. Drat the man. If she could announce a betrothal it might lessen the censure she was certain would follow shortly. "And my very dear friend. Mr. Granger, this is Lord Kinellan —"

"Gareth, eighth Marquess of Kinellan." The supercilious lord was certainly full of himself.

"And my cousin Jane's particular friend." Maria glared at him and continued. "She has had to put off her visit to his lordship's estate in Scotland ever since the spring, as she was helping me with my copious troubles."

"Sir." Kinellan moved a scant inch in a bow.

"My lord." Hugh's nod was as brief.

"Lady Kersey, I will tell you frankly that I am here to escort your cousin to Castle Kinellan, without any further ado. If your" — he gestured to her and Hugh — "assignations are always so much in the public eye, I daresay we may have to insist on a wedding to save your reputation, my lady."

"That is out of the question, my lord." Pulling himself up to his full height, which made him eye to eye with Lord Kinellan, Hugh stuck out his chin, as if daring the man to draw his cork. "Much as I would wish to marry the lady, I must decline if I am to save her reputation."

The truculent look on Kinellan's face

softened, replaced by curiosity. "An interesting argument to proffer when trying to keep a lady from ruin. Can you explain further, Granger?"

Hugh exchanged a look with Maria. "I'm afraid not at this time, my lord. Suffice it to say that I would make an offer to the lady if my prospects were not currently in a hobble. When I am able to tell you more, my lord, I will. The lady knows all the particulars, but has sworn herself to secrecy."

"Even more intriguing, Granger. I can perhaps see why the lady finds you amusing. But that still does little to forward my cause, which is to take Lady John back to Scotland with me. She will, undoubtedly, refuse to go, citing her cousin's circumstances as the reason." Kinellan's frown went straight down his nose. "In which case I will propose that Lady Kersey pack her bags and accompany her cousin to my estate." He beamed at them, convinced he had hit upon the perfect plan. "There is nothing to keep Lady Kersey here." A glare at Hugh kept both of them quiet — for the moment. "She and her cousin will have a fine time celebrating the holidays in Scotland. You have never done so, have you, my lady?"

Stunned by this sudden reordering of her

life — without so much as a by-your-leave — Maria had had enough. "No, my lord, I have not done so, and I am afraid I will not remedy that situation this year either. My traveling to Scotland is out of the question."

"Indeed." Lord Kinellan fished in his jacket pocket and produced a quizzing glass, which he applied to his eye and scrutinized Maria. "You stand up for yourself. Not something one usually sees in one so young. They are most often happy to be told what to do." Nodding, he dropped the quizzer back inside his coat. "Even though it may prove inconvenient for me, I find myself approving of you, my dear." He glared at Hugh. "Which makes your good behavior toward the lady even more paramount."

The tapping of running feet down the corridor alerted Maria that Jane was approaching. Now perhaps she would put Lord Kinellan and his high-handed ways in their place.

"Kinellan? Is it really you?" The door swung open and Jane rushed in, then stopped so abruptly at the sight of Maria and Hugh that she stumbled on the carpet. Maria grabbed her to keep her from plowing headlong into his lordship.

"Maria! Mr. Granger. What are you —" Her gaze pivoted to the distinguished gentleman who had turned toward her voice and now regarded her with hungry eyes. "Kinellan."

The husky desire in Jane's voice told its own tale to Maria.

Jane and Lord Kinellan moved as one toward one another, with an intensity that was striking to witness. Kinellan caught her in his arms and was lowering his head when Jane stopped him, her face turning bright red. "Kinellan. We are not alone."

"It has been almost a year since I saw you, Jane. I don't give a damn who is in this room." He sank his mouth onto hers and her protests ceased.

Maria moved closer to Hugh and as if in accord, they turned away, but not before Jane wrapped her arms around Lord Kinellan's neck and pulled him even closer to her.

Much as Jane might insist she had no deep affection for Lord Kinellan, her reactions in the past few moments told another tale.

"Should we leave?" Hugh whispered in her ear, tickling it with his warm breath.

"If I thought we could get away with it and they wouldn't find us, I would say yes. However —"

"Maria, Mr. Granger." Rather breathless, Jane's voice nevertheless called them back.

They turned to find Jane standing beside Kinellan, his gaze still on her with an avid gleam. "I beg your pardon for that most inappropriate" — frowning, she glanced up at Kinellan, who grinned back at her — "display. But as Lord Kinellan said, we have been long absent from one another due to various circumstances." Here she glared at Maria.

Well, that was Jane's decision. Maria raised her chin, refusing to be made guilty for a choice that had been Jane's alone. "And now those circumstances no longer seem to exist, my dear. I am settled here at Kersey Hall, under the protection of the earl and countess. You should feel free to pursue your own, um, pleasures."

"And leave you alone to do the same, I assume, Lady Kersey?" Kinellan raised his eyebrows, as if daring her to say more.

Jane cocked her head at Lord Kinellan, then swiftly brought her gaze to bear on Maria. "To what does he refer, my dear?" She shot a severe look at Hugh. "Why are you and Mr. Granger here? Saunders said only that Lord Kinellan waited for me."

Maria opened her mouth, not at all sure what was going to come out of it this time.

"I was shown into this receiving room to discover Lady Kersey and Mr. Granger locked in a sensuous, and very heated embrace." Lord Kinellan apparently did not mince words.

"Maria! Mr. Granger." The shock in Jane's voice was actually comical. Had she truly thought Maria would not act on her feelings just because Jane disapproved?

"I must beg your pardon, Lady John." The perturbed look on Hugh's face wasn't as severe as his anger at Lord Wetherby had been; however, the grim set to his jaw told her he was deeply displeased with Kinellan. "His lordship surprised us during a private moment, for which I have also begged his forgiveness. As you yourself understand, it is rather uncomfortable to be subjected to witnessing such intimacies between two people."

Smothering a smile, Maria took his hand and squeezed it.

"I do not, however, apologize for the sentiments I had just expressed to Lady Kersey regarding our future lives together. We had just agreed to marry —"

Hugh might as well have set off an explosion. Everyone began talking at once, except Maria, whose anger grew with each passing word.

"Mr. Granger, you have no right to ingratiate yourself with my cousin by making a proposal of any nature."

"Granger, you and I will talk about this ill-conceived plan, this instant, sir."

"My lord, I am sorry, but I need not speak to you, nor ask your permission for anything." Hugh looked from one to the other. "Nor you, my lady, although you are Lady Kersey's kinswoman."

"I am considering the welfare of my cousin, Mr. Granger." Jane had stepped forward, bringing her considerable poise and stature to bear. "I have sworn to keep her from making a third disastrous marriage."

"And you believe if she marries me she will come to regret it?" A tightness came into Hugh's voice.

"I am not prepared to make that exact pronouncement, Mr. Granger, although I believe your circumstances may be uncertain at the moment."

"The lady is well aware of my circumstances, my lady. She has deemed them insignificant enough to have formally declared her affection for me." He returned his gaze briefly to Maria, giving her a gentle smile before continuing. "I will tell you, however, that we are not formally betrothed, although we have both expressed the wish to marry. The circumstances surrounding my brother's condition are, as you say, uncertain. Therefore, we have agreed to a waiting period in order for Maria to finish her mourning and for my brother's inevitable end. After that, we will know our path more clearly."

Silence followed Hugh's pronouncement as Jane and Kinellan looked warily at one another.

"That actually sounds like a fair plan, my dear." Nodding, Kinellan crossed his arms.

"But will they adhere to it?" Jane shook her head, avoiding Maria's eyes. "You interrupted an amorous tryst not half an hour ago. When I leave, what is to stop other, more sensual assignations?"

"You will have our word, Lady John." That tension was back in Hugh's jaw, but he remained civil in his address, thank goodness. Maria hated to think what Kinellan would do were Hugh or anyone else to disparage her cousin. "The word of a gentleman and a lady."

"I am sorry, Mr. Granger, and I do not disparage your honor when I say I know my cousin, and while you may be able to hold steadfast to your convictions, I fear Maria will be inclined to give in to temptation once I am gone and she is left to herself."

Her cousin's distrust of Maria's ability to

resist Hugh's advances hurt deeply, although she had to admit there might be more than a grain of truth to the statement. If she and Hugh ever found themselves alone, she would likely be the one who wished to throw caution in the air and indulge in intimacies best left to those duly married.

Perhaps intuiting Maria's reluctance, Kinellan spoke up. "I suggested Maria accompany us to Castle Kinellan for the holidays. She could return in the spring when her mourning period is completed and they could judge then whether or not their affection is deep and true or merely a convenience based on proximity." His gaze took in Jane and the hunger returned to them. "We have not seen one another for some ten months and yet our affection is as strong as it was the last time we met." He turned his gaze to Maria and his eyes were filled with compassion. "If you and Mr. Granger can manage thus for the next several months, I would wager you will go on well together into eternity."

The chatter broke out once again, louder than before.

"There are other things to be considered, Kinellan."

"Your point is taken, Lord Kinellan,

however —"

"Does no one wish to hear what I have to say?" Maria raised her voice until the others quieted. She looked around the small circle, Jane and Kinellan looking daggers at Hugh, who had turned apologetic eyes to her.

"Go on, my dear." He squeezed.

"No one in this room has the right to tell me what I can and cannot do." Staring down Jane, who had opened her mouth but closed it before speaking, Maria released Hugh's hand and stalked over to her cousin. "But I will tell you that I will not be journeying to Scotland with you and Lord Kinellan."

"But my dear, I believe you should."

"What?" She whirled around to face Hugh, standing patiently with a rueful smile on his face. "You wish me to go?"

"No, my love, I do not want you anywhere but with me." He came forward and took her hands. "But I believe your cousin is right. If we are together here on the Kersey estate, the temptation for us to meet clandestinely will be great. I am strong of will" — he tipped her chin up so she must look squarely into his eyes — "but I am no saint. No matter our resolve, I fear we will break our word. Then not only will your reputation be in jeopardy, but we may have to marry when we should not." He raised her hand for a kiss. "Trust me, my love. All will be well in just a little while."

Tears threatened, but Maria willed them back. Even though Hugh's argument made sense, she wanted to be with him, be close to him, see him whenever she cared to. And that desire was exactly what she could not do. It had been the same with Alan when she had stayed with Jane at Lord Sinclaire's. She and he had been together constantly, which had led to more intimate encounters, which had subsequently led to her pregnancy and marriage. This marriage must be different if they were to have a chance of happiness.

"Very well. I shall go to Scotland with you, Jane." She looked only at Hugh. "But the very moment you know something about your brother and the estate, you must let me know. I will be in the next coach leaving." She glared at Kinellan. "Even if I have to drive it myself."

"I promise you shall know of the determination the moment I do." Hugh's dear face was hopeful, though sadness lurked deep in his eyes.

Quickly she reached up to him, gave him another swift kiss that lingered on her lips, then fled the room. She would be dutiful and go because Hugh wished it, but in her heart she feared it a mistake. Too many things could happen to conspire to keep them apart. Together they could make a stand. Divided they would be more likely to fail. Lord, please let her be wrong.

The moment Maria hurried from the room, the tension seemed to drain from Lady John's entire body. "Thank you, Mr. Granger. I am afraid my cousin would have put up a more strenuous fight had you not intervened."

"Do not thank me, Lady John." He hadn't intended the harsh tone, but if it gave the woman pause, so much the better. "I would not have advised Maria to leave had I not believed it the best thing for her to do." He nodded at Lord Kinellan. "His lordship, however, made a good point about removing Maria from a situation that might pose a risk to her reputation." He paused, went to the door and closed it before speaking again. "I agree that she should leave Kersey Hall at least for a time. Not necessarily to remove her from my sphere, but from Lord Wetherby's."

"Who the devil is Lord Wetherby?" Kinellan barked and Lady John put a restraining hand on his arm.

"Lord Kersey's heir." The lady gave him a knowing look. "There was an incident this morning that has apparently alarmed Mr. Granger."

"It should alarm you as well, my lady. Your cousin finally confessed to me that the 'bird' attack was a fiction she told in order to mask Lord Wetherby's true intent, which was to ravish her."

"Dear lord." Clutching her throat, Lady John stared at him helplessly. "Why did Maria not tell me?"

"Perhaps she didn't think you would believe her. Luckily, she was able to thwart his intent, wounding him sufficiently to ward off the attack. However" — Hugh stepped closer to them — "I do not believe it will be the last one. Wetherby has been rebuffed once. With some gentlemen of his character, that kind of behavior only encourages them until they succeed. I therefore believe Scotland will be the safest place for her until we can marry. Although if circumstances go against me, then I do not know what the best course for Maria will be. I will gladly give her and her child the protection of my name and champion them in any way necessary." He shook his head. "But if I cannot provide a decent home or living for her and the child, then I cannot take them from a life that offers such things."

"Thank you, Mr. Granger." The words were heartfelt, for the lady now looked at him with more respect than previously. Perhaps she understood at last how deep his devotion to her cousin ran. "We will discuss our departure and make certain you are able to say goodbye to Maria before we leave. I suspect Lord Kinellan will wish to wait a day or two before attempting the return journey."

"A day or two only if we don't wish to be bogged down in snow throughout most of the journey." Kinellan sounded gruff, but his manner toward Hugh had also undergone a subtle change.

While they had been talking, darkness had fallen. "I must go see to my sister. She will be worried if I do not appear for dinner." Hugh bowed. "My lady, my lord."

With no further ado, Hugh opened the door and headed down the corridor. The situation, while not perfect by any means, was a great deal better than when he had entered the receiving room. He and Maria were at least pledged to one another, tenuous though that declaration might be. He'd write to Littles this evening to see if there was any change at all with Kit.

In the last letter the butler had sent, he'd

written that the doctor himself was amazed at the tenacity Kit showed in clinging to life. Although his usually robust brother had wasted away to skin and bones during the last two months, he had not yet decided to give up the ghost. A blessing and a curse, but one that was ultimately in God's hands.

Hugh strode out the front door, a lantern in his hand to light his way to Wingate. "Come on, Kit." He spoke under his breath, almost as a prayer to whoever would listen. "Come back to the living. I want you to meet the woman I'm going to marry and give us your blessing." In the best of all possible worlds, that was how it should be. Otherwise, he might lose her entirely.

CHAPTER EIGHTEEN

Monday morning dawned clear and cold, with no hint of snow in the air. A perfect day for a last outing with Maria.

The decorating of Kersey Hall had begun after breakfast and he'd walked his sister there to help with the festivities. However, having to stand about within arm's length of Lord Wetherby and not plant him a facer would have been harder than riding bareback with a burr under his backside. Instead, he'd decided to spirit Maria away for some time alone before she left tomorrow. He'd been thinking all yesterday what he and Maria could do so that she would have good memories of their last day together. And with the weather cooperating, it was a perfect day, in Hugh's estimation, for ice-skating.

He'd just sent Bella inside the Hall and handed a note to Saunders to give to Maria. He'd already told the grooms to have their horses saddled so they could ride out to the pond near the dowager's house. It should be frozen solid after the last cold snap, making it excellent for his purpose. The skates were stored in the tack room in the stable — Bella had visited him last year and they had had such a grand time skating, he'd decided to keep the skates handy for the next winter's use.

The groom had just brought their horses — Galahad, and Lily, a chestnut mare — when Maria came through the front door. Beautiful as always, today she looked even more brilliant in a light gray riding habit that caught the morning sun, making her seem to glow. God, but he would miss her.

Determined not to succumb to melancholy on this of all days, he smiled broadly and came toward her. "Good morning, my lady." First names were for use only in private, but they would be private soon. "I thought you might like a special outing this morning."

"Good morning, Mr. Granger." Her smile dazzled him, although just looking at her red lips made him want to taste her once again. "An outing sounds wonderful."

"I warn you, the ride may be a bit chilly." He held his hands out and tossed her up onto Lily.

"I'm sure I won't mind." Her eyes crinkled at the edges, as if she were laughing at him, daring him to keep her warm.

He'd be happy to oblige.

"Where are we going?" She adjusted herself in the saddle, settling her right leg over the pommel and pulling her skirts down over it.

"Now that would spoil the surprise, wouldn't it?" He swung up on Galahad, checking to make sure the package with the skates in it was secured behind the saddle. "Don't worry. It's not far."

"I am waiting with great anticipation, sir." She gathered the reins and looked expectantly at him. "Lead on, Mr. Granger. *Tempus fugit.*"

"Yes, it does, my lady. Let us go, by all means." He tapped his horse's flank and the roan moved off at a fast walk. Lily followed close behind and when they reached the smooth driveway, he touched the horse again and they swung into a canter.

Maria flashed him a smile as she drew even with him. She had an excellent seat, though of course she'd learned to ride here, a little over a year ago. The former Lord Kersey had taught her to ride, along with other things, so he gathered.

He refused to think of that. Rather, he

preferred to dwell on her generous nature as with the Tates, her kindness when dealing with children or animals, her gentle wit — though sometimes it came out quite sharp as well. These were the things that had made him love her. That he would miss most about her when she had gone.

Turning the horse down the driveway that led to Francis House, he wondered what she thought he had in store for her. He glanced to his right to find her grinning widely. Of course she would think he was bringing her here for a tryst. Wanton woman. Just last night they had promised her cousin and Lord Kinellan they would wait until they were married to engage in intimacies beyond a kiss. Well, he didn't think they could withstand such a promise if she were to stay at Kersey, but since she was leaving in the morning, today seemed safe.

They flashed past the circular driveway and continued on toward the formal gardens. From his vantage point atop the horse, Hugh could see the pond about a quarter mile beyond, shining brightly as the sun reflected off the ice. Excellent.

Pulling Galahad down to a trot and then a walk, Hugh brought them to a stop right at the end of the irregularly shaped pond.

There were bulrushes thick at the far end, with overhanging trees, now leafless. Nearest to them was the overturned log where he and Bella had sat to lace on their skates last year. There was also a place to tie the horses so they could crop the little bit of grass still left. An idyllic spot for their last day together.

Hugh dropped to the ground, then helped Maria down as well. She slid down into his arms, every part of her touching every part of him it seemed. The minx would try his patience for certain. He gave her a stern glare. "You had best behave, young lady. I made a promise to your cousin not to compromise you before we could marry."

"I think I will take my chances with Jane's wrath if it means I can be close to you, my love." She gave a coquettish laugh and Hugh groaned. Best divert her away from this dangerous topic.

"Here is your surprise." He waved toward the frozen pond.

"I see." She looked askance at the pond, then at him. "I will admit I am surprised, for I cannot fathom a single reason why you would have brought me here."

"Ah, but here is the other part of the surprise." He untied the parcel from behind the saddle and brought out two pairs of —

"Ice skates!" Maria darted forward, taking one up, but being mindful of the blade. "I used to go ice-skating all the time at my parents' house. There is a river nearby that would freeze when the weather was cold enough." She turned a gleeful face to him. "How did you know?"

"I didn't." Grinning like a fool at her look of pure pleasure, Hugh thanked whatever angel had whispered in his ear to take Maria skating. "I hoped you had skated before, but I would have been happy to teach you if you hadn't."

"Well, let's see who knows what." She dropped down onto the log and began to tie the skates onto her shoes. "Last one onto the ice has to pay a forfeit."

Lord, and didn't he know what her forfeit would be if she won the wager.

Hugh sat down to strap his skates on as well. The process wasn't terribly difficult, just lengthy. He fumbled with the straps, his fingers stupid as he tried to hurry.

"One skate on!" Maria laughed and began on the other one.

"No fair. You have smaller fingers that work better than mine." Cursing under his breath, Hugh buckled the first skate on and reached for the second, although he doubted he could catch up with Maria now.

"Done!" Pink cheeked, she laughed again as she stood before him, showing him first one and then the other skate. "Do you need some help with your laces, my dear?"

"No, thank you." His words came out a growl, which made Maria laugh all the harder.

"Come." She held out her hand and helped him up when he was finished. "I cannot wait to skate again. It has been an age at least. I had to have been ten years old."

"Well, I hope it comes back to you, but if not, I will be here to save you." He grinned as they made their way toward the pond's edge.

"My hero." She clutched his arm in mock terror.

He pushed aside some frozen vegetation, creating a path to the ice. "Hold my hand."

She gripped it tightly and followed him to the edge.

"Wait here and let me sound out the ice. It's been so cold recently I don't think it has thinned, but best be safe."

Maria nodded gravely, her brows drawn inward. "Do be careful."

He set his skates on the smooth ice and pushed off. Each year it came back to him, as if he skated every day of his life. Cautiously, he struck out for the center of the

301

pond, watching for slushy spots or cloudy patches of ice. That meant it wasn't frozen hard enough. But everywhere he looked the ice was clear. No air bubbles, no cracks, just solid, clear ice. Perfect. "I think it's good," he called, turning toward the bank. "Come on out." He waved to her even as he started back.

Maria set her skates on the surface and pushed off. She wobbled for a moment, her arms flailing as she fought for balance.

Hugh hurried toward her, then something seemed to change.

Suddenly, she remembered her balance and her strokes became strong and even. She threw back her head and laughed, then struck out to meet him. Grabbing his hands, she assumed the skater's position, right hand over left, and their feet began to glide in unison.

"I see it came back to you." He steered them down the center of the pond toward the bulrushes at the end, then turned to head back up the far side.

"It did. This is so marvelous. I did not realize how much I had missed it until I started to skate." Maria's excitement was infectious. He'd not thought of skating since last year, but now the thrill of the speed — almost like flying — seemed one of the most exhilarating things he'd ever done. "Take my hands like this."

He clasped her hands, left in left and right in right, until they faced one another. Then he began to spin them around, faster and faster until the world sped by at a dizzying pace.

Maria leaned her head back, laughing up to the cloudless sky, her face more beautiful than he'd ever seen it.

He slowed them down until they stood facing one another, panting. "I love you." Hugh managed to get the words out before he sank his mouth onto hers. The kiss was quick — they were still both gasping for breath — then a gulp of air, then he kissed her again. Longer this time, pressing against her even as he wrapped his arms around her and drew her to him. Another breath and he settled in for a lengthy kiss that he deepened, delving through her lips, into her mouth, tasting all the entrancing flavors that were uniquely her. God, he would never get enough.

Slowly, he came back to his senses and broke the kiss, albeit reluctantly. Maria nestled her head on his chest, as though it was the most natural thing in the world to do on the middle of a frozen pond.

"Do you still want me to leave?"

"You know I do not." Existence here without her would be the worst form of torture.

"Then I won't go." She raised her head to look at him, love shining in her eyes. "We can get married, Hugh. I can live with you and your sister and my daughter at Wingate. If only we think about it, we can find a way to be happy."

"My love, what do you think Lord Kersey will do when he finds out that I have married his kinswoman without so much as a by-your-leave? I wager I will find myself without a situation, therefore no house, no means to support any of us." He hated to extinguish the hope in her face, but the harsh reality of their plight could not be mitigated. "Our best plan is the one we agreed to last night."

"But I don't want to leave you. Not even for the time it takes me to go from here to there." She struck out toward the far shore.

"Maria, come back." He set out after her, but she swung around toward him.

"I won't do it, Hugh. I won't go. There must be some other way we can be together without another wretched scandal raising its head." She looked so distraught, so forlorn, where moments before she'd been all smiles and laughter.

"Come back, my love. We can talk about it before we go back to the Hall." It was more of a perfunctory concession. He'd thought about nothing else for the past days save how to make everything come out right. Nothing, save her leaving or Kit dying, would end their torment.

"Promise me, Hugh. Promise me we will be to —" Maria's foot slid backward toward the bulrushes, broke through the ice and plunged her into the depths of the icy pond.

CHAPTER NINETEEN

Hugh stared in horror as Maria screamed, just before her head submerged beneath the dark water. Without thought, he threw himself down on the ice, spreading his weight over its surface, his head over the hole where she had disappeared. "Maria!"

Her head broke the surface and she screamed again.

He grabbed her shoulders. "I've got you. I've got you, Maria."

Eyes wide, she clutched at his arms, her nails digging into his coat sleeves until he thought she would rip the thick material.

"Ah . . . ah . . . ah." She panted for breath, the panic in her face giving way to terror. "Help me, Hugh." Her voice was little more than a whisper.

"I've got you." He squeezed her shoulders. "Listen to me. Are you touching the bottom? This pond is not very deep at all."

She stilled, then nodded her head. "I . . .

f . . . feel it."

"Good." He took a stronger grip on her. "I want you to push off from the bottom toward me. Quickly, love. Push now."

She tensed, then lifted as he heaved and pulled her back up onto the ice. Still panting, she clutched his arms as he slowly slid them onto the more solid ice in the middle of the pond. "Easy, now. I've got you. Are you hurt?"

Staring at him, Maria didn't respond at first, then shook her head as violent shivering overtook her. "C . . . c . . . cold, Hugh."

"Here." He ripped off his jacket and pulled it around her, then picked her up and skated frantically for the shore. In moments he deposited her shaking figure on the log, then pulled off his skates and hers, all the while assessing the situation. "We need to get you out of the cold."

The dowager house stood a quarter mile away, best make for that. Inside he could build a fire and get her warm again. The horses, still quietly cropping grass nearby, were the best bet, if Maria could ride. "Come on, love. We're going to Francis House."

Still shivering, Maria nodded and tried to stand, but she shook so hard her legs wouldn't support her.

"Here." Hugh picked her up and ran to Lily. "Can you hold on to the pommel? I'll lead the horse if you can just hold on."

Teeth chattering, Maria nodded, her whole body still shaking uncontrollably. Once in the saddle, she leaned over and wrapped her arms around the horse's neck and groaned.

"What's wrong?" Hugh had been leading Galahad to the log to use it as a mounting block, but dropped the reins and ran back to her.

"Warm." Her cheek pressed against Lily's mane, her arms hugged the huge neck, absorbing the animal's warmth as best she could.

"I'll have you warm as quick as can be, love." He grabbed her reins, scrambled up on Galahad, and started off at a trot. Unsure of how strong her grip on the horse was, he dared go no faster. Still, they arrived at the kitchen door of the dowager house in almost no time.

Hugh leaped down and ran to the door. He had no keys to the house with him, but that was of little worry. Using his elbow, he broke the windowpane, glass tinkling on the stone floor inside. He reached inside, lifted the latch, and the door swung inward. He hurried back to Maria, still clinging to the horse for dear life. "Come, sweetheart. Let's get you before a warm fire."

He had to pry her arms from around the horse's neck, and pulled her into his arms. She shook so hard he staggered as he carried her into the house and sat her down before the fireplace. "Are you all right?"

She nodded, but continued to shiver.

"I'll get some tinder and start a blaze in a minute."

Searching around the kitchen, however, revealed that the servants had taken every scrap of wood or else it had been used in the last days the house had been open and not replaced. Nothing remained with which to build a fire.

Maria sat huddled in his jacket, bent over, her arms wrapped around her. She needed to get out of her wet clothing and sit before a fireplace blazing with heat. But where? At the least he could take off her soaking boots. He bent and unlaced the brown, muddied half-boots, then pulled them off, emptying out a deal of water onto the floor in the process. Now he needed to see about something dry for her to wear. "I'll be right back, love."

His words brought no response, which alarmed him greatly. He tore out of the kitchen, taking two steps at a time to the ground floor. Racing for the front staircase to the first floor, he sped past the library, music room, and receiving rooms. They had been little used when Maria and Jane had lived here, so likely had nothing to offer, although if he couldn't find wood anywhere, he'd come back to the library. At least books would burn.

On the first floor he hurried into the dowager's chamber to see if anything had been left there. The room had been stripped and swept clean. No bedding remained, but the bedcurtains still stood around the four-poster bed. Should he pull them down to drape around Maria? Poking at the fireplace, also without a stick of firewood, a growing sense of dread filled him. If he couldn't get Maria warm and very shortly, she could catch an ague or a severe chill. People died every day from such ailments. He'd never forgive himself if he lost her due to his own foolish actions.

He opened the door to the bathing chamber wide to allow enough light to come in so he could see. The windowless chamber was small compared to the bedroom, but then it had been built with a mind to keeping the heat in. Feeling for the small fireplace used to heat water for the bath, his hand met with the box that held the wood.

Bless the lord, it still held several sticks. He quickly filled his arms, then paused. This room was small and would hold heat well. What better place to bring Maria? If he started the fire now, the chamber would be cozy by the time he brought her here.

After shoving the wood into the small grate, he grabbed the tinderbox and quickly struck a spark. The fire leaped into life and Hugh said a prayer of thanksgiving. A swift search of the chamber revealed two more stashes of wood, enough to keep the fire going for at least an hour or so. He checked one more time to make sure the fire blazed, then ran from the room to fetch Maria.

Huddled over and shivering so hard the chair clattered on the wooden floor, Maria barely seemed to notice when he scooped her up in his arms once more and carried her to the bathing chamber. There was no place to put her, save the bathtub, which was porcelain and cold. He'd have to improvise something, then set about finding her some dry clothing, though that seemed a hopeless cause in the bare household.

"Maria? Maria!" She still had not responded by the time Hugh got her to the bathing chamber. Body shivering and teeth chattering all the way, she'd lain like a block of ice in his arms. Somehow he had to get her wet things off and get her warmed up.

The fire had heated the small room appreciably by the time they arrived. He stood her in front of the fireplace, then ran back to the bedchamber and yanked at the bedcurtains. The rings that held them to the frame popped and shot all over the room, but the thick material came away in his hands. Striding back to the warming room, he doubled the fabric and lay it in the tub. "Now, let's get those wet clothes off you, sweetheart."

Thanks to the fire, her shivering had lessened. Still, she was soaking wet. She'd never feel warm while she wore those garments. But how would he get her out of them? And what could she wear while they dried? They intended to marry, true, but Hugh wasn't prepared to strip her and leave her naked.

His own shirt had gotten wet when he carried her, but it would dry quickly if held before the fire. She could wear that — more for modesty's sake than warmth, but it would serve.

"Maria, take off my coat."

She shook her head and clutched the jacket more closely.

"You can have it back, and my shirt as well, but we need to take off your clothes so you can get warm."

She eyed him suspiciously, then gave a ghost of a smile. "I . . . I knew you . . . c . . . couldn't k . . . keep that p . . . promise."

"Good lord, woman." Hugh shook his head as he peeled the damp jacket off her. "I'm trying to save your life, not seduce you."

"C . . . could do both."

A chuckle escaped him. Maria was nothing if not persistent. At least it showed a return of her spirit, so much better than the awful lethargy that had frightened him earlier. "Let's get you warm before we think of doing anything else."

Stripping off her dripping pelisse was easy, although she shook harder and inched closer to the fire. Proceeding to remove her gown, however, he hesitated. He was about to cross a Rubicon from which he'd not return. If discovered, they risked censure and their marriage became a certainty, no possibility of appeal if his circumstances changed for the worse. But if she died, none of that would matter in the least.

With unsteady fingers, he unbuttoned the little silver buttons, each carved into a rose, that ran down the bodice of her riding habit. The material, a fine wool, was damp and cold to the touch. It came away, revealing a

313

very pretty pair of embroidered stays over a sleeveless linen chemise. He swallowed hard and his nether regions stirred despite the cold.

"You c . . . can gawk later, Hugh." Maria rubbed her arms where the gooseflesh had the hairs standing at attention. "Help me with the skirt fastening in b . . . back." She turned around and he untied the skirt and underpetticoat, which fell sopping to the floor. Kicking them away, she wobbled on unsteady legs, then inched closer to the fireplace and held her hands out. "You need to stoke the fire while I unfasten my stays. Thank goodness these close in the front."

Glad of something to do other than stare at her luscious body, Hugh grabbed more wood and poked up the fire before dumping the logs in. Sparks flew upward and heat poured out into the room.

A glance over his shoulder showed Maria standing only in her chemise now, the thin material clinging to her, showing every delicious curve or shape. Perhaps that thin material would dry while on her. And she could have his shirt as well, to help hide her many temptations. Pulling his shirt out of his breeches, Hugh let the folds fall around his hips, then unwound his cravat, which he draped over the tub rim. He grabbed the back of his shirt and pulled it over his head.

"Ooh, Mr. Granger. What a nice, strong back you have." The teasing sound of Maria's voice raised his spirits. If they could get her warmed up, with a little luck, she would not take cold from this incident.

"Why, Lady Kersey. You say the nicest things." Smiling, he waved the shirt in front of the flames to dry it even more. "I hope you mean —"

He turned to hand her the shirt and stopped, his heart hammering in his chest.

Not only had she removed her stays, but her chemise as well, standing before him naked save for her stockings and garters. His mouth dried and his cock surged against his breeches.

More lovely than he had ever imagined — and he had imagined her naked before him many times in the past weeks — she reminded him of Botticelli's *The Birth of Venus.* Her smooth skin, pale in contrast to her dark, rosy nipples, made him long to run his hands all over her. Breasts that would fill his hands and stiffen his member gave her a rounded form above, while her generous hips provided like curves below. While the dark, thick triangle at the apex of her thighs beckoned him to explore its secrets. Hugh drew in a ragged breath.

"Dear God."

She rubbed her arms, making her breasts bob up and down. "I've thought of another way you can help me get warm."

"Maria." He couldn't allow this to happen. "We cannot do any such thing. You know we cannot."

Grabbing the shirt he still held out to her, she reached up and removed two pins from her hair. It cascaded down over her shoulders in snaky, wet strands. She shook out his shirt, then wrapped it around her hair, squeezing the water from it, then rubbing it vigorously, seemingly unaware of the way her breasts jiggled and bounced with every movement.

His cock kept track of every motion, it seemed, bumping against his breeches insistently until it lay hard and ready, seeking a way out.

Letting the shirt drop to the floor, Maria left the warmth of the fire and walked toward him.

He backed up as far as he could, until his bare back hit the cold tile wall.

"Maria, please. We promised."

"More fool us then." She draped herself against him, sliding her arms around his neck, her breasts pressed skin to skin against his. "Love me, Hugh. Please love me."

He groaned, but didn't try to push her away. How could he? He'd almost lost her forever. Her body still shook with cold. He should be willing to do anything to keep her safe and warm, no matter if the task was odious or pleasurable. That this task would be immanently pleasurable shouldn't matter, shouldn't make him feel guilty.

She burrowed against his chest and he slipped his arms around her. "You are a very stubborn lady."

"And you are a stubborn man." She smiled against his chest. "I imagine we will have more battles than this one because of it." A chill shook her. "I'm just glad I won this one. I really am terribly cold, Hugh."

"Sweetheart." He lifted her into his arms, and grabbed the material out of the tub. "I hate to take you from the warmth of this room."

"Transfer the fire to the bedchamber fireplace. It won't be as warm as this room, but it will take the chill off it." She grinned up at him. "We can produce the rest of the heat ourselves."

With a sigh, Hugh stalked into the bedroom and threw the ripped bedcurtains onto the feather mattress. He laid Maria on the material, then ripped the other curtain off the rails and draped it over her.

She drew the soft fabric around her and snuggled into it.

It then took only moments to scoop the fire into the bucket for ashes and transfer it and the remaining logs to the main fireplace. Soon it was roaring, and the cold of the room retreated. Hugh turned back to the bed where Maria lay, following his every movement.

"Come to bed, my love." She raised the makeshift blanket, invitingly.

She'd still not stopped shivering, even though the fire and cover had helped. What she needed, wanted, was Hugh's big, hot body pressed against her again. The body he was revealing this very moment before her. Hungrily, she waited to see all of him.

His strong chest and shoulders were a delight to the touch, smooth and warm when she'd draped herself against him in the bath chamber. Now she wanted more.

He sat on the edge of the bed, taking off his boots, building her anticipation until she squirmed beneath the cover. Didn't he know how much she wanted him right now? From his reaction to seeing her *au naturel* — she'd felt that hardness press against her earlier — she assumed he wanted her too. So why was he taking so abysmally long?

At last he turned around and oh, yes, without a doubt he wanted her. His shaft jutted straight out, full and hard and magnificent. She raised the covers again and he dove between them.

He pulled her to him, wrapping her in his arms as if he would engulf her entirely, pressing all of him against her. As she'd suspected, his body was hot, heat pouring off him in waves, like a blazing bonfire. For a moment she simply reveled in the warmth, her body relaxing at last into the safe haven. He did not shrink from her cold limbs at all, but tried to rub every part of her that needed his warmth.

Her shivering finally stopped, though her stomach trembled for a completely different reason. Staring deeply into his blue eyes, now darker than she'd ever seen them, she wanted to stay like this always, warm and intimate with this man. She lowered her mouth to his, touched his lips briefly, then sucked his bottom lip between her teeth to nibble on it.

He moaned deep and long before pulling free and rolling her onto her back, bringing him on top of her, his weight pressing her deep into the mattress. Dropping kisses on her lips, her chin, her jaw, her neck, he wound his way down her body, her temperature rising at every touch of his mouth. Disappearing beneath the covers, he continued his caresses, where she could not see. Suddenly, he sucked her nipple into his mouth. Half gasp, half moan escaped her, bringing her head up off the mattress. While his mouth played with one breast, his fingers stroked and tweaked the other one, hardening the tip until she thought she might explode with the pleasure of it.

His head emerged from the covers, his dark curly hair charmingly disheveled. "You do not get off so easily, my lady. Will you guide me in, if you please?"

"I am more than happy to help, sir." She slid her fingers along the hard muscles of his abdomen, over his slim hip, and down to where his member stood ready. Slowly she stroked it, up and down, wanting its raging heat inside her now.

He raised up and she positioned him right at her opening, then shifted her hands to his buttocks and pulled him toward her. Like the finest silk, he slid smoothly in, filling her completely.

Happy beyond belief, Maria moaned as he began to thrust inside her, long slow glides that reached all the way to her core. A tension began to spiral deep within her, a pressure she'd only experienced a few times before during her brief marriage to Alan. The faster Hugh stroked, the tighter wound she became until the tension reached a critical tipping point. This was how she was supposed to feel when she was with a man, but so seldom had.

"Hugh, Hugh!" she cried as she shattered around him, pulsing deep within.

He continued to thrust, faster and faster until, with a great cry of release, he shuddered inside her, filling her with his hot essence. After a moment he slumped on top of her, but immediately rolled over onto the bed, spent and panting.

Maria sagged into the mattress, totally spent, immeasurably happy, and finally, completely warm.

CHAPTER TWENTY

Drowsing in Hugh's arms, Maria could think of no place she would rather be. Certainly not in the Highlands of Scotland where, if she allowed Jane and Lord Kinellan to guide her, she would be for the better part of the winter with little or no contact with Hugh. She ran her hand over his forearm and was rewarded by the squeeze of his embrace. Undoubtedly, after this morning's activities, the situation had changed once again, as she had known it would. Still, she wasn't sorry. This is how their life should be, would be if his brother's life did not have so much of their future hanging on it.

She turned to face Hugh, resolved not to think about the uncertainties of her life, only the things she knew to be true. That Hugh loved her, and she loved him. That despite anything that happened with his brother, she and Hugh would be together.

And therefore, she would not be leaving for Scotland in the morning.

Hugh's eyes opened, only halfway at first, then a frown touched his brow. "What are you thinking, my love? You're frowning." He kissed her forehead right where it joined her nose. "I hope it does not mean you are having second thoughts?"

"Absolutely not." She slid her arms around his neck and snuggled down beside him. No one had ever made her feel so warm and safe. "Although I was thinking that things have now changed."

"Indeed they have." Raising up, he kissed the tip of her nose. "I hope that is not a surprise to you."

She smiled into his neck. "No, it is not. I'm actually quite glad that things have changed between us. And because they have, I do not see any reason for me to go to Scotland."

"Why did I think that would be your first thought after we shared intimacies?" He continued a trail of kisses down her neck.

"Because it is true. The major reason I was going with Jane and Lord Kinellan was to keep this from happening." Peeping underneath the cover, she clucked her tongue and shook her head. "Tsk, tsk. Now it would be like shutting the stable door after the steed is stolen."

"It may have been one reason, but not the only one, if you remember. There is also the notion that we should keep you away from Lord Wetherby. That has not disappeared." With a sigh, Hugh lay back on the mattress, staring at the canopy overhead. "If we could marry now, then our problems might be solved. But like it or not, the matter of money must be taken into account."

"It is my own fault, I suppose." Maria ran her hand over Hugh's bare chest. "If I had only waited and let my father make settlement arrangements before my marriage to Alan, I would at least have something we could perhaps have lived on. But I was afraid he would not marry me if we waited, and the result of that folly is that I have nothing. Alan didn't even have the decency to provide for me and his child in a will. Jane said he could have made a bequest if he'd wanted to. He was so sure the child would be a boy, I suppose, that he didn't think he needed to make a will."

"He did make a will, Maria."

"What?" She raised up in the bed to stare at Hugh. "Why would you say that?"

"Because I witnessed it." Hugh sat up as well, his head cocked, a frown furrowing his brow.

"That's impossible. Mr. Clarke, the solicitor, would have told me." Hugh's words made no sense whatsoever. If Alan had made a will . . . "When did you sign the document? Soon after he inherited the title?" That was the most likely time a will would have been made.

Hugh shook his head. "He asked me and Mr. Chambers to sign a paper on the morning of the duel." He swallowed and looked away. "About an hour before he died."

"But why was I not told this?" Why had the solicitor lied to her? "Mr. Clarke assured me that there was no will that benefitted me or little Jane. It was one of the first things we asked once we understood there was no male heir."

Flopping back onto the bed, Hugh punched the mattress. "Blast it to hell. I beg your pardon, my love. It was the junior clerk."

"What are you talking about?"

"That morning in April, Lord Kersey had us sign the paper, then gave it to me. I was leaving that morning for London on business and he asked me to take it to the solicitor's office." He flung his hand over his head. "The foolish clerk mislaid the will. It did not come to Mr. Clarke's attention until the current Lord Kersey had been found. He asked me about it when he came to Kersey Hall two weeks ago."

"April?" Astonishment gave way to incredulity. And anger. "You have known about this will since April and did not think to tell me about it?"

"Maria, please." Hugh shook his head and tried to take her hand, but she crossed her arms across her chest. "I did not know for certain it was a will until two weeks ago. That morning I signed it I hoped it was something to benefit you and your child. But the late Lord Kersey did not take me into his confidence about it. It was not until Mr. Clarke told me it was a will that I knew for certain."

"And you could have told me about it two weeks ago. Why would you wish to keep something like that from me?" Fighting to hold back tears, Maria sniffed and wiped her eyes with the tail end of their covering.

"I swear to you I did not. Here, get back underneath the cover. You'll freeze again." Pulling the curtain around her shoulders, Hugh scrambled from the bed and stoked the fire. "This is the last of the wood. We shall have to leave shortly." He disappeared into the bathing chamber. When he returned he had his shirt on and her still wet clothing in his hands. "We should have hung these up to dry at least a little."

"Why did you not tell me, Hugh?" An outlandish fear gripped her that Hugh hadn't wanted her to have an inheritance. That way he could plead financial difficulties as a way to keep from marrying her.

"My love, I didn't know that Mr. Clarke hadn't told you." He dropped the clothes to the floor and took her into his arms. "In fact, I assumed he had, especially when immediately afterwards you moved from this house back to Kersey Hall. I thought the will had contained some kind of stipulation that would allow you and Jane to always live on the estate."

"So you don't know what is in the will?"

Hugh shook his head. "Mr. Clarke showed me the page with the signatures on it, nothing more. Nor did he divulge its contents to me." He kissed her and held her tight, soothing her fears. "But I think that if he did not tell you, you need to go to London and find out."

"Absolutely. Just think, if I have even a small inheritance, we may be able to marry regardless of your brother's circumstances. Will you take me?" The prospect of spending the several days' journey to and from London with Hugh made her take heart afresh.

"I do not think that would be wise, my love. First, I am still employed by Lord Kersey. My duty to him will keep me here. Second, we do not need him to know about this business, as any will favoring you would consequently not favor him."

"True." She burrowed closer to him. "I will tell this all to Jane. She will devise a plan, I'm sure."

"Now come." He kissed her and drew her to the edge of the bed. "We must make you look as disheveled as possible, without making you so uncomfortable that you freeze. Take the top curtain and wrap it around you." Picking up her sodden riding habit, he tossed it onto the remaining curtain and proceeded to roll it up in the material. "This will wring some of the water out of your clothing, but it must be damp enough that people at the Hall will believe you fell through the ice." He looked at her apologetically. "It's going to be a rather cold ride back to the Hall."

"I will be fine. And all we need tell them is the truth — with one short interlude left out." Her cousin's rule always held true. "Let's see if we can get my chemise a little drier. No one will see that save my maid, and she is very loyal."

The afternoon shadows had begun to

lengthen across the lawn by the time Hugh tossed Maria, shivering in the cold wet clothing once more, up onto Lily and they set out for Kersey Hall by the shortest route possible.

As they drew up in front of the house, grooms appeared to take the horses.

"Call Lord Kersey and Lady John Tarkington this instant," Hugh called to a footman on duty at the front door. He then helped Maria crawl down off Lily, almost as frozen as she had been earlier. The ride had been an agony of icy wind on the wet clothing. Shivering, she let Hugh help her up the front steps. As they approached, the door opened and a bevy of people spilled out onto the portico.

"What has happened?"

"Maria? Maria, are you all right?"

"Granger, what the devil is going on?"

Everyone spoke at once, so Maria answered none of them. She gazed about until she located Jane and steered herself through the throng and into her cousin's arms.

"Maria, what happened to you?" Jane's worried face peered into hers, looking for some accident or illness.

"I f . . . . fell through the ice. On the p . . . pond." She leaned on Jane's shoulder and whispered, "I will be fine. Get me to my room. We must talk."

Maria had to give her cousin credit. If there was some sort of emergency, even if she didn't know the particulars, Jane would rise to the occasion every time.

"Let us through, please." Her arm around Maria, Jane pushed through the crowd of people, all of them asking what had happened. Ignoring everyone, acting like a general with victory in sight, she escorted Maria through the gauntlet of nosy friends and relatives, reaching the front stairs without a single encounter.

When they finally reached Maria's room, Jane called for Hatley, who immediately stripped her mistress, popped her into bed, and sent for the bathtub and hot water with the same military efficiency Jane had showed. Lying snug between clean sheets, Maria truly appreciated such competence.

As soon as the maid had gone to oversee the bath, Jane sat on the end of the bed, and fixed Maria with a steely eye. "What happened, Maria?"

Tell the truth, but not the whole truth. They had agreed.

So Maria launched into the excitements of the day, omitting only her interlude with Hugh in the dowager's bed in Francis House. She ended with the news about the possible will and requested her counsel on the matter. "Jane, I cannot think why Mr. Clarke would not have contacted me if Alan's will had contained a bequest to me."

"I cannot see any reason why he would withhold it from you either, my dear." Tapping her lips, as was always Jane's way of signaling she was thinking. "Although someone might well have a reason to keep it from you."

Panicked, Maria sprang up in the bed. "You don't think Mr. Granger would do such a thing, do you?"

Jane waved her worries away. "Of course not. He has nothing to gain by doing so. Quite the opposite, in fact, if you do marry. Which I gather you may now be forced to do. You've been in his bed, haven't you?"

"I have no idea what you mean." Maria sank back down beneath the covers. Of course Jane would know. Maria'd almost never been able to conceal anything from her cousin.

"I am quite sure you do, my dear." Jane tossed the statement at her cousin and waited.

Wishing she had said nothing to Jane, Maria pulled the covers over her head. "Leave me be."

"I am afraid that is out of the question

now, my dear." Jane peeled the blankets back from Maria's face. "If you have taken Mr. Granger as your lover, everything has changed."

"Why would you think I have done such a thing when we expressly said last night that we would not do any such thing?" Lord, but she wished Jane was not staring so intently at her. Like a cat waiting to pounce on an unsuspecting mouse who had not told the whole truth.

"That promise was not worth the breath it took to make it." Jane scoffed, waving the pledge off like an unwanted dish at dinner. "Kinellan may have been fooled by it — a very gullible man, I will tell you — but not I." She peered at Maria again. "Are you denying that you have taken Mr. Granger as your lover?"

"No." The word was spoken very low.

"I did not think so."

"But how did you know?" Maria was truly puzzled as to how Jane had found her out.

"You look very different, my dear, than you did this morning." Smiling, Jane touched Maria's cheek in a caress. "Happier, more relaxed. Satisfied."

Maria blushed, her cheeks now the warmest they had been all day.

"But this means our strategy must now

change as well."

"How?"

"For one thing, it may be better if you marry now rather than waiting. It will afford you more protection and there will be less talk if you end up increasing again." The look Jane gave her made Maria wish to slink beneath the covers and never emerge. "As we will be journeying to London tomorrow — please remind me I must tell Kinellan this before the morning, he dislikes it so when I change his plans at the last moment — we can send Kinellan to the Archbishop of Canterbury for a special license. Then you and Mr. Granger can be married at your convenience."

"Something tells me that Mr. Granger is going to object to talk of the marriage before his affairs are settled with his brother." That seemed to be a sticking point with him. She understood it, after a fashion, but could not agree to it. Not after this afternoon's interlude.

"He may not have a choice if his brother lingers much longer. Your safety and reputation are more important than his pride, or independence, or whatever it is that is making him so obstinate."

"He is a stubborn man, to be sure."

"Then he will need to learn to give in

333

more graciously and more often."

Laughing as the door opened and the bathtub was carried in, Maria laid her hand on Jane's. "Thank you, Cousin, for all your help and advice guiding me through widowhood twice now. You must be an expert."

Shaking her head, Jane rose and headed for the door. "Enjoy your bath. Relax as much as you can, because after tomorrow, you may have precious little to rejoice about."

CHAPTER TWENTY-ONE

Mr. Hezekiah Clarke might not have been a nervous man by nature; however, today he seemed to be suffering from some disorder that gave him the perpetual fidgets. Maria, Jane, and Lord Kinellan sat in Mr. Clarke's private office, an intimidating audience for a normal solicitor to be sure, but for a man whose clientele included dukes, archbishops, and members of the royal family, they should have been nothing out of the ordinary. But today, it seemed, Mr. Clarke was nervous.

"Can you tell me, Lady Kersey, why you have finally decided to inquire about your legacy?" The little man with the round glasses glared at her, though he gripped his pen so tightly the goose quill creaked under the strain. He sat behind a large, spindly legged desk, piles of papers and files on either side of him.

"Because until day before yesterday I had

no idea my late husband had made a will leaving me anything." They had all agreed — after Maria insisted — that Maria would speak to Mr. Clarke herself. Only if the interview seemed to be getting out of hand was Lord Kinellan supposed to step in.

"That simply cannot be true, my lady." Mr. Clarke shook his head vehemently. "I have sent you two letters at least since November, informing you of the will and asking you to come to London at your earliest convenience to discuss your plans for managing the properties."

"What properties, Mr. Clarke?" Torn between excitement and exasperation, Maria shot a look at Jane. Did she really have an inheritance? Gooseflesh rose all along her arms. "I tell you again that I have received nothing from you since your letter informing me that Lord Kersey had been located and when he would be taking possession of Kersey Hall. That was in October. There was no mention of a will."

"Because the will had not come to light at that time." Pursing his lips, Mr. Clarke shook his head. "It wasn't discovered until about the middle of November, at which time I traveled to Kersey Hall to discuss its ramifications with you and Lord Kersey."

"Which you certainly did not do, Mr.

Clarke. I have never met with you until this morning. Do you deny that?" Wide-eyed, she again shot a glance at Jane. Had someone posed as her at that meeting?

"No, of course not, Lady Kersey. I was informed by Lord Kersey of your continued grief and seclusion at the time. But he assured me he would inform you of the will and advise you that I would be contacting you by mail regarding its contents." As if the idea was just dawning, Mr. Clarke leaned forward, the multitude of little lines in his face thrown into sharp relief. "Did Lord Kersey neglect to inform you of my visit?"

"Of course he did, Mr. Clarke." The infuriated voice of Lord Kinellan boomed in the small space. "Why on earth would he?"

"What do you mean, my lord? Lord Kersey gave me to understand —"

"That he would tell the woman who stood to inherit property he himself believed to be his?" The disgust in Kinellan's face transformed him from a handsome man to a demonic one. "Why would he tell her if he stood to lose a substantial amount by doing so?"

"But his lordship didn't know the contents of the will." Mr. Clarke's face paled as his alarm rose.

Kinellan waved that away. "Probably didn't matter. Either he would assume the worst, or he is petty enough to deny Lady Kersey even the meanest of bequests." The marquess glared at the solicitor until Mr. Clarke shrank back in his chair. "You should have insisted on seeing the dowager countess, if only briefly. No one is ever too bereaved to give their solicitor five minutes of their time."

"But I wrote to her ladyship."

"Obviously intercepted by Kersey." Jane's vehemence seemed no less than Kinellan's. "And if you detailed her inheritance in those letters, then Kersey knew exactly what he stood to lose."

"Oh, no, my lady." The quickness of the denial indicated the measure of Mr. Clarke's guilt. "I never quoted any specifics from the will in those letters. They merely urged a meeting to discuss the will."

Kinellan shrugged. "That probably alarmed Kersey enough for him to treat the matter as urgent and take action."

"What action could he take?" Maria's head was in a whirl. "Mr. Granger said that just after Lord Kersey's meeting with Mr. Clarke, I was invited to move back to the

338

Hall. Did that have something to do with it?"

Jane and Kinellan exchanged a candid look before Jane spoke. "Quite possibly, my dear. Your moving back to the Hall would have put you in closer proximity to Lord Wetherby."

"Lord Wetherby?" The afternoon was becoming more and more confusing. Jane must be wrong about this part of it. "What does he have to do with it?"

"Kersey wanted his son to marry you, my lady." Lord Kinellan obviously was not a man to mince words. "And when you showed no interest in him, he likely gave instructions for Wetherby to make the marriage happen any way he could."

With a gasp, Maria grasped her throat. "The day in the woods gathering greenery. Lord Wetherby . . ." She dropped her gaze.

"He tried to ravish you, according to Mr. Granger." Kinellan shook his head. "It's a wonder Granger didn't beat the man senseless then and there."

"I lied to him, my lord. I too was afraid of what Mr. Granger might do if he knew the true circumstances." Trying to make herself small on her seat, Maria clasped her hands in her lap and stared fixedly at them. "I believed Lord Wetherby simply wanted to have his way with me. I never thought he was trying to force a marriage."

"Because you didn't know you had anything of value in your possession, my dear." Grasping her hands, Jane turned to Mr. Clarke, who'd been following the exchange with a look of shock on his pale face. "Can you please tell my cousin what her husband left her, Mr. Clarke?"

"As I said in my letters, which I am sorry you did not receive, my lady, the bequest is substantial." From the folder before him, Mr. Clarke withdrew several sheets of blotched foolscap — blotted and crossed out passages abounded — that had been folded and sealed, although the seal was gone. "Thanks to the canny purchases of the fifth Earl of Kersey, your late husband's uncle, three properties were acquired during his lifetime and were therefore not part of the earldom's entailment. In addition, that same earl was a great collector of artwork, all also not bound by the fee tail." Mr. Clarke looked directly at Maria, who grasped Jane's hand. "All told, my lady, with land, jewels, and artwork, I would estimate the bequest includes at least half the earldom's assets."

Unable to say anything, much less move, Maria stared at Mr. Clarke, waiting for Jane or Kinellan to do something. The silence continued, however.

"My lady?" Quickly, Mr. Clarke rose and went to the door and opened it. "Mr. Gaines, a pot of tea and four cups as quickly as you can." He returned to his chair behind the desk. "I know this may be a shock, Lady Kersey, but the tea will be here shortly."

"*May* be a shock, Clarke?" Lord Kinellan's voice finally rang out.

The spell broken, Maria turned to Jane, sitting ashen beside her. "Is it really true, Jane?"

"Oh, I assure you it is, my lady," Mr. Clarke broke in. "I cannot give you exact figures as to the value of everything, but I daresay it is close to fifty thousand pounds."

Silence resumed until the clerk entered with the tea.

Mr. Clarke hastily poured, and once Maria had sipped the brew, well sugared against the shock, the world came back into focus.

"What must I do, Mr. Clarke? I have no idea how to go on." She looked at him blankly.

"Today there is little you need to do. If you wish to continue to be represented by this firm, there are several documents to sign. You will need to establish a bank account. I can make suggestions or perhaps his lordship can. Do you stay long in London?"

She hadn't thought about that eventuality because she'd never dreamed she would need to take care of such matters. If only Hugh were here, he would know what to do. "Lord Kinellan? What are our plans?"

Taking out his pocket watch, the marquess glanced at it and sighed. "I had hoped we could finish this business today and leave early tomorrow. Will that be possible, Clarke?"

"I believe we can finish by this afternoon." He smiled at Maria and his eyes behind his spectacles gleamed. "Let us begin with a formal reading of the will, my lady."

"The snow seems to be holding off." Giving a great yawn, Maria stretched as best she could in the swaying carriage. "Do you think we will arrive at Kersey Hall before dark?"

Because Lord Kinellan had feared bad weather, they had left London at the ungodly hour of seven o'clock. No wonder she was tired.

Beside her, Jane too stifled a yawn. Her cousin apparently had gotten less sleep than Maria. She and Jane had shared a room last night, so it had not been hard to miss her cousin slipping out of the room when Maria had been drifting off to sleep. She'd not returned until just before the inn's maid had arrived with warm water.

Lord Kinellan, opposite them on the backward facing seat, seemed to be hiding a yawn as well. "I beg your pardon, Lady Kersey. What did you ask?"

Maria had to bite back a smile. "Only if you thought we'd arrive before dark."

"We have had good roads with little traffic and therefore have made good time." He peered out the window and nodded. "With a little more luck, we may arrive in time for tea."

"Not that I wish to take tea with any of the Kersey family." Fuming again at the thought of Lord Kersey's perfidy, Maria gritted her teeth and wished she could at least plant Lord Wetherby a facer. Why should men be able to have all the fun? "We shall need to stop at the inn in Sudbury to make arrangements for the night. I will not spend one more hour there than I have to."

"Did Lord Kersey think it strange that we were going to London?" Staring with wide-open eyes, trying to stay awake, Jane's head drooped occasionally in a doze.

"I didn't tell him where I was going. I simply asked the nursemaid to bring me

Jane and told Hatley to pack for two days."

Kinellan's brows shot up and he grinned. "Our little Maria has learned how to stand up for herself. I like that in a woman."

"I don't know how much I can stand up to anyone." Drawing the lap blanket more snugly around her, Maria sighed. "I may have a great amount of property now, but I don't know anything about them at all. I don't even know where the properties are located, although I have the directions written down. Nor do I know where the art is stored." Beseechingly, she turned to the marquess, whose head was beginning to droop as well. Certainly a marquess would know what to tell her. "What do I do, Lord Kinellan?"

Stretching out his long legs in the cramped space, Lord Kinellan looked like nothing so much as a colt unfolding its unruly legs. "First, you must accept the fact that your life has been forever changed. You are an heiress, Lady Kersey, and as such you will have great freedom. The freedom to live anywhere you wish, entertain lavishly, travel on the Continent, hire the best nursemaids and governesses for your child. All of this and more is now possible and is your decision to make."

Unbelievable. To be able to do all of that,

to decide her own course, when previously she'd been allowed to decide almost nothing, was exhilarating. She and little Jane could live a life almost without care. Her parents could have a new house, servants, her father the best care possible. "It sounds too good to be true."

"Well, but there is another side to such good fortune."

The carriage hit an icy patch and slithered to the side of the road.

Maria grabbed the seat to keep from being pitched into Kinellan's lap. "What do you mean?"

The marquess shrugged and glanced at Jane, fast asleep on the seat beside her, her head propped on her hand, unaffected by the jostling of the ride. A smile tugged at his lips, a tenderness in his face she'd never seen before. He reached over and gathered her cousin in his arms, bringing her to sit alongside him, and moved her head to his shoulder. At once she nestled into him, a smile on her lips, and continued to sleep.

"Where were we, my lady?"

"I think perhaps we can dispense with the titles, if it is all the same to you, my lord. Please call me Maria." She nodded to the sleeping Jane. "You are likely to be my kinsman soon in any case."

He peered at the sleeping woman in his arms. "That is, unfortunately, not a foregone conclusion. Your cousin is an obstinate woman, brought on, I believe in part, by the financial security of her widowhood. Her ability to do as she pleases has made her so independent she doesn't always think of what may or may not be the best course for her."

"Has she refused to marry you then?"

"She has avoided the question, I suspect, because she has a true fondness for me. Or at least I hope that is the reason." He settled Jane more securely in his arms. "Do you still wish to marry Mr. Granger after receiving your newfound wealth? You now have the means to live the rest of your life unencumbered by a husband."

"Of course I wish to marry him." What an odd question for Kinellan to pose. "Now we do not have to wait for his brother's . . . demise." That would be a godsend in itself. She'd hated to think they'd just been waiting, like a pair of vultures, for the elder Mr. Granger to die. "We will be able to marry and start our lives anew, together, immediately."

"Then you must have proper settlements drawn up this time. I suspect Mr. Granger will insist upon it, as whatever is not stipulated as yours will, upon your marriage, revert to him."

"You said before that there was another side to good fortune. Is that one of them? That I must guard it at every turn?"

"If you wish to keep it, my dear, then yes. You will have people, complete strangers, suddenly cozying up to you, begging your assistance. If you are to keep your fortune, you must learn to say no to them."

"But there is so much . . ." She could do so many things with her newfound wealth.

"There won't be if you do not set rules on the spending of it. Given his current occupation, I suspect your future husband will be very good at that." Kinellan glanced out the window. "We are slowing, probably at Braintree to change the horses." He smiled at her. "Not much farther."

Perhaps another hour or so and she'd see Hugh again. She'd missed him dreadfully and it had only been two days. But now they need not part, ever again. As the carriage pulled into the coaching inn, light flakes of snow began to fall, a reminder that the holiday season would soon be upon them.

Despite the sorrows of the past year, this coming Christmas would be the best she'd ever known. With a new husband and new-found means with which to celebrate, the coming season of peace on earth and joy to all mankind would be one she would likely never forget.

Chapter Twenty-Two

Lights were blazing in Kersey Hall when Kinellan's carriage pulled up to the front door. Figures bobbed and twirled in one of the upstairs rooms. The Christmas house party had begun the day before and seemed to be progressing well. Maria doubted it would continue so.

Kinellan handed her and Jane down from the carriage. "Will you go find Hatley and Nurse, please, Jane. Tell them to pack our things immediately. I don't care if they have to stuff them in a flour sack, by the time I finish my talk with Lord Kersey, I want us to be able to leave."

"I will take care of it, my dear." Jane looked wistfully at her. "I only wish I could witness your conference with Lord Kersey."

Kinellan lifted the knocker and let it fall. "I promise to give you a full report, my dear."

Chambers opened the door. "Lady Ker-

349

sey, Lady John, Lord Kinellan. His lordship will be pleased."

"I highly doubt that," Kinellan muttered as they entered.

After handing her pelisse to the butler, Jane headed directly for the stairs.

"Where is Lord Kersey?" Maria pulled off her coat and gave it to a nearby footman. "With his guests?"

"Yes, my lady. In the family drawing room."

"Ask him to please attend me in the blue receiving room. Tell him . . ." She shot a look at Kinellan, who nodded. "Tell him it is a matter of grave importance that I speak with him."

"You will not be joining the party, my lady?"

"No, Chambers. I plan to have one of my own." Hesitating only a moment over that cryptic reply, the butler bowed and left.

"This way, my lord." She led Kinellan into the room where they'd met so abruptly three days ago.

"A room that has seen its share of interesting conversations, I'll wager." Kinellan headed straight to a sideboard and poured himself a drink. "I'm sorry there's no sherry, Maria. I daresay you could use some fortification as well, what with the cold ride and the coming interview."

"Thank you, no." Maria twisted her hands together, still uncertain what she was actually going to say to Lord Kersey. "I believe my anger at his treachery continues to warm me just fine."

With a chuckle, the marquess downed his drink and set the glass on the sideboard. "I've rarely looked so forward to a woman speaking her mind. It's much more entertaining when one is not the target."

The door opened and Lord Kersey entered, a broad smile on his face. His cheeks were a bright pink, from the exercise of the dancing or from his cups, was unclear. Maria would wager on the latter.

"Cousin Maria!" The jovial host headed straight for her and took her hands. "We believed you would not return for some days yet." He glanced at Kinellan. "My lord. We weren't exactly sure where you had gone."

"I've been to London, to see Mr. Clarke."

Kersey dropped her hands as though they had suddenly caught fire. The underlying color seemed to leech out of Kersey's skin before her eyes, leaving hectic red blotches on his cheeks and nose. "You did?"

"Yes." Needing to put some distance between them, Maria strolled to the fireplace. "He was quite surprised that I knew

351

nothing about my husband's will, or of his own visit to Kersey Hall over two weeks ago." She turned to face the scoundrel again. "Of course, he assumed you were indeed the gentleman he mistook you for and would actually give me the letters he sent telling me of my inheritance."

"Cousin Maria." His now leering smile made her skin crawl. "You were still distraught over your husband's death. I didn't want to worry you over financial matters at a time like that."

"The only time I felt truly distraught, my lord, was when your son tried to ravish me in the woods." Anger bubbled up from deep within her. "I believed at the time he acted simply from lust, but now I understand the true depths of his despicable plan." She stared into Kersey's wide, horror-filled eyes. "Your despicable plan to have him compromise me so I would have to marry him and forfeit all my inheritance to my new husband."

"Cousin . . . Maria." The earl trembled, his hands shaking so badly he seemed to have developed palsy. "It was never that. Anthony has been attracted to you from the day you met. Unfortunately, he does have a reputation, well-deserved I'm sorry to say, as a rake. Gentlemen like that allow their passions to rule them."

"I'd hardly call someone with such savage, animalistic behavior a 'gentleman,' my lord." From the sideboard, where he'd poured himself another drink, Kinellan scowled at Kersey with such intensity the earl cringed. "You should have taken a horse whip to him the first time he tried to assault a woman."

"Fortunately, I managed to escape his advances. And as I am quitting Kersey Hall this very night, I expect never to see your son or you again, unless it is at some public function." She glared at him. "In which case I pray you, do not address me if you see me. I will not be speaking to either of you."

"Cousin —"

"Do not call me 'cousin.' " Fury rising, Maria darted toward him and he jumped back. "I refuse to claim kinship with someone who would try to take my inheritance from me, and by such brutal and nefarious means."

"My lady, please calm yourself." Worry lines had popped out on Kersey's forehead. "Certainly we can come to some amicable agreement?"

"Agreement about what?" The man was mad if he thought she would agree to anything he proposed.

"Your inheritance, of course." The earl twisted his hands together.

"What agreement can you possibly imagine I would come to with you about my rightful legacy?" Her words dripped venom.

"Your husband had no right to leave you . . . that legacy." Kersey puffed out his chest. "The loss of that property could destabilize the earldom."

"What property are you talking about?" Maria fought to keep her countenance. "How would you know what was in that will, my lord? Mr. Clarke said he did not share its contents with you."

"I don't know, exactly. But anything taken from the earldom will weaken both it and the Kersey heritage. Your husband —"

"My late husband was a rake and a cad and a thoroughly irresponsible man. Just like your son." Glaring at the earl, Maria stalked toward him. "That will was possibly the one selfless thing he did in his entire life. And Mr. Clarke assures me that all the properties listed in it were not part of the entail and therefore within his legal right to bequeath to me for my maintenance and that of our child."

"Properties?" A fine sweat had broken out on Kersey's brow. "He left you more than one?"

A snort of amusement from Kinellan brought a smile to Maria's lips as well. Time to leave.

"Lord Kersey, I will bid you adieu. You showed me what I believed to be kindness, but was actually a ploy to steal my future. Therefore, I am removing to London until I decide *which* of my properties I will be residing in permanently. Enjoy your Christmas party." She pulled on her gloves. "Your greenery in the hallway is quite lovely. And when the party is done, if you decide to come to London to further your celebration, be sure you bespeak your lodgings beforehand. For I can assure you, the Kersey townhouse will be occupied."

The stunned earl staggered backward.

Heart beating so hard she was almost dizzy, Maria took Kinellan's arm and he escorted her from the room. Now to find her cousin, her child, and her maids. She couldn't wait to scrape the mud of this place from her shoes forever.

Excitement growing as the carriage neared Wingate, Maria gave Jane's hand a squeeze. "Ouch." Her cousin snatched it away, shaking it. "Do restrain your exuberance, my dear. I will need the use of that hand without broken bones."

"I cannot help it, Jane. I cannot wait to tell Hugh about this miraculous change in circumstances." She'd thought of nothing else, save her harsh words for Lord Kersey, almost since they left London. The surprise on his face would be one of her fondest memories in the years to come. Years together with him.

The carriage rolled up to the little manor house, where a light shone in a single room. Probably a sitting room where Hugh and his sister would read or talk in the evenings after dinner. Soon it would be the three of them, talking, laughing, sitting companionably. In years to come, little Jane would be with them and later their own children together. Just as her family had been when she was growing up.

When the carriage stopped, Kinellan helped her down. "Would you like us to go with you, my dear?"

Jane poked her head out the door. "It will be a shock to him, Maria. As much a one as it was for you. Perhaps we should accompany you."

"Thank you, but no. I want this to be a private moment between us." She could picture Hugh's astonishment, then delight. He would take her in his arms and kiss her as if they stood under the mistletoe. A moment in their lives they would remember forever.

Maria straightened her pelisse, adjusted her hat, took a great breath and marched to the door. Her knock brought the butler, and she was shown in immediately. "May I speak to Mr. Granger, please?"

"Yes, my lady." He divested her of her coat and hat. "Will you come this way?" He showed her into a small, neat receiving room, done in dark greens and reds. Very festive for this time of year. "I'll tell Mr. Granger you are here."

Nodding, she walked to the fireplace, where a fire had been recently banked, and held out her hands to the glowing embers. Excitement seemed to have gotten the better of her, for she now seemed to run hot and cold. Her hands were like ice, but her body burned like a furnace. Was this the way it was supposed to be when life turned into a fairy story? All her dreams were about to come true.

"Maria."

She whirled around but Hugh was already at her side, enfolding her in his arms.

"Lord, but I'm glad to see you." He hugged her to him, and the wonderful feel of him pressed to her once more brought tears to her eyes. "Have you just — you're crying." Leaning back to peer at her face, he cupped her face. "What is wrong, my love?"

"Nothing." She wiped her eyes with the back of her hand. Why did she never remember a handkerchief? "I missed you so much is all. I didn't know quite how much until now."

"Here." He produced one of his handkerchiefs, and the scent of citrus — now permanently linked to him in her mind — filled her head. Blotting the tears, he carefully patted her cheeks dry. "Now, come with me to the drawing room. Bella and I sit there after dinner."

"Can we stay here? I have news from London I would like to tell you alone."

"Of course." He led her to the damasked sofa and sat beside her, holding her hand in a gentle grip. "What is it, sweetheart?" His deep voice had softened. "Was Mr. Clarke's news disappointing?"

"Oh, no, Hugh." Maria couldn't contain her smile. She'd been waiting so long for this moment. "The news is impossibly good, better than I could ever have dreamed." Leaning against his shoulder, just to feel his warmth, she laced her fingers through his. "I never thought I would say this, but Alan has finally made amends for the callous way he treated me all during our marriage. In the end, I suppose, he wished to leave this world with his conscience, not completely clear, but at least at peace, having knowledge that our child and I would be taken care of in any eventuality."

"I am glad of it, my love." He squeezed her hand and it radiated throughout her. "I remember him that morning, very somber, not at all like his usual devil-may-care self."

"Do you think he knew he would not return from the dueling ground?"

"I think he did. Sometimes a man knows when his luck has run dry." Slipping his arm around her, Hugh leaned his head against hers. "Did anyone tell you that he died well?"

She shook her head. "No. No one wanted to tell me anything for fear it would harm the baby."

"I spoke to his second, after I returned from London. He told me that Lord Kersey seemed calm, even poised as he took his position. When the handkerchief dropped, he raised his weapon in good time and fired. The bullet lodged in Lord Remington's shoulder, but didn't wound him badly enough that he couldn't shoot. So Lord Kersey stood there and waited some seconds, without flinching, while Remington took careful aim before shooting him in the heart."

The image of the golden-haired man she had worshiped for such a short period of time, struck down in a crumpled heap, brought back the tears. She pressed her face into Hugh's shoulder and sobbed.

"Do not cry, my love. It was a good, clean death. A gentleman's death, met bravely." He handed her his handkerchief. "And a quick one, which Remington must have come to envy."

"Why?" Maria dabbed at her eyes. She'd never thought she'd cry over Alan again.

"The wound in Remington's shoulder became inflamed. They amputated his arm, but the infection couldn't be contained. He died, quite probably in agony, two weeks later."

A shiver ran down Maria's spine. This was not supposed to be the topic of conversation this evening. She blew her nose and sat up. "I don't want us to talk of death, Hugh. I want us to talk of life, our life together."

"We will, my love. But you have not yet told me your good news." Raising her hand, he placed a kiss on the back, his lips warm and alive.

"The will Alan made bequeaths me three unentailed properties, including the Kersey townhouse in London, an artwork collection that includes a Rembrandt, and half a dozen pieces of jewelry."

As she spoke the pressure on her hand increased. Hugh's eyes had widened until his blue eyes swam in a sea of white, then he shook his head and slipped his hand from hers. "This is true? This is what I signed in April?"

Slowly she nodded. His lovely deep voice had a gruff ring to it. Of course, he would take some time to appreciate what this meant. The shock of such a large legacy, now hers and little Jane's, must wear off a bit before he could see how neatly this smoothed their path. "Isn't it marvelous, my love?"

Hugh swallowed, but didn't answer.

"Hugh? Are you going to come back —" His sister, Bella, spoke as she came into the room. "Oh, Lady Kersey." She curtsied, then frowned at her brother. "Hugh, why have you not brought Lady Kersey back to the drawing room? I can ring for more tea."

"Not at the moment, Arabella." His voice had softened when he spoke to his sister. "Lady Kersey and I have several private things to discuss. We will come to you as soon as we are done."

A worried frown appeared on Bella's

361

brow. Perhaps she'd caught the strange tone in Hugh's voice as well. "Very well. I hope to see you shortly, my lady." With another quick curtsey, his sister left.

"Hugh, what is wrong?" The cold trickle of fear that had begun to flow through Maria's veins became a flood. Why was Hugh not as elated as she about this unprecedented boon? "Don't you understand? We can now marry, without fear of poverty. The income from this fortune will support us for our entire lifetimes. My child, my Jane, will be an heiress of the first water. Your sister as well. We can give her a dowry that will rival any titled lady's." She grasped his hands, then shrank back, stunned to find them cold as death. "Dear lord. Hugh, my love. What is the matter?"

"No, Maria." He rose, shaking his head. "We cannot do this."

"Cannot do what?" Leaping to her feet, Maria went after him, following him to the fireplace. "What is it you think we cannot do?"

"Marry." Running his hand through his hair, Hugh suddenly squeezed the ends, as if he would pull the hair off his head. "We cannot marry, Maria."

"What do you mean? Of course we can marry. We love one another, and now, by

362

the grace of God, we have ample means."
Fear twisted her heart. Why would he say
such a thing?

"If we marry now, it will seem to some as
if I had a hand in Lord Kersey's death."

"But you didn't." The man wasn't making
any sense. "Lord Remington challenged him
and killed him. All you did was sign the
will."

When he turned to her, she gasped. The
harsh planes of his face that had never stood
out before, were now plainly visible. When
he hung his head, a sense of guilt seemed to
emanate from him. As though he couldn't
look at her. "I signed the will that left his
widow a fortune. And then I married the
widow."

"Hugh, that's ridiculous. No one will
think anything of that." Dear lord, was he
serious? Did he mean not to marry her
because of the money?

He raised his head, his eyes bleak. "You'd
be surprised what people will say. Especially
when I turn up penniless because my
brother was declared a suicide." Clenching
his jaw, he closed his eyes, his mouth working as though some great emotion struggled
to escape him. "The last I heard from The
Grange, Kit has taken a turn for the worse.
He will not take any food. Usually the

servants could get him to swallow at least some gruel or soup. Now they can barely get a spoonful of water to go down."

"I am so sorry, Hugh." Hesitantly, she placed a hand on his shoulder. "We've known for some time that this was inevitable. Perhaps he's decided it is time for him to go."

"And with him goes any hope of a good life for any of us." He shrugged off her hand. "Mr. Lambert, the surgeon who attended Kit from the beginning, wrote to let me know that the local magistrate spoke to him about Kit's case. The magistrate knows he will have to rule on the cause of death, and wanted Lambert's opinion."

"Do you know what Lambert told him?" Gasping in a breath of air, Maria held it against the answer she did not want to hear.

"Under the circumstances, what else can Lambert say other than *felo-de-se,* the taking of one's own life." Hugh let out a sigh and crossed his arms over his chest. "We will lose everything." Gazing at her, he walked a few steps until he stood directly in front of her. "Including our ability to marry."

"No, Hugh." She grabbed his arm. "I don't care, do you hear? I don't care what people may say about you signing that will.

I don't care what they may say because your brother, in a fit of melancholy, tried to take his own life and eventually died from the wound. All I care about is that we are together because I love you." This time she wouldn't be able to stem the tide of tears, no matter what she did. "Can't you see that?"

"I can, my love. And I told Lord Kinellan the other evening, I would have to be the strong one of the two of us. I swore I would do anything to protect you or your child." He grasped her hands, kissed them, then gazed into her face. "Including giving you up."

"No." Maria shook her head, slowly at first, then faster, tears flying from her cheeks like drops of rain. "No, Hugh, no."

"I must, my love. If you and little Jane are to have a chance at life, it cannot be with me. Go now." He kissed her forehead and released her. "Take the chance that God has given you and do not look back."

The tears streaming down her face blinded her and when her vision cleared, he was gone. Jane and Lord Kinellan were there, buttoning her pelisse, guiding her with arms around her shoulders out the door and into the carriage.

Jane settled her against the seat, her arms

tight around Maria. "There, there, my dear. We will be at the inn shortly. Hatley will take care of you and I will be there if you wish to talk about . . . anything."

Maria shook her head. All the talking had been done and the stubborn man whom she loved more than anyone in the world save her child, had won. What could she do if he wouldn't agree to marry her? Nothing. She could stay and try to change his mind, but if his brother was truly dying, then Hugh had grief enough to contend with. She'd not make his burden heavier by hounding him in his time of sorrow.

Her own grief was heavy enough to bear. And the only thing to help her shoulder it was hope. Perhaps, in time, her absence would outweigh Kit's passing and its consequences. Then he would see that love was the only thing that truly mattered, and return to her. Love and hope must sustain her until then.

CHAPTER TWENTY-THREE

Snow had been falling steadily since early morning, turning the dirty streets of London pristine under a fluffy white covering. Maria sat in the window seat overlooking the park, little Jane on her lap, laughing and trying to catch the snowflakes. Children ran and slid out in the park. Two little girls were lying in the snow making snow angels while their brothers engaged in a snowball battle. Everyone was happy and laughing, even Jane.

But not Maria. With Christmas scarcely a week away, and all the Christmas cheer to gaze at right outside her door, she'd have thought she would be more firmly in the holiday spirit than she was presently. She'd settled into the London townhouse, in fashionable Belgravia, with a minimum of fuss. Of course, as Kinellan said, when one could pay, one could get one's way.

She smiled, recollecting his droll expression when pronouncing that adage. In the week they'd been in London she'd grown very fond of Jane's *amour*. The lucky woman had better hold on to that one with all her might. Not that Jane was in any danger of Kinellan straying from her. He had eyes only for her cousin. Lucky woman.

Bouncing little Jane on her knee, Maria stubbornly refused to think of Hugh again. Not that her resolve meant very much. She thought about him at least three times every day, which meant he was not occupying all of her time as he'd done on the first days of her residence. Then the only time she'd not thought about him had been when she dropped into an exhausted sleep. Now the sharp ache in her heart whenever she brought his dear face to mind, had been replaced by a dull one. Perhaps one day, years from now, it would disappear entirely. She didn't quite believe that, however.

The biggest problem currently was that she had too much time on her hands. She spent most of her days gazing out the window, thinking about things she shouldn't. Like ice-skating. One day a group of young people had gone by the window, chatting merrily, their skates slung over their shoulders or tucked neatly under an arm. Instantly, she'd been transported back to that day skating on the dowager's pond — and the luscious interlude in bed after Hugh had rescued her. She'd sat in the window for an hour until Jane had dragged her in to tea. But she had no appetite.

With Christmas only a week away, she really should rouse herself. Some evergreens around the house might put her in a more festive mood, but decorating was for parties and she wasn't cheerful enough for anyone. She had asked her parents to join her in London, but her mother said the journey would be too much for her father. They had begged her to come and bring the baby, but Maria had postponed that visit until after the New Year. Irrational as it might be, she wanted to celebrate her first Christmas as an independent widow here, in her home. Unfortunately, it would be a very lonely holiday. Jane and Kinellan were here, her cousin promising to remain indefinitely. The marquess's response had not been in the spirit of the season, but had expressed his own sentiments very succinctly.

Still, they would be here to celebrate little Jane's first Christmas with Maria. The house should look more festive. "Nurse." Maria had only to raise her voice slightly and Nurse Celeste appeared. A young woman who had not been a nursemaid before, but who had helped raise five brothers and sisters into their adult years, Celeste seemed genuinely fond of her charge.

"Here, take her, Nurse. She probably wants a bottle and a nap." Maria stifled a yawn. "As do I, I'm afraid." Well, not the bottle, but the nap, definitely.

"Very good, my lady." Celeste picked little Jane up in well-practiced hands and headed off to the nursery.

Sighing, Maria rang the bell for more tea. What else was she to do? Still in mourning, she couldn't attend parties or balls. A concert might do, but she'd never enjoyed music as most people did. And books had begun to pall. Everything she wanted to do, lay miles away in the country — rides and walks in the woods, friends to visit, tenants to check on. None of those were available to her here, save the rides and walks, although instead of the woods around Kersey Hall she would have to substitute Rotten Row or some of the carriage haunts in Hyde Park. Certainly not the same as the unrestricted avenues around the Hall. Perhaps this afternoon she and Jane could at least walk in the small park opposite. Anything to keep her from moping around.

Jane accompanied the entry of the tea tray. "Why so gloomy, Cousin?" She seated herself across from Maria and helped herself to a biscuit. "We must do something to raise your spirits. You don't want to go to church on Christmas Day with a Friday-face, now do you?"

"No, but I cannot seem to find anything to raise my spirits. Christmas at home with my parents was always a joyous time of year. We made a big outing of going into the woods to bring in the greenery. Mama's sisters and their children would come to the house for Christmas dinner, so there would be lots of conversation and stories. We children played games like blindman's bluff and find the slipper. Then of course there was the snapdragon." Maria bounced up in her seat, excitement in her for the first time in days. "Oh, that was so much fun, even with the burned fingers." She laughed and sighed. "Why can't it be like that this Christmas?"

"It can be, my dear. But in order to do so, you will need to invite your friends to Christmas dinner. Better yet, ask them to come several days before Christmas and make a house party of it. You have the room here." Jane gestured to the townhouse, which had six bedrooms.

Maria's excitement ebbed as quickly as it

had surged. "But I don't have any friends to invite."

"Nonsense." Tasting her tea, Jane made a face and hastily added more sugar. "You have Charlotte, Elizabeth, Fanny, and Georgie. Who could ask for a livelier group once you add in husbands, children, and three more babies? Little Jane will be beside herself with new playmates."

"They are really your friends, Jane." Maria's shoulders slumped. "I was always the outsider in their little group. I'd never have met them had you not invited me to Charlotte's party in the first place."

"But you have become one of us, my dear. Doubly so, as we called ourselves The Widows' Club. You have had a much worse time of it than any of the rest of us." Jane set her cup down and took Maria's hand. "We were a comfort to one another during the darkest days of our lives, and we will be the same for you, no matter the sorrow."

"Do you truly think they would come?" Hope flared in Maria's heart. The women of The Widows' Club had taken her in once. And although they had disapproved of her marriage to Alan, they had all supported her when they heard about his death, sending cards of condolence and letters to help her through her grief.

"Why don't you write to them today?" Her cousin smiled and helped herself to another biscuit. "I heard from Elizabeth just before we left Kersey Hall that she and Georgie were to travel to Blackham Castle for the holiday, although Elizabeth was not particularly sanguine about passing the holiday with Lord Blackham. They will likely be quite happy to alter their plans and come to London instead. And Charlotte and Nash are not even a day's journey from Town."

"I suppose there might be a chance those three would come." Now that the possibility of a merry Christmastide was within her grasp, Maria didn't want to get her hopes up too high. To have the plans all fall apart would hurt abominably. "But I doubt we can expect Fanny to journey so far in such weather." The snow outside had thickened until she could scarcely see the trees in the park.

"You forget, my dear. Kinellan is here." Jane's smile grew wide and wicked. "I will ask him to write to Lathbury suggesting they come as well. I will almost guarantee that barring a blizzard, Lord and Lady Lathbury will appear with their children and his young sisters. You will have a house full of Christmas cheer in less than a week."

Suddenly the prospect of spending the yuletide in London seemed joyous once more. She might not have the one person with her she wished for most, but she could have friends and family with her to celebrate a new beginning to her life. She rose from the window seat, turning her back on the snowy scene. "I will write them all directly so the letters can go in the afternoon post."

"Very good, my dear." Smiling with anticipation, Jane picked up a lemon tart. "Nothing like friends and food to guarantee everyone will have a good time."

Saunders opened the door to Hugh's office early one afternoon and handed him a letter, sealed with a black wax wafer. "This just arrived in the afternoon post, Mr. Granger."

Even though he'd been expecting this announcement for weeks, the black seal sent a shiver of dread coursing through Hugh. "Thank you, Saunders."

"I'm sorry, sir." The compassion in the footman's face somehow made the news Hugh was about to receive real in a way it had never been before.

Hugh nodded and Saunders slipped out.

"Ah, Kit. I pray you are finally at peace." He lifted the seal and unfolded the page.

Two brief lines told of his brother's passing. And that Mr. Lambert had informed the magistrate both of the death and the suspected cause — a self-inflicted pistol shot to the jaw. Life in Lavenham was about to get ugly.

Carefully, Hugh refolded the letter and slipped it in his pocket. It was early yet. He and Bella could quickly pack what was necessary and leave for home within the hour. First, however, he'd need to inform Lord Kersey that his absence from Kersey Hall would be required for some days. He dreaded this interview almost more than the coming procedure with the magistrate.

Lord Kersey had been in a rare mood since last week when Maria delivered her little surprise. Saunders had been on duty at the party in the drawing room, but had been called downstairs to fetch more punch for the ladies. He had heard raised voices in the receiving room and had managed to linger long enough to hear most of Maria's harangue. Lord, what he wouldn't have given to have been able to hear her — and see Kersey's face when he learned his easy life had just become a deal harder.

All week Hugh had walked a tightrope, in an effort to keep his relationship with Maria from Kersey's notice. How anyone who looked at him didn't guess the truth, he could not fathom. Each time he thought about her, which was constantly, he would stop and stare into thin air, remembering a particular moment he had been with her: in the garden in October, the tea party with his sister and her cousin, the morning they'd spent in the dowager's bedchamber. He didn't allow himself to recall that memory unless he was alone. Embarrassing things sometimes happened when that memory was particularly vivid.

In any case, news that Hugh had won the affections of the new heiress would not likely bode well for him, or for the job that now stood between him and destitution. Any excuse to sack him or any other non-essential servant would be welcomed, he suspected. The fact that the house party that was supposed to last until the New Year had been shortened to the day after Christmas showed that Kersey was fully aware of the scope of the properties over which he no longer had control. Thus the lord's evil temper had shown itself in new ways. What he would say when Hugh asked permission to leave was anyone's guess.

Winding his way down the corridor, Hugh sought out Chambers as the one person who would know where Lord Kersey was currently drinking. On the way to the butler's pantry, he cocked his ear as he passed by the library. The unmistakable clink of glass on glass suggested he'd found his man. He pushed the door open and strode in.

Lord Kersey stood by the sideboard, a decanter of brandy in one hand, a well-used glass in the other.

Not the best time, perhaps, to ask for a leave of absence, but then these days there wasn't a good time to ask his lordship anything.

"Granger. There you are." Kersey staggered forward a step. "By God, where the hell have you been hiding?"

"I've been in my office all morning, my lord. Totaling up the incomes from the outer tenant farms as you requested." It had been a waste of time as the figures remained the same as the ones he'd totaled last month and in October as well.

"And?"

"No change, my lord." Hugh hesitated, then went on. "There won't be a change until the cabbage and leek crops are harvested in late January. That is the way the rotations have been staggered since I came here to work for the old earl."

"Damned tenants. Why can't they produce

crops year round?" He stared blearily at Hugh. "Can't they plant year round?"

"They can and do, my lord. But to get the best yields, there are periods when fields have to lie fallow, to allow them to recover from the previous planting." Clenching his fist at having to explain the idea of crop rotation to a drunken man who would not remember it tomorrow, and would likely ask yet again, Hugh focused on shifting the conversation to his request.

"Too many fields not producing anything. Too many tenants not producing anything." Lord Kersey's head came up and he stared at Hugh, a snarl on his lips. "And why in God's name haven't you gotten rid of that family on the farm that's supposed to be rented by now?"

Hugh's heart sank, all his other worries melting away as the plight of the Tates came quickly forward. "I put the notices up, my lord. There have been no inquiries to my knowledge."

"Then your knowledge is limited, Granger. A letter arrived yesterday asking if the tenancy was available." Kersey poured another glass full. "I instructed Chambers to answer the man in the affirmative. He'll be here, ready to move in on Saturday."

"On Saturday, my lord? With so little

notice, the Tate family will scarcely have time to find a place to move into." All Hugh could think, even with disaster looming for the Tates, was that he had failed Maria one final time.

"That is no concern of mine." Kersey took a long pull of his drink. "They should have made provisions long before now."

"But my lord —"

"Saddle up and ride out there now. Tell them they have two days to vacate the tenancy or their things will be tossed into the yard. Is that clear, Granger?" Kersey's voice boomed in the enclosed space.

"Yes, my lord." Hugh closed his eyes and imagined the fountain out in the garden, Maria in her pale gray gown, shimmering like a star, and her adamant stance that the Tates be given a chance to recover from Mr. Tate's death. As Maria had been given a chance.

"Very well then." Kersey motioned him out of the room, slopping brandy over his hand. "Get on with it."

"No, my lord."

"What?" The earl tried to focus on Hugh once more.

"I said no, my lord, I will not turn a good tenant out of their place when they still have three years to run on that tenancy and able bodies to work the fields." God, but it felt good to say that to Kersey's face.

"You are insolent, Granger. And on account of tenants who wouldn't give a tinker's damn if you starved or not."

"I think they would care, my lord. But you obviously don't care about them." The rush of power at being able to speak his mind to a man who had been, in a few short weeks, a tyrant and a tormenter, was exhilarating. He imagined Maria had felt something like that when she confronted him last week. "And as I refuse to be your henchman for this particular execution, I hereby tender my resignation, effective immediately."

"You cannot do that, Granger!" The earl's face turned a bright red, his eyes almost starting from their sockets. "I have not dismissed you from my employ."

"Lord Kersey, you no longer have the right to do so. I am not your employee as of one minute ago." Hugh grinned at the man, who looked from one side of the room to the other, as if searching for someone to tell him how to make Hugh behave. "I take my leave of you, my lord." Hugh bowed, turned, and hurried from the room, all the while anticipating the tumbler of brandy being hurled at the back of his head.

In the corridor, Hugh hurried back to his

office. There were several of his belongings he wanted to retrieve, and he'd need to inform Saunders of his departure. The footman had been a good ally. He would miss him. Opening the door, Hugh made a quick inventory of everything that belonged to him. He could not tarry here. Bella must be informed and the house emptied as speedily as possible, lest they find their things put out on the lawn next to the Tates' possessions. His sister would likely be too concerned with Kit's death to care much about his losing the position at Kersey. Until they were out on the side of the road along with the tenants.

Still, one idea kept a smile on Hugh's face all the way back to Wingate: Maria would have been pleased and proud of him.

CHAPTER TWENTY-FOUR

Late December
London

"What did I tell you?" Jane stood beside Maria in the townhouse's entry hall, surveying with apparent satisfaction the pandemonium that had ensued upon the arrival of Fanny and Matthew, Lord and Lady Lathbury, and their entourage of servants and children. "I knew they would come. Merry Christmas, Cousin."

"I don't think I shall ever doubt you again, my dear," Maria whispered, then swept Fanny up in a strong embrace. "Merry Christmas, Fanny. It is so good to see you. Thank you so much for coming."

"Oh, we wouldn't have missed it." Fanny bussed her cheeks, then turned to Jane, not only her friend but her sister-in-law. Both their husbands, brothers, had perished at Waterloo. "Jane, dear." They embraced. "I see you still have Kinellan on the string.

Best get him to come up to scratch while we are here. Christmas is a lovely time of year for a wedding."

"And so convenient, don't you know, since all The Widows' Club will be here." Tall and darkly handsome, Matthew, Fanny's husband, followed behind her in the impromptu receiving line. "Maria, so good to see you again." He engulfed her in his embrace, almost making her lose her breath. Lord, how did he not crush Fanny in their more intimate moments?

"And Jane" — he moved on to her cousin — "we have missed seeing you at Kinellan's for most of the year."

"I am well aware, Matthew, of where I have and have not been." She hugged him fiercely. "Don't think for a moment Kinellan has let me forget."

He laughed and put his arm around his wife. "I don't think he's let anyone do that. You really must marry the man, Jane, so we can stop his fussing about your absence."

Jane cut her eyes toward Maria. Time to move the guests along. "If you would follow Mrs. Cheever to your room, Fanny, Matthew, you can freshen up and join us in the large drawing room."

"Are we sharing a room?" Matthew cocked his eyebrow at his wife.

"I am afraid so, my lord." Maria led them to the front staircase where the housekeeper waited. "The townhouse has only six bedrooms."

"Good." He winked at Maria and bent to whisper, "Much better to have less running back and forth between rooms in the dark of night."

Maria giggled and followed them up the staircase to the first floor, Jane just behind her. They turned at the first landing, heading for their other guests already in the drawing room. She could hear animated chatter as they approached the door.

"Wrotham was blanketed in snow last week, such a picturesque village in winter."

They entered to find their friends Charlotte, Lady Wrotham, and Elizabeth, Lady Brack, on the end of the long green-and-white-striped sofa nearest the fireplace. Nash and Jemmy, their husbands, were at the far end of the room, deep in conversation.

"But the roads are so rutted this time of year," Charlotte continued. "We were fortunate that the travel here took only the best part of yesterday. Kitty traveled much better than I had anticipated a baby would."

"We would have arrived before you, but Jemmy's father would keep on and on about the castle Christmas traditions we would be missing, and making us promise to have little Nes back at Blackham for the ushering in of the New Year. A very big occasion for a firstborn son of the Cross family, apparently." Elizabeth sipped her tea, then glanced toward her husband, a fond smile on her lips.

"Are Fanny and Matthew here?" Charlotte set her tea down quickly, looking eagerly at the door. "I have not seen them in an age, it seems."

"They have gone to their room and should be along quite soon." Maria rang the bell for more tea, then settled herself in the Queen Anne chair that matched the sofa.

Charlotte and Jane exchanged glances.

"I would say later, rather than soon, my dear." Jane laughed and snared a fairy cake. "Fanny and Matthew have never waited overlong to christen a new bed."

"Jane!" For some reason her cheeks heated at the thought of her friend availing herself of marital pleasures while the rest of them sat talking downstairs.

"It is nothing but the truth, isn't that right, Charlotte?"

"I would have to say so, Jane." Grinning and trying to hide it, Charlotte picked up her cup, took a sip only to find it empty, and replaced it on the tray.

"Elizabeth" — Maria hastened to change the topic before her Christmas party became a scandal — "I heard you call your son Nes, is that correct? What an unusual name."

"His true name is what is unusual. Onesiphorus."

"Oh, my." Never had she heard such an outlandish name. "Where did you come up with that name?"

"It is my father-in-law's given name, and as he had objections to our marrying, we bargained with him — approve our marriage and we would name the child after him if it was a son. And as there is no other title available to him, we had to come up with a least objectionable nickname. So Nes it is." She shrugged. "I've become accustomed to it."

Tea arrived and talk turned perfunctory in front of the servant.

"You have truly captured the Christmas spirit in this room, Maria." Elizabeth gazed about the room with admiring eyes.

From the moment she'd written invitations to her friends, Maria had planned to have this one room be cozy and festive. Even though traditionally greenery was only brought into the house on Christmas Eve, Maria had followed the example of Lord

Kersey — much as she hated to admit it — and arranged the decorations in this room well before the usual day. She'd ordered fir, holly, ivy, rosemary, and mistletoe brought in, then she and Jane had tied festive bundles to place on windowsills or mantels and draped garland wherever she could attach it. The mistletoe ball, decorated with tiny red and white ribbons, hung prominently over the entrance to the room, although no one had noticed it yet.

"Thank you, Elizabeth. I wanted us to be joyful this Christmas." Never mind that her own joy had been cut short, her friends would make the difference in her life now.

"Good afternoon, all." Fanny and Matthew crossed the threshold, stopped and looked above them.

"Ha, caught you." Matthew grabbed Fanny to him, bent her over his arm, and kissed her long and thoroughly. When he finally righted her, Fanny's smile reached from ear to ear.

"Do you have any more mistletoe around the house we can sample?" she said to Maria, with a laugh.

"Here." Matthew reached up and plucked a white berry from the ball. "I will see to it you have a collection of these before the night is over."

"If you would kindly move out of the way, Lathbury, there are others of us who would join the party." Kinellan's voice rang out jovially.

Matthew obliged by taking Fanny's hand and leading her into the room.

No sooner did he move than Kinellan said, "This way."

The door was filled by another couple, the lady in a dark green gown with gold medallions scattered over it and a tall, handsome gentleman in buff and blue. "Come along, Lulu." Georgie tugged on the lead and a bouncy King Charles Spaniel trotted into the room.

"Georgie!"

The women rose at once and converged on Georgie, now the Marchioness of St. Just.

The hugging and kissing that ensued between the members of the former Widows' Club threatened to get out of hand, until Rob, Marquess of St. Just, waded in to rescue his wife.

"Ladies, I beg of you to allow Georgie to be seated, please." He escorted the blushing Georgie to the sofa, Lulu leading the way, plumed tail waving proudly.

"You do not have to make a spectacle of me, Rob." Georgie sat glaring at him, though she smiled all the same. "He wants people to notice how delicate I am because he is inordinately proud that I am finally increasing."

Another great cry, this time of congratulations, went up. The ladies clustered around Georgie, chatting excitedly, asking questions, giving advice, while the men gathered together at the sideboard, Kinellan handing out congratulatory drinks and raucous jokes being made *sotto voce* at Rob's expense.

Maria, however, hung back, suddenly an outsider in her own home. These ladies were her friends, yet they all possessed something that she did not — a husband, or in Jane's case, a gentleman of significance in her life. Only Maria was alone, in sharp contrast to everyone else at the party. If only Hugh could have been here, her happiness could be complete. No, that would only be true if they were actually husband and wife. A wave of loneliness engulfed her. Never would she find the contentment all her other friends shared, because the one man she loved was not here to complete her happiness. Would never be here to do so.

Tears started from her eyes and she fled to the fireplace before anyone could see. She wiped the tears on the back of her hand, half expecting to be handed the folded handkerchief, smelling of citrus and Hugh. He'd always done so before, but not now. And probably never again.

"Maria?" Jane, of course, had seen her leave the group. "What is wrong, my dear?"

Throat swollen with unshed tears, she could only shake her head, and wish for that handkerchief.

Miraculously, a square of linen appeared before her. She gasped and looked up into Kinellan's face, filled with compassion. "Fashionable ladies' gowns have but one design flaw. They do not have pockets in which to carry one's handkerchief. So I thought you could use mine for the time being."

"Thank you." Her nasally voice sounded terrible, but there was little she could do about that until the tears stopped. She wiped her eyes, suddenly aware of the silence in the room. Looking over her shoulder brought the realization that every-one in the room was watching her.

Fanny was the first of those on the sofa to come to her. "What is wrong, Maria?"

She tried to simply shake her head, but Fanny would stand for no nonsense.

"If there was no reason to cry, your cheeks would be dry and your nose wouldn't be red." She led Maria back to the sofa and sat her down next to Georgie. "Why are you so unhappy, my dear?"

With a shuddering sigh, she tried to pull her wits together. "Until very recently, I believed that I would be getting married soon."

"You were?" Fanny's eyebrows rose extremely high and she turned to Jane. "And you didn't write to us?"

Jane shrugged. "I was not privy to it until quite recently, and then . . . other events took precedence, so I could not correspond as I would have wished."

"But, Maria." Georgie laid a hand on Maria's. "Aren't you still in mourning, or rather half mourning, for the late Lord Kersey?" She looked pointedly at Maria's purple gown.

"I am, although we were planning to wait until my mourning had passed and his . . . circumstances had settled down." A tear spilled down her cheek and she caught it with Kinellan's handkerchief, still hoping to smell the scent of citrus.

"What happened to change your plans, my dear?" Elizabeth looked encouragingly at her.

"This." Maria waved her hand at the room. "It finally came to light, eight months after he died, that Alan had made a will

391

benefitting me and little Jane." She glanced from face to face. "Greatly benefitted me and Jane. To the point I thought I would never want for anything ever again." She sobbed. "I was wrong."

"My dear." Charlotte put her arms around her. "You cannot mean that when your betrothed found out about your fortune he refused to marry you?"

Too distraught to speak, Maria nodded.

"I know it sounds odd," Kinellan broke in, "but there are extenuating circumstances having to do with his family and an incipient scandal. The gentleman wished to shield Maria from possible censure, and thus withdrew his suit."

"Have you written to him since you parted?" Fanny began to pace in front of the fire.

"No. I didn't write because I was afraid he either would not answer at all, or rebuff me once more." Maria sniffed. "I didn't think I could endure that again."

"Perhaps it is time that you did so." Fanny paused in her pacing. "You were certain of his affections?"

"Oh, yes." Nodding vehemently, Maria cut her gaze over to Jane. "Quite certain."

Fanny must have caught that glance because she moved closer to Maria and bent down to whisper, "Is there the possibility of a child?"

Biting her lip, Maria gave a brief nod. She'd not gotten her courses last week as she should have. It could be nothing, but the last time she'd missed them, she'd been increasing.

At that confession, Elizabeth spoke up. "Then you must write to him, my dear. If there is the possibility he is to be a father, you must let him know. No matter what scandal hangs over him, it will be nothing compared to the ruin you will endure should you have a child out of wedlock."

The circle of friends had sobered. All were nodding in agreement, some with a look of sympathy in their eyes.

"Who is this gentleman you would marry, Maria?" Georgie cocked her head like a bird contemplating a treat.

"His name is Mr. Hugh Granger, the steward at Kersey Hall." Maria pulled and twisted Kinellan's already abused handkerchief. "He is one of the most kind, thoughtful, and handsome gentlemen of my acquaintance. In fact, he rescued me when I fell through the ice while we were skating."

Gasps from all her friends brought forth that tale, with some obvious omissions.

"Well, Mr. Granger sounds terribly interesting and romantic, my dear." Georgie had followed the tale avidly.

"Says the woman who married a pirate." Elizabeth laughed at her sister-in-law.

"A want-to-be pirate, although he did steal my heart." Georgie grinned fondly at her husband, standing with the little knot of men who had gone back to their brandy.

"That merely makes him a thief, dear." Fanny perched on the chair opposite the sofa.

"But he has a ship." Georgie patted her lap. "Isn't that right, Lulu?"

"Yip." The little dog sailed into Georgie's lap and Georgie stroked her silky coat.

"Careful, my girl. You won't be able to do that much longer." Georgie turned back to Maria. "Maria, I think you should go immediately and write to Mr. Granger. Invite him to the party, but only hint that you have something important to say to him, something you must say to him in person."

"If he's got a brain in his head, he'll know what you wish to speak to him about." Fanny rose, her gaze going straight to Matthew, a subtle smile on her lips.

The others stood as well, bringing Maria reluctantly to her feet. Her reasons for not writing to Hugh still held. Another rejection and she would likely never recover. But her friends were correct. She needed to let him know, even if vaguely, that there was a new consideration when talk of their possible marriage was concerned.

Inviting her friends had been the perfect idea. She must remember to thank Jane for it. At least now, if she was able to stand face-to-face with Hugh once more, she would not be alone. Perhaps in more ways than one.

CHAPTER TWENTY-FIVE

For the third time, Anthony, Lord Wetherby, tried to tie his cravat in an American knot, but the damned cloth kept creasing, making it look like a mathematical knot, which was too common. Every other gentleman in London seemed to use that particular knot. He would rather be unique. People took notice of the one-of-a-kind. Especially the ladies. Of course, he wasn't in London at present, but it would still behoove him to attract what attention he could here in the country.

But he had to tie the damned knot first. In frustration, he jerked the length of cloth from around his neck and it slithered to the floor. "Phipps!"

His valet came at a run from the dressing room, another white cravat in his hands. "May I assist you, my lord?"

"Yes. Get on with it." He stood perfectly still while his man tied the knot with ease.

"Will there be anything else, my lord?"

"Make sure my Hessians are polished to a shine and ready for the ride this afternoon. And I'll wear the claret coat and the green-and-red-striped waistcoat. Add a bit of holiday to the ensemble."

"Very good, my lord."

"The navy blue for now." Anthony held his arms back and Phipps slipped the coat neatly over them, then snugged it down over the shoulders, creating an excellent fit. A final look in the mirror, a slight adjustment of the shirt sleeves, and he deemed himself fit to be seen this morning.

Hurrying down the stairs to the breakfast room, he passed the table where the post was kept.

A footman was tarrying there. Odd. "You, footman. What's your name?"

"John, my lord." The man turned to him, shoulders back, suddenly straight and tall.

"What are you doing with the mail, John?" Anthony peered closely at the servant, but the man stared straight ahead. At least he was well trained.

"I was told to check the incoming post for letters addressed to Mr. Granger. They are to be forwarded on to him in Lavenham, my lord."

The hairs on the back of Anthony's neck

rose up. Certainly his father had given no such order after Granger's insolence. "Who told you to do that?"

"Charles, my lord, the first footman."

"Charles. I see." He'd find that footman as soon as he dispensed with this one. "And have there been any letters for Mr. Granger?"

"No, my lord."

"Hmm." Nothing there then. "Very well. You may go, but you are relieved of this duty as of now, do you understand?"

"Yes, my lord." The footman turned to go, sliding something into his pocket as he did.

"Wait." Anthony grabbed the lad by the arm. "What did you put in your pocket?"

Without a word, John brought out a letter and handed it to Anthony.

He snatched it from the servant's hand, peering at the handwriting. Addressed to Mr. H. Granger, Wingate, care of Kersey Hall. And in a feminine hand. He looked at the footman. "You're dismissed, John. Go to Mr. Chambers and tell him to give you your wages, but no reference." A smile broke over Anthony's face. "Tell him to ready Charles's as well. He'll be down as soon as I can find him."

"Yes, my lord." John turned on his heel and strode toward the kitchen.

Turning the letter over, Anthony wafted it toward his nose. No scent. Unfortunate, but the woman quite likely couldn't afford perfume. The letter was sealed in black, unusual except for use by those in mourning. Perhaps the woman was obsessed with Princess Charlotte and in mourning for her. A glance around the corridor showed no one in sight, but then you could never be too careful. He stepped into the small blue receiving room and shut the door.

Anthony went to the desk by the window and pulled the seal from the folded foolscap. Unfolding the letter revealed a single sheet, written only straight across. Hardly a love letter then. Those could run on for pages, as he'd had the bad luck to know. He raised the letter to read the few lines.

My dearest Hugh,

A love letter after all? He read on, his jaw slackening with every word until his mouth stood wide open at the signature.

Your beloved Maria

Dropping down onto the conveniently placed desk chair, he stared at the missive, his head whirling. Granger had been trysting with the little widow all along, right under their damned noses. But obviously hadn't married her. Which, given her new-found wealth, was undeniably strange.

He returned to one particular sentence. *I particularly wish to speak to you in person, about something of a delicate nature so I dare not write it.* "I'll be damned. The little widow is increasing."

How had he let her slip through his fingers? And why had none of the family known of her and Granger's *tendre*? Father would be absolutely furious when he found out, and likely blame it all on Anthony again. As if he hadn't tried his best to compromise her, at the very risk of his life.

Tapping the end of the letter against the desk, he let his thoughts wander. Was there some way to turn this to his advantage?

Tap, tap, tap. Had the widow told anyone about her "delicate condition"? The start of a scheme began to form. It would work best if she hadn't told a soul, but even if she had, he had confidence in himself and other considerable skills in deception that could be brought to bear upon dear Cousin Maria.

He folded the letter and shoved it in his inner coat pocket, then rose and quit the room. So much to do. But first, to find his father and inform him that Anthony would be spending Christmas in London.

The night before Christmas had been the merriest evening Maria had spent in ages. They had moved the furniture in the drawing room, clearing enough space for them to have dancing. Each of her friends had performed on the pianoforte, so while that lady played, Maria had partnered that lady's husband. She found Jemmy the easiest to follow, and Kinellan too tall to make it comfortable to stand up with him. Rob had twirled her wildly around the room, but Nash, was quite the most accomplished dancer. Of course, after the altercation with Alan last autumn — in which Nash had drubbed him but good — she still felt the need to walk on eggshells around him.

Despite the laughter and fun, however, Maria still couldn't help wishing for a partner of her own. For Hugh. She'd heard nothing from him, as she'd feared. Tomorrow was Christmas Day. If he'd wished to come to see her, he would have done so by now.

Her heart tried to flutter, but she forced air deep into her lungs, quelling the agitation. She'd have to learn to live without him, as she'd done with William. Strangely, now, her first husband's face was lost in memory. If she concentrated she could remember the way his unruly hair stuck up, or how he laughed when she tickled him, but no complete image of him remained. Would it be that way with Alan? With Hugh?

"What shall we do now, Maria?" Elizabeth had come to her side, perhaps sensing her melancholy. She would have to be a good hostess and do better.

"I thought either cards or charades?"

"Oh, let it be charades."

The voice that wafted above the chattering guests froze Maria in her place.

"I am very good at charades."

"Lord Wetherby, my lady." Her butler's perturbed tone spoke volumes about his opinion of Anthony.

As one, Jane and Kinellan rose from the sofa and rushed to Maria's side, although there was certainly no danger from his lordship in a room filled with her friends. Still, she was glad of their nearby presence. Maria stepped forward and curtsied. Best find out why the scoundrel had come, before asking the gentlemen to throw him out. "Merry Christmas, my lord. To what do we owe the honor of this call?"

He grinned and sauntered toward her. "I had decided to spend Christmas in London after all. Even with Father's guests, the country had become deadly dull." When he finally stood before her, he made a grab for her hand, but Kinellan jerked Maria aside.

"A simple bow will do, Wetherby." With a smug grin Kinellan demonstrated. "It is fairly easy to accomplish if you practice long enough."

"I see you have got it well in hand, Kinellan. How hard could it be?" Anthony turned once more to Maria. "My lady." He executed a perfect if somewhat florid bow. "I remembered Father saying you were planning to spend Christmas in the Kersey townhouse, so I thought while I was here I should come wish you a Merry Christmas."

"And having done so, my lord, I hope you will be on your way. As you see, I have guests." She motioned to her friends behind her, all staring at the interloper with avid interest.

"Ah, would you be so good as to introduce me, my dear. Friends of yours —"

"As you will not be staying, Wetherby, I see no need for introductions." Crossing his arms over his chest, Kinellan glared at Anthony, for the world as though he was itching to go several rounds with him at Jackson's saloon.

A narrowing of his eyes was the sole

response to the taunt, but Anthony then addressed himself once again to Maria. "In that case, my dear, that leaves only the other matter I wished to inquire about."

On her guard around the blackguard, Maria frowned and shot a glance at Jane, who looked blank and shrugged. "I know of no other matter between us, my lord."

"The child, Maria," he whispered, though loudly enough everyone surely heard him.

"Lady Jane?" A sudden chill raced through Maria. Had he done something to her daughter before sauntering in here? Her legs threatened to buckle, and she grabbed Jane's arm. "Jane, go to the nursery. Make certain —"

Before she had even gotten the words out, Kinellan had run from the room. Charlotte, Fanny, Elizabeth, and Georgie all clustered around her and the gentlemen surrounded Anthony, wearing very un-gentlemanlike expressions.

"I don't know who you are, Wetherby" — Nash had positioned himself in front of the scoundrel — "but none of us will stand by and allow you to threaten or harm Maria or her child."

On Anthony's right stood Rob, his mouth grim as death, and on the left, Jemmy, blocking the door. "He's going nowhere,

Nash. Never fear."

"Gentlemen, you misunderstand." The softness of Anthony's voice made Maria's skin crawl. "Ladies, do not distress yourselves. I was not referring at all to Maria's daughter."

Maria had had enough of Lord Wetherby. She should have just made good on her promise to his father to give either of them the cut direct when she saw them again. "Then who the dickens do you mean?"

"Why our child, of course, Maria."

Though unable to speak, Maria's mouth had dropped open, her brow furrowed in an attempt to make some sense out of his words. Her friends, however, wore curious expressions, as if they might, heaven forbid, give some credence to his claim.

Finally, she said, "You must be mad."

"I assure you, I am not." His face bore the expression of a repentant rogue, who has definitely sinned and enjoyed it, but would have you believe he is sorry now. An expression Anthony had apparently cultivated and could produce at a moment's notice. "Do you not remember? We agreed that if you found yourself increasing, you would write to me and we would make arrangements to marry."

"Get out!" Maria strode toward him

exactly as she had done to his father. "This is now my house, not Kersey property. You will get out now before I have the footmen fetched to throw you out."

"You don't need to wait for footmen, Lady Kersey." Rob spoke up and punched Jemmy in the arm. "We're old hands at moving unconscious bodies, aren't we, Brack?" He gave Anthony a fiendish glare. "We'd be happy to oblige you this instant."

"Maria." Anthony seemed to ignore all the threats, but maintained a calm and soothing manner. "You haven't even told me if you have suspicions. However, if you didn't have any you would have said it straightaway." He grinned at her and her stomach turned. "Do you think you are carrying my child?"

"No." It took every ounce of strength of will to refrain from pummeling his smirking face. "There is no way on this earth that I am carrying your child because I have never, ever been intimate with you, Lord Wetherby, and never will be. So take this little scheme of yours and try it on some other woman. It will not work on me."

"I can produce proof, if you insist."

"You can do no such thing." The man was mad. What proof was he going to produce? The rock that smashed his face when she dropped them to the ground during the mistletoe gathering? Would he bring in the imaginary bird to testify what it had seen? "It's preposterous. It never happened for there to be any proof."

Her friends, however, had begun to eye her askance. Dear lord, why would they not believe her? "Then show it to me."

To her astonishment, he reached into an inner pocket of his jacket and produced two black jet jeweled hairpins. She looked closer. They looked just like the ones she had been wearing when —

"I found these in the dowager house after you left."

Her hand going to her throat, Maria gasped. Dear God, he knew. Anthony knew about her tryst with Hugh the day she fell through the ice. They had been in such a hurry to get back they had left the chamber somewhat disarrayed. She'd missed the hairpins later that night, but didn't remember where she might have lost them. Now she knew.

"Are they yours, Maria?" Fanny asked, her gaze darting from Maria to Jane to Anthony.

She should simply lie to Fanny. Say they were not hers. Or tell the truth, as Jane had stressed all along. Her friends already knew about Hugh, knew that Anthony was spouting lies. So why were they sending questioning glances her way? The gentlemen were carefully avoiding her gaze now. In a case like this, did everyone assume the man was telling the truth and the woman was lying?

And suddenly Maria was running. Out the door, up the stairs, down the corridor to her bedchamber. She raced in, heart pounding, then whirled around and slammed the door. Suddenly drained, she leaned against the door, laid her head on the panel and burst into tears.

How was she to prove to everyone that she'd been in the dowager house with Hugh, if Hugh was not here to defend her against Anthony's lies?

CHAPTER TWENTY-SIX

"Twenty-seven, twenty-eight, twenty-nine, thirty." The soothing ritual hair-brushing had helped calm Maria once more after the disastrous events of the evening. At least her friends had rallied around her after she'd left in tears. According to Jane, Anthony had been escorted from the house by the gentlemen of the party. Not quite by the seat of his pants, as Rob and Jemmy had hoped, but forcefully enough that he had gotten the idea he was not welcome. Jane had reported this information to her later, when she'd come up to check on Maria before she went to bed.

Putting the brush down, Maria picked up a pot of hand cream and spread a bit of it on her skin and began to work it in. The small nightly rituals always helped her to relax and hopefully to have a good night's sleep, although that might be stretching it tonight.

A slight tapping on the door, made Maria sit up quickly and grab her robe. "Who is it?"

"Jane. Can you open the door?"

Her cousin had presumably gone to bed over an hour ago, but Maria dutifully opened the door, finding Jane, tea tray with tea and biscuits, in hand. "What are you doing?"

"I thought a little Christmas repast would not be amiss." She set the tray on the low table in the part of the bedchamber furnished as a sitting room, with sofa and chairs, and poured two cups. "Here, have a biscuit." She took up one, thin and crisp with chocolate sprinkled on top. "I think Cook may have been hiding these for tomorrow, but as it is after midnight, it is tomorrow."

"I am not particularly hungry, Jane."

That apparently made no difference to her cousin, who thrust the biscuit into her hands with the admonishment, "Eat."

Dutifully, Maria bit into the biscuit, and quickly decided Jane's idea had been sound.

"Have you thought any more about what you plan to do about Wetherby?" Jane stirred milk into her tea briskly, avoiding looking at Maria.

"There is nothing to do about him, Jane.

He is lying, pure and simple. And unless Hugh arrives, it is only his word against mine."

A scratching at the door made Maria exchange glances with Jane, who frowned. "Who is that?"

"I don't know." Throwing her robe around her shoulders once more, Maria called again, "Who is it?"

"Elizabeth and Georgie."

Wide-eyed, Maria opened the door to find Elizabeth bearing a plate of biscuits and Georgie a bottle of milk and several cups on a tray.

"What are you doing here?"

"We thought after the incident with that horrible Lord Wetherby, you needed fortification," Georgie said as the pair made their way in, putting their tray and plate beside the tea things.

"But I see Jane has beat us to it." Elizabeth sat down next to her. "Are these chocolate biscuits?" She snared one and bit into it. "These are delicious."

Smiling at this outpouring of love, Maria sat by Georgie on the sofa nearest the crackling fire. "Won't you have something, Georgie?"

Her friend looked askance at the sweets. "I fear I have lost all appetite for sweet

411

things since I began increasing, which is most inconvenient because I love to eat them but now they make me violently ill."

"No biscuits for Georgie." Jane moved the plates away from their friend. "We were just discussing what Maria must do now that Lord Wetherby has tried to compromise her, yet again."

"He has tried it before?" Elizabeth looked aghast. "Isn't it terrible when the most attractive men are also the most evil?"

"You find him attractive, Elizabeth?" Jane's eyebrows rose. "I find that quite surprising."

"Well, I didn't say I would be attracted to him, but some women might."

Another knock on the door brought giggles from Maria and Jane. "Shall I guess who this is?" Maria headed for the door again.

"Too easy." Taking up one of the sweets from Elizabeth's tray, Jane contemplated the heart-shaped cake. "Guess what they are bringing instead."

Grasping the door handle once more, Maria opened it on Charlotte and Fanny, who looked at the gathering and burst out laughing. "May we join the party?"

"Please, come right in." Maria gazed at her friends as the last two settled into the sofa, setting their offerings on the table and grabbing cups of tea. She'd never have believed these women could include her so completely in their circle. As she'd told Jane, they seemed more her friends, but that apparently wasn't true. A feeling of warmth and closeness, of being included and belonging for the first time in a long time would make this Christmas one of the most special she had ever known.

"We now have chocolate as well as tea and milk, Maria. And Fanny managed to procure some cherry tarts." Jane waved her back over to the table. "You need to eat and keep your strength up."

Slowly, Maria made her way back to the group, laughing, talking, and eating with great abandon. "I need to ask you something, ladies, because I do not think it was my imagination. And it may very well have a great bearing on how I will need to proceed with regard to Lord Wetherby's accusation."

Her friends quieted down immediately, looking gravely at one another.

"What is it, my dear?" Elizabeth put her hands in her lap, her attention fixed on Maria.

"When Lord Wetherby said that I had been intimate with him, but I denied it, who did you believe?"

The ladies looked at one another, a low murmuring running through the group.

As she expected, her cousin spoke up first. "Of course I believed you, my dear. But then I have special knowledge of the situation since I was there. I know both Lord Wetherby and what he's capable of, and Mr. Granger and his character. Two more different men could not be found, I must say."

"I believed you, Maria."

"I believed you."

The affirmations continued around the room until Charlotte was the only one who hadn't spoken.

Dreading this last comment, Maria nodded to the woman sitting silent in the wingback chair. "Charlotte?"

She swallowed and looked into Maria's eyes. "I . . . wondered, Maria. But only because Lord Wetherby looks so much like Alan Garrett."

"He does, doesn't he?" Elizabeth nodded.

"So I wondered if perhaps, because of that, you had found him attractive for a while but . . . not anymore." Color had risen in Charlotte's cheeks. "I hated to doubt you for even a moment, my dear. But I remember what Alan was like, how attractive he was." She lowered her gaze. "How persuasive he was."

"I noticed that the moment I met him, Charlotte." Maria knelt by her friend's chair. "Anthony even uses the same bergamot scent."

Charlotte made a face.

"I know, it was awful. But I can assure you, his resemblance to Alan was the first thing about him I found unattractive." She patted Charlotte's hands and rose. "I would never have become intimate with him, especially not after I fell in love with Mr. Granger."

"So what do you plan to do, my dear?" Fanny spoke up. "If he goes about spreading these lies, people who don't know the truth will absolutely believe them. Society will judge that the child, if there is a child, is his."

"Which is why I have decided that after Christmas I will go back to Kersey Hall, find Mr. Granger, and tell him what has happened, or what may have happened. If there is a child I shall know it for sure in a few months' time. Then we will hopefully decide to marry." That would be her nightly prayer for the next few weeks. "But whatever happens" — Maria looked around the room at the friends who would support her decision no matter what — "under no circumstances will I marry Lord Wetherby. Even if all Society believes the child to be his, I will not tie myself to such a dissolute man."

"Well, let us all pray then that Mr. Granger can be found and persuaded that whatever the circumstances, he belongs with you." Fanny rose, pulling her shawl around her shoulders. "And as we will all be going to church in the morning, I think we should take our leave now. Good night, my dear." She bussed Maria's cheeks. "Pleasant dreams. And Merry Christmas to us all."

"Merry Christmas, Fanny."

The chorus of Christmas cheer continued as her friends left her to seek their own beds.

Yawning, Maria closed the door, buoyed up by her friends' wishes for her happiness with Hugh. That would be her primary prayer tomorrow in church, and every day thereafter until somehow she and Hugh could be together.

CHAPTER TWENTY-SEVEN

"It's snowing!" Nose pressed against the window, one of Matthew's young sisters pointed out the window as Maria came downstairs Christmas morning.

"I see it is. It's very pretty, isn't it?" The snowfall made the old sooty snow that had lingered around Town fresh and new again. A good omen for her, perhaps?

"Merry Christmas!" Maria called as she entered the full breakfast room. Every place seemed filled by her guests, who were chatting excitedly.

"Merry Christmas!" The deafening response reverberated down the corridor, making Maria smile as she took a seat just vacated by Lord St. Just.

"Do not let me run you away, my lord." She nodded to a footman who had deftly cleared the marquess's plate and brought Maria silverware and tea.

"I'm going to check on Georgie. She was

417

feeling a bit queasy this morning, but is still hoping to be able to go to church." Rob hurried away, a concerned frown puckering his brow.

Such devotion would have been nice during her own pregnancy. She shook her head and spread her napkin over her lap. Perhaps the next time would be different.

Breakfast was a merry affair, with spirited conversations punctuated by hearty laughter. The older children were ready for church, but more excited about the presents promised in the afternoon before Christmas dinner.

Maria sat back and drank in the good cheer all around her. It gave her hope that everything would work out for her and Hugh. She had to believe that if she was to be able to carry on each day.

The clock on the mantel struck ten o'clock and Maria rose. "I believe we will need to leave now in order to account for the snowy walk this morning."

There was a flurry of activity as her guests called for maids, footmen, valets, and nursemaids in an effort to prepare for the outing. Within fifteen minutes, however, everyone was waiting in the entry hall. At last Rob escorted Georgie downstairs. She was pale and leaned on his arm, but she smiled and called, "Merry Christmas," as they reached the ground floor.

Immensely proud and happy, Maria led the throng out into the snowy wonderland, her Christmas morning so far everything she could have wished for. The church service was solemn and beautiful, the message of the Christ Child forever familiar, and brand-new. As she had promised, she sent up a fervent prayer for Hugh and her to be together as husband and wife. When the bells rang, peal after joyous peal, at the end of the service, it proved the perfect benediction to the morning's worship.

The walk back home seemed shorter, with the children running through the snowy streets, stopping to fashion and throw snowballs at each other. Jemmy and Rob joined in, pelting each other with a quickness that soon covered their jackets in snow. Their antics kept the whole party laughing until they turned the corner into the street where Maria's house was located, to find a lone figure leaning against the railing.

Her first glance at the man's figure made Maria's heart give a huge thump and she gasped. Hugh had come after all. She darted forward, outdistancing the others only to pull up short when she recognized the lounging figure.

"Lord Wetherby." Disappointment so sharp she could taste it filled her mouth. "Merry Christmas."

"Merry Christmas, Maria. I am invited to Christmas dinner, am I not? I left rather suddenly last evening and did not hear the invitation." He had straightened and now stood smiling down at her with a smug grin.

"I would think the suddenness of your leaving would have given you a hint as to the answer to your question." No sooner were the words out of her mouth than she regretted them. Here she had just come from church, from the message of peace on earth, and her first words spoken to someone were rude. Even if he deserved them, she was better than that. "I beg your pardon, Lord Wetherby. That was uncalled for on Christmas. It is early for dinner, but will you come in for a cup of wassail?"

"With pleasure, Maria."

She cringed when he spoke her name so familiarly, and when he offered his arm in escort she ignored it. There was only so much she could tolerate in the name of Christmas. As the others arrived behind her, she mounted the stairs, followed closely by Lord Wetherby. The subtle murmur that went up when her friends recognized Wetherby made her shrug, though she continued into the house.

"Thank you, Fuller." The butler took her coat and hat as her footmen stood ready to take the outer garments of the rest of the party.

"Well, what do we have here?"

Abruptly someone seized her, turned her around, and pressed their mouth to hers. The overpowering stench of bergamot gave him away. Wetherby, rot his heart. She squirmed and pushed against him. Had the man gone completely mad to do this in front of all her friends?

Just as suddenly she was ripped from Wetherby's embrace and shoved aside into someone else, who turned out to be Jane. Her head spinning, Maria could only ask helplessly, "What has happened?"

Jane's only reply was to smile broadly and point her finger.

Her guests had been making so much commotion Maria had not noticed a fight had broken out in her entry hall. Well, more of a skirmish that was extremely short-lived. It came to an abrupt halt when the unknown pugilist threw a punch that connected squarely with Wetherby's nose. The lord went down as though he were a felled oak and lay still on the parquet floor, bedaubed with blood here and there.

The mysterious combatant turned toward her, a smile on his handsome face that threatened to split it in two.

"Hugh!" Maria launched herself at him, wrapping her arms around him, holding on, never wanting to let him go.

"My love," he whispered, hugging her back, enfolding her in his strong arms.

"I didn't think you would come." But he had come. He was here. She burst into tears.

"Don't cry, love." He chuckled as he fished out a handkerchief and handed it to her.

Kinellan approached them, approval in his eyes. "One of the better pieces of Christmas entertainment I've ever witnessed." He patted him on the back. "Well done, Granger."

"Thank you, my lord." Hugh nodded, but kept his attention on her.

"Did you get my letter?"

"No, I'm sad to say." He nodded at Wetherby, who was beginning to groan. "He intercepted it before Saunders and his accomplice could get it."

"I don't understand. Why could you not get your mail yourself?"

He glanced around. "Could we perhaps speak someplace more private?"

"Of course." Reluctantly, she unwound

herself from him but grabbed his hand. "First, let me take care of this." She nodded to Wetherby, now moaning and struggling to rise. "Fuller, will you get the footmen to assist Lord Wetherby outside? I am not sure if he had a carriage or not, but he needs to leave my property in whatever means he has available."

"Yes, my lady." The butler looked as if he'd been given a substantial vail.

On the verge of taking Hugh somewhere private, she looked around at all the expectant faces of her guests. She could not in good conscience leave them in suspense. "My lords and ladies, I make known to you Mr. Hugh Granger, of whom you know a little. If I can pray your patience for a little more, I will introduce him to each of you shortly."

Wide smiles and nodding heads were her answers and she thankfully took his hand. "Come with me."

She led him into the smallest receiving room, the closest one that would give them a private moment. The door had barely closed when he seized her face in both hands and brought their lips together in a hungry kiss.

Oh, but she had longed for his touch so much she might never get enough. The sureness of his hands, the tenderness of his lips, the sweet sensation of his mouth on hers sent chills all through her. Wanting nothing more than to stay like this, intimate and loved, for all time, she settled herself against him and surrendered to the exquisite pleasure of his kiss.

Much later she emerged from the warmth of surrender to find them on the small sofa, still entwined in each other's arms. "Oh, my love, I missed you so much."

"No more than I have you." He smoothed back loose strands of her hair, his touch like silk on her head. "There has not been a day gone by that I did not think of you. Wondering what you were doing, if you had found another to interest you, almost drove me mad."

"How could I find another when the only one I want is you?"

"You did look rather enamored of Lord Wetherby when I came out of this room, where the butler had put me, to find you in the embrace of that rogue."

"Hugh" — she sat up and swatted at his arm — "how can you say I looked enamored? The wretch seized me for no reason at all, and commenced kissing me." She shook her head, still baffled by Wetherby's actions. "It is not the first time I have thought him a lunatic."

"I think I can shed some light on his motives, my dear. Other than the obvious ones having to do with lechery." His eyes twinkled. "He caught you underneath the mistletoe."

"Oh, no." She clamped her hands over her mouth. "I'd forgotten I'd instructed Fuller to suspend a mistletoe ball in the entry hall. I had concentrated most of my decorating efforts in the upstairs drawing room. That is where most of the Christmas party has taken place these past few days." She laid her head on his shoulder. "I've wished so many times that you could be here."

"I am sorry I wasn't, my sweet. As I said earlier, I did not receive your invitation because Wetherby intercepted it."

"You were saying you had someone retrieve your mail? But why?"

"Because I left Kersey Hall not long after you did. I received word that Kit had died, so I took Bella and went back home to The Grange. Just in case you tried to contact me, I arranged for Saunders to make sure any mail that arrived for me was actually delivered. When your letter went astray, Saunders made certain I knew it. But once everything with Kit's death had been settled, I had planned to come here to London to find you."

"Hugh." She squeezed his arm and noticed for the first time the black armband he wore. "I am so sorry about Kit. Even though we knew it would happen, it seems such a shame."

"I believe he is at peace now." Hugh looked into the fireplace and sighed. "But of course his death brought troubles of its own."

"The inquest." What Hugh had feared so long.

"It truly looked hopeless at first. The physician's report was conclusive that he had tried to take his own life." Clenching his jaw, he continued to stare into the fire.

Hesitating, but needing to know, she steeled herself to ask, "Did they rule it suicide?"

She still would not care about any scandal attached to the forfeiture of Hugh's family estate, but he would. It must have hurt abominably to witness his brother being put on trial.

Oddly enough, Hugh's grim expression lightened. "By God's grace, the magistrate ruled it an act of great melancholia, brought on by being thwarted in love. At least they got that right." A small smile touched his lips. "The thing that actually swayed the magistrate most against a ruling of *felo-de-se,* was the fact that Kit lingered so long after the shooting."

"Indeed, that is strange." Providential, but a decidedly odd ruling. "What was his reasoning for that?"

"He said that Kit clinging to life for so many weeks proved that he wished to live, not die. Therefore, the gun must have fired accidentally while Kit was using it for some other purpose. So his death was officially ruled an accident." Threading their fingers together, Hugh gave them a kiss. "Kit is now at peace, buried with the rest of our family in the Lavenham churchyard."

"So there will be no scandal?" Could she finally breathe a sigh of relief?

"No scandal. Our family estates are intact and even now being transferred to my name."

Thank God. Her prayers of the morning had literally just been answered. "So that objection to our marriage is forever gone?"

"Yes." He leaned his forehead against hers. "In fact, I now have no objections whatso-ever to our marriage."

A rueful smile twisted her lips. "You do not still feel guilty for my husband's death because you merely signed his will?"

Leaning back against the sofa, he pulled

her head to lie on his chest where she nestled comfortably.

"I must admit I still think it peculiar that my signature helped give you the inheritance that I will now share in, but I have spoken of it to my solicitor in Lavenham, and he says while it may seem odd, it is perfectly legal." He hugged her, then sat up, holding her hands tightly. "If people talk, I'll just refuse to listen to what they say. If it means we can be together and happy, then I will not let it stand in our way."

"Does this mean you are proposing to me, Mr. Granger?" What she had longed for so much was finally coming to pass. Her eyes teared up.

In answer he slid to the ground on one knee. "Lady Kersey, will you do me the great honor of becoming my wife?"

"Yes, oh, yes." Flinging her arms around his neck, Maria burst into tears. Finally, she would have the chance for her happily-ever-after marriage, to the only man on earth she was sure could make her happy.

"My love, you really must carry your reticule if you are going to cry so often. I have quite run out of handkerchiefs."

Laughter at this moment was very sweet.

He kissed her long and thoroughly. "Now this is how one should celebrate Christmas."

She raised her eyebrows in what she hoped was a seductive way. "I think I have a better idea."

His eyes darkened. "Do tell."

She grabbed his hand and rose from the sofa, then led him to the door. Peeking her head out, she quickly concluded everyone must have gone to their rooms or the drawing room. Perfect. In moments she had them racing up the staircase, hand in hand. On the first landing she slipped down the corridor, still miraculously empty of both guests and servants, and into her suite of rooms.

She drew him to the bed, then said simply, "Love me, Hugh."

"With pleasure, my love."

Drowsy and warm, Maria lay cradled in Hugh's arms, contemplating how much longer she could steal him away for herself. Christmas dinner was due to begin at three o'clock sharp and unfortunately, as hostess, she must be there. How much more she would prefer to stay in bed with Hugh, but duty would call them all too soon.

They had spent the better part of the afternoon in bed, exploring, tasting, touching one another, learning what each one liked, and what drove them wild. Why she wasn't still asleep after so much vigorous activity was a mystery.

"Is it time to dress for dinner?" His breath tickled behind her ear.

"The clock struck two just now." She scooted back toward him, so her entire length pressed against him.

"Shall I take that invitation as a no?" He nuzzled her neck, producing gooseflesh all over her body.

"I think we may indulge once more. We do need to make up for lost time. Ahh, like that."

He'd drawn her leg up and over his, then entered her with a quick thrust that filled her completely.

Hugh, she'd found, was a rather inventive lover, never doing the same thing twice. Life with him was going to be very satisfying.

Thrusting vigorously now, he slid his fingers down to her mound, brushing through her curls to find the little nub he knew just how to play with to bring her to pleasure time and again. Circling his thumb around her as his thrusts pounded deep inside, caused the tension at her core to coil quickly.

Moaning deep in her throat, Maria pushed back against him, straining to reach the tipping point into pleasure. A little bit more . . .

a little bit more and she shattered deep inside, pulling him farther in even as he cried out, spilling his hot seed once more.

Relaxing into the mattress, Hugh disengaged, then rolled her over to face him. Panting, he pulled her to his chest, his heart hammering loudly in her ear. "I have a confession to make."

"What?" She was panting too, although the drowsiness threatened to take over.

"I may not be able to walk into dinner."

Maria giggled. "I may not either. Do you think the hostess can be indisposed tonight?"

"If it were any dinner but Christmas, perhaps."

"Then you have to get up too. We can lean on one another."

Hugh chuckled. "And you know where that kind of behavior will lead."

"Right back here." She kissed him and sighed, perfectly content. "What a wonderful thought. But first we have to get up."

"Shall we do it together?" He sat up, bringing her with him.

"Always."

EPILOGUE

Christmas night the festive family drawing room was full of Maria's friends once more, with one precious addition that made the company complete.

Georgie sat at the pianoforte, playing "God Rest Ye Merry Gentlemen" as everyone stood around the instrument singing carols. Later there was to be dancing and cards, and last but not least, the snapdragon. Tomorrow everyone would have singed fingers, but tonight they would have fun.

As the carolers began on "Hark! The Herald Angels Sing," Maria took Hugh's hand and quietly led him over to the tea table.

"Can I help you with something, my lady?"

She shook her head and poured tea into two cups. "There is one thing we have not had a chance to discuss."

"And what is that?" He stirred milk into

his tea, then sat on the sofa next to her.

"Since you never got my letter, I need to tell you that it invited you to this party, but it also said that . . . that I had something in particular of a private nature I needed to discuss with you." Maria stirred her tea, and waited.

"Of a private nature that you need to discuss?" He jerked his head up so quickly the hot tea slopped over the rim of the cup and splashed into the saucer. "Maria, are you telling me —"

"Shhh." She cut her eyes over to the singers, but no one seemed to mark her or Hugh. "I only suspect so. It is too early to truly tell, but . . . well, my courses are very late. And that has only happened once before."

"A baby." A silly grin pulled at his mouth. "Our baby."

Relief coursed through her. She hadn't known if he would be pleased to have a child so soon. "Yes, if there is a child, it will be our child." She bit her lip. "But there is a concern."

"What do you mean?" Alarm wiped away the happiness that had been in his face moments before. "Is there something wrong? With you? With the child?"

"No, nothing is wrong in that respect. But

433

in another attempt to force me to marry him, Lord Wetherby may put it about that the child is his."

"The cur." He made the words sound like the foulest curse. "When did he spout this lie?"

"Yesterday, and only to us; however, after today he may put it about in hopes of casting doubt between us." *Cur* was too good a name to call him. "But you know that it is not true, don't you?"

"Of course, I do."

The response was so quick she blinked. "You do? I mean, you should, but why are you so sure?"

"Because once I realized he wanted to compromise you, I set several servants to watching him. If they ever saw him with you, they were to stay where they could see you and come to your aid if need be." He smiled brightly. "I hope you will like having a husband who thinks two steps ahead."

"I see I shall have to be on my guard. But what servants did you employ?"

"There were quite a few. Charles Saunders, your butler at Francis House; John Freer, a footman; Hatley."

"Hatley was part of your 'spy ring'?"

"No one else would be as close to you. If Wetherby had been bold enough to come to your chamber, Hatley was instructed to raise the alarm for fire. That would have gotten everyone out of their beds and foiled whatever plot he might have had." He sipped his tea and relaxed back into the seat. "I am only glad that such measures never became necessary." Hugh's face became sheepish. "I do have a matter to discuss with you, not of a private nature, but one I hope you will approve of."

"What is it?" This sounded curious.

"Saunders and Freer lost their positions because of their work for me, so I have offered them employment on one of our properties."

"Well that certainly sounds fair. And it does seem we have enough to accommodate them." She'd like to help the two men who had been helping her unbeknownst.

"The Tate family as well?"

"The Tates?" A sinking feeling made her stomach roil. "Did someone apply for the tenancy?"

"It is a long story that I think you will quite enjoy, but another time. But yes, the family was evicted from the tenancy, so I took them to The Grange. I don't have a vacancy there, so we may need to make other arrangements for their employment, but, the point is, they have a roof over their heads and the promise of work they will be suited for." He took her hand and rubbed it, warming her all over. "I knew you would wish to know they were doing well."

"Yes, I did." He did know her very well indeed. Love for him welled up in her heart. "When can we be married? I don't think I can wait another day."

"Well, you may have to wait a day or two, until I can procure a special license, but I think we may be able to find something to do to make the time pass." Hugh reached into his pocket and pulled out a sprig of mistletoe, berries still clinging to the little branch, and held it over his head. "Do you have any ideas about that, my lady?"

"Yes, I believe I do." Laughing, she leaned forward to give him a kiss. One of many, many kisses under the mistletoe at Christmas and throughout the New Year. For all the rest of their lives.

ABOUT THE AUTHOR

Jenna Jaxon is the author of the House of Pleasure series, as well as the historical romance trilogy Time Enough to Love. She lives in Virginia with her family and a small menagerie of pets. When not reading or writing, she indulges her passion for the theatre, working with local theatres as a director. Visit her at jennajaxon.wordpress.com.